# The GLASS HOUSE

## MONIQUE CHARLESWORTH

**POSEIDON PRESS**
NEW YORK

Copyright © 1986 by Monique Charlesworth
All rights reserved
including the right of reproduction
in whole or in part in any form
Published by Poseidon Press, A Division of Simon & Schuster, Inc.
Simon & Schuster Building
Rockefeller Center
1230 Avenue of the Americas
New York, New York 10020
Originally published in Great Britain in 1986 by Hamish Hamilton Ltd. Published by arrangement with th
author. POSEIDON PRESS is a registered trademark of Simon & Schuster, Inc.
Text designed by Irving Perkins Associates
Printed in the United States of America
1   3   5   7   9   10   8   6   4   2

Library of Congress Cataloging-in-Publication Data

Charlesworth, Monique
The glass house.

I. Title.
PR6053.H37218G5   1986      823'.914      86-25446
ISBN: 0-671-63091-1

*for my mother*

# Chapter 1

Victor had had the oddest feeling for some time. It was the sensation of being followed, of being watched. Even in the dark underground garage, as he climbed into the big Mercedes and sniffed the aromatic new leather, he felt impelled to look over his shoulder. There was nobody there; no other car but Herr Wachtel's dark green Jaguar. Nobody sprang from the shadows to menace him. And yet he looked and every time shook his head at the absurdity of it. Victor was not a nervous man, nor was he fanciful.

Another thing: in the streets, the placid, well-ordered, elegant thoroughfares of his city, he had begun to notice something he had never seen before. Children; the odd small boy walking purposefully across the Alster/Kennedy-Brücke, head bowed, trudging along with no mother or elder brother in sight. Two or three of them loitered near the flag poles on the Jungfernstieg. In summer, the tourists queued there for excursions on white, glass-topped motor boats, but now the wind was chill and he wondered, on his morning walk, that they should choose such an exposed position for their games. A child of ten or eleven, a boy who surely must have been playing truant from school, had stopped him yesterday, asked the time politely and then run away before he could reply. Victor, a courteous and good citizen, would never refuse such a request.

A whole tribe of them had preceded him on the way to the bank, dodging in and out of doorways, springing noiselessly on thick-soled sports shoes which seemed far too large for their spindly legs. They were thirteen or fourteen, that awkward gangling age, with that faintly threatening air such juveniles had when out in packs, causing the mid-morning lady shoppers to clutch their bags a little closer. They did not shout or call to each other, but wheeled and swept among the pedestrians like bats using radar to swoop and turn, never quite touching anyone. Then all, as upon a signal, had suddenly raced away around the corner. They would have bats' voices, he thought, angry adolescent squeaks, and wondered why he had never noticed them before.

Unmarried and childless, Victor had little interest in the younger generation beyond the show of tolerant benevolence expected of uncles. He held this honorary position in a dozen households and his arrival always caused a certain amount of jostling and thrusting, a certain smiling eagerness to be the first to greet him. Like all good uncles, he generally had some small present in his pocket, something to keep the children quiet while the parents sipped an aperitif. He did not like or dislike children, and, being quite unmoved, knew exactly how to deal with them.

These adults-to-be kept impinging upon his consciousness. There they were again, three boys at the zebra crossing as the big motor idled. They did not cross and one of them stared impudently at him through the tinted glass. He was old enough to have a child the age of this adolescent with his arrogant stare, his shoulders hunched in the dark blue anorak, delicate pink ears protected from the cold only by the long, fair, girlish curls tucked behind them. A pretty boy, a profile as delicate as a girl's, smooth cheeks unblemished by a pimple or hint of a beard. There was something uncanny about that unblinking gaze that sought Victor out; something familiar. The car glided away and it was not until he reached the dual carriageway that the faint twinge of recognition fixed itself more exactly. Of course, Victor thought, that is how I looked as a boy. Those effeminate curls were the colour of his own military crop, except that the stubble over his ears was whitening. He had seen that piercing look, that vague, sulky defiance long ago in an old photograph album. He had stood thus, now sharp, now staring sullenly at the camera, but he had been younger. Nine, ten at most.

That album, like all the rest, had not survived. Victor had no family treasures, no yellowing snapshots on his lacquer sideboard. He saw again the heavy brown leather book with its delicate, interleaved pages which crackled as they were turned. How odd, he thought, for such a memory to surface from the void. Perhaps he was getting old. He smiled at the notion of an old, toothless Victor mumbling on about boyhood days. Unthinkable, impossible, for Herr Genscher, so much a man of today, ever to degenerate to such senility.

Victor never spoke or thought about his past. It was like a country he had visited once and disliked, a cardboard stage-setting peopled with unpleasant characters. Not for him the tearful reunions of old Kumpeln or the back-slapping Bierfest with strangers who once carved their initials at the next desk. There was no scrap of nostalgia in him for that common fabrication, the childhood idyll. He observed the children of his friends, who seemed to inhabit a sunny, false fantasy world of books and games, a jolly fairy-tale of princesses and talking animals, which seemed as unreal and distant to him as the dark wastelands of his childhood. They seemed to him to play at innocence, to pretend a naïvety that only story-book children had. He, playing the friendly uncle, credited them with more sense and saw the sly looks behind the dutiful Knicks and proffered hands. His friends might sigh for their lost youth, but Victor would not have been a child again for anything in the world.

These street-corner kids, alert and prematurely wise, looked as though they belonged to the real, the darker realm, he thought. And then, hooting down and humbling an upstart Karmann Ghia, he shrugged off these absurd notions. Only old men brooded about their youth, he thought, and it was for old women, grown nervous, to see a threat in every shadow. He was at the very prime of life.

There was no denying a touch of vanity in Victor. Not, heaven forbid, the preening ways of the dandy, whose comb

3

was forever leaping from the back pocket into the hand; not the anxious, frowning looks that middle-aged men gave themselves when they passed those huge mirrored wardrobes in Bornhold's splendid display, that quick turn and reassessment of the thinning patch. He did not need to indulge in that dip and bob of the head. Victor's was an above-averagely handsome face; his suits, of fine English worsted, were not, yet, cut to conceal a paunch. He saw himself pleasantly reflected in the plate-glass doors of the restaurant and in the smile of the lady manageress. She tilted her head flirtatiously, leading him to Herr Walther. He belonged to the secret society of the attractive, who acknowledged each other with glances as unmistakable as a Masonic handshake. Pretty women, meeting Victor, inevitably examined his right hand and, noting the absence of a ring, always smiled in a certain way. They were his milieu, not these hitherto invisible half-people, these gangs of baby thugs so unaccountably roaming the city centre.

'Grüss Gott!'

There he sat, stout and jovial, nicely wedged into the plush green alcove, the bottle already uncorked, one pudgy hand outstretched with an apologetic smile as if to say I would get up, but you see how difficult it is for me.

'We must hurry,' he said. 'Unfortunately I fly this afternoon to Bonn, more verdammte Ostpolitik. Can you see old Adenauer turning in his grave?' and he chuckled at the thought. 'It's an interesting moment to get into this game, my friend, I think that I shall miss it in my little house in the woods with only little birds and animals to shoot at and no humans,' and he let out a breath of premature nostalgia, looking hard at Victor over the rim of his glass.

He had round, rosy little cheeks like a doll's, a gleaming egg of a head which shone under the green-shaded lights, and a Humpty-Dumpty body, but with no hint of fragility. His round stomach was unfashionably circled by the dark cloth of enormously high-waisted trousers, further supported by braces, which gave him the air of a Tyrolean on his Sunday off. His comfortably spread legs, like the rest of him, had long forgotten the sensation of being crossed.

4

'Ah, but you'll spare the wildlife for six months, won't you, if the deal goes through?' Victor said amiably. 'I shall need an adviser, a consultant for a time. Let the pheasants fatten for a season. It will be worth your while.'

Herr Walther nodded his head; he was pleased, but wouldn't show it. He made a point of bestowing even the inevitable as a favour. He never took his round little eyes from Victor's face.

'First the deal must go through. The half-year figures are a disaster, circulation's down fourteen per cent and everybody is nervous. This time I think the journalists will accept a package even if it loosens their control, especially if the alternative is, Gott behüte uns, Herr Springer.'

He aimed a mocking smile at Victor, who smiled back. His was a privileged initiation into the rites of his chosen world; a view from the top. He noted the newspaper man's pleasure in hyperbole as characteristic of his type. Victor was going to learn to play with the unfamiliar vocabulary and alternately to abuse and placate a difficult, but gifted staff.

'Your advantage, Herr Genscher, is one of surprise. We will present you as a non-political proprietor, an old-fashioned liberal of the old school. He's a businessman, we'll say, one with impeccable credentials. Even so, it won't be easy. You understand, of course, that the editorial board alone can select the new editor?'

Herr Walther had a brisk and confident manner, exuding authority, just as his solid bulk denoted a massive strength. He was not the sort of man who cared to be contradicted. He had the unyielding heart and all the stony impenetrability of a rent-collector in a bad district; he would get his money, whatever happened. He was unstoppable. Victor, loth to interrupt, agreed with his statements by nodding. He gave him full rein.

'Good, good, that's impossible to change, you see. Now the crux of the matter is the initial share purchase. You must have my ten per cent, as quickly as possible, we cannot move too fast.'

'Today, if you like,' Victor said mildly and the fat man gave him a beaming smile in which gold teeth glinted. He held a small piece of paper, but seemed not to need to refer to it.

'Excellent. Now, you take an option to buy the new rights issue, and when you put that together with my modest holding, the editorial staff's percentage goes down by ten per cent to just under thirty. Of course my ten per cent is then reduced to about six, but you then hold 31, which gives you control. Done! And you have the cash to relaunch, even to begin to modernise production. And you still have the lease-back on the building to negotiate. That's your business of course. I shall merely be your honoured consultant,' and he raised his glass to that notion. They toasted the new empire.

'Yes, good, it's very acceptable,' Herr Walther said, easing himself further into his niche. 'I think we can persuade them. I flatter myself I have a little influence,' and he smiled modestly. 'Now the ticklish bits are the redundancies and the wage agreement, that's where your real problems begin,' and, looking round him, but discovering nothing more threatening than a waitress in a bright red and green dirndl, he lowered his voice to a confidential tone. Security was one of Herr Walther's favourite words.

'We present the package at a surprise general meeting. No speculation before hand and a week for them to decide. Boum!' and a fist thumped down on the grass-green table-cloth.

Now it was time to order. Herr Walther asked for fried pork chops, fried potatoes and the token salad his wife always insisted upon; he would follow this with a plate of Salzburger Nockerln and soft, Limburger cheese. Fats were his passion; fed on pork, Wurst and salami, rich gravy, butter and melting cheeses, he had acquired a permanent, slightly greasy sheen. His wife thought that his huge, pale buttocks and almost hairless, tapering legs looked just like a pig's, an obscene comparison she tried to avoid making by dint of turning her back, always, as he undressed.

'I don't see how, with the right management, it can fail,' he went on, wiping his mouth. 'Not if you have my shares and the cash in your hand. I, of course, shall introduce you. A little speech, I think, stressing the inviolable nature of editorial integrity, that sort of thing. Here, I've prepared this. Rather a

persuasive little word, tell me what you think.' Conspiratori-
ally, he slipped a piece of paper across the table. He smiled
through bulging cheeks when Victor did, scanning the lines.

'Pop!' Herr Walther said, leaning back to aim an imaginary
weapon at his jouranlistic adversaries. 'We'll hit them right in
the pocket, where it counts.'

Victor came as a godsend to this greedy man. Behind his
bonhomie, this tough old bird was truly delighted with the
solution he believed he had manufactured personally to solve
his problems. Victor had his measure; he had had him bagged
for a long time. He slipped the paper into his pocket before
calling for another bottle and a fingertip just grazed something
there: a small, rectangular card.

The white car wended its way through the afternoon traffic
heading towards the Ost-Weststrasse and Victor was glad to
turn off at Holstenwall, where it eased a little. He was a
confident man, a man on the brink of achieving an ambition, a
man quite without nerves. And yet: there was one little thing.
A trifle, an oddity, the regular daily appearance in his postbox
of a small printed card. It was the cheapest kind of business
card, vaunting the prowess of a martial arts specialist, offering
lessons in the grubby backstreets of Altona. A joke, of course,
on the part of one of Victor's sporting pals, one that no longer
raised a smile when, day after day, the card insinuated itself
into his pile of letters. Victor's postbox did not only contain
business items; he was accustomed to find pale, pastel-tinted
faintly scented letters there, but these were the only aberration
he tolerated.

This card bore a name, of sorts: Meister Judo. It offered a
telephone number, an address and a crude sketch of a man
sitting cross-legged. He wore the loose white coat and pyjama
trousers of his calling and from his mouth issued the words,
'Self-defence the only defence! For sport, for recreation, for
your security, learn with Meister Judo. Ages 8 to 80 accepted,
private tuition available.'

This card did not find its way into Rommer's box, nor into
that of Herr Frisch; its offer was made to Victor alone.
Wheezing, mumbling, faintly annoyed and apologetic, the old
caretaker had shrugged his shoulders at it. Perhaps, when he

took the rubbish down, somebody slipped in; he could not, after all, inhabit his glass box all day without a break. There were chores to do. Disagreeably conscious of failing his employer, while loth to exert himself in any way, Herr Frisch had promised to keep a lookout. His hunched, retreating back adopted an attitude of defeat before the event, and sure enough, no card-dropping miscreant had been spotted.

Something about this card made Victor uneasy. He took it from his pocket now, a slip of pasteboard which arrived grubby, with curling edges flaking into their separate parts, as though it had been used to clean a particularly filthy set of fingernails. Later in the day, Herr Tiedemann noticed it in the waste-paper basket, picked it up and examined it with his habitual curiosity before he, too, discarded it.

Herr Tiedemann was an upstanding, thorough, precise, conscientious old gentleman, letting no detail escape his careful attention. Whatever interested Herr Genscher neces-sarily enthralled his venerable, albeit junior colleague; all the more so since his employer had taken to leaving the office for two to three hours to transact unknown business elsewhere. For it was business; even Herr Genscher's relaxed and congenial lunches with acquaintances turned out to be busi-ness, sooner or later. Was he taking judo lessons? Herr Tiedemann could hardly believe that this was the case but, just to be certain, made an excuse to enter the inner sanctum and examined his boss's features sharply and in vain for any signs of recent exertion.

Nobody worked late at Rommer's. On the dot of six there was a click as Fräulein Schmidt turned off her machine and covered it carefully, rearranging the mighty Olympia on its thick felt mat in the exact centre of her desk which she then locked, departing carrying her wastepaper basket which she aligned at the door in a suitably inferior relationship to those of Herr Brinckmann and Herr Goldberg. She had the small pleasure of wishing Herrn Genscher, who descended the stairs with her, a pleasant evening.

Herr Tiedemann, who had dawdled busily through another day, was already walking smartly towards the Hauptbahnhof, his daily constitutional flushing his sallow cheeks, and Victor, who had forgotten his briefcase, leant to unlock the boot of his car.

Against the dark, carpeted interior, the white was at first glance a startling contrast. Somebody had scattered dozens of the cards inside; they had even found their way into his leather case. He straightened in stiff-backed anger, the shiny new anti-theft key dangling in his hand. Now this was a violation. He would throttle the intrusive bugger, den beschissenen Judomeister.

He left the busy brightness of the Königstrasse as it hurried through Altona aiming with all possible speed for the salubrious suburbs, and drove slowly down the Beckerstrasse. It was one of those narrow, straight side streets where the houses formed one long row in the same dirty grey stone, the symmetrical lines of windows staring unsympathetically at their counterparts broken only by the intermittent claims of Astra, Stella Maris and Pilsener Jever.

It was twenty past six and yet few windows were lit behind their net curtains and there were still a number of urchins idling in doorways, the sort who liked to run a key down the sides of cars, especially if they were new, making their mark in anticipation of owning something rather similar when they grew up to be hoodlums. Victor parked under a street-lamp two streets away and walked back, leather soles skidding slightly on the icy tarmac.

The judo school was next to a taxicab business, where a number of men lounged on old armchairs half-reading sporting papers while they eyed the faded blonde who worked the switchboard. Meister Judo, the window proclaimed in see-through angular capitals, the remainder of the glass being sprayed black. An amateur had executed this legend in tape which had left long white snail marks and further gleams of light seeped through small scratches and spots where the colour had worn off. A bell jangled distantly as Victor opened the door and stumbled on the unforeseen step.

It was a kind of anteroom, a narrow corridor no more than two metres wide with half a dozen chairs against the wall opposite. A large framed testimonial of some sort hung on the plastic which was pretending to be wood, the large red seal flattened against the glass. The door at the far end opened and an old woman shuffled out and thumped herself down on the chair behind a small table there.

'You're late,' she announced severely. 'The lesson has begun,' which was already clear to Victor from the loud thumps and shrieks which had accompanied her through the doorway.

'I am thinking of taking a course,' he said mildly and she looked him over, assessing the rich fabric of his coat through cunning old tortoise eyes which had a whitish rim around the iris and which struggled against the further handicap of overhanging pouchy eyelids.

'Private of course,' she said. 'You'll be wanting a private course at your age. Beginner?' and she drew from the desk a faint Gestetnered sheet, containing information which had left the page at the bottom, the whole surmounted by the familiar sketch, also askew, so Meister Judo looked as if he was toppling over. She fished spectacles out of a pocket and peered at it.

'Two hundred Deutschmark the beginner's course, private,' she said, jabbing with one stubby finger at a number on the page. When this met no protest she rose, with an effort, pushing the yellow heels of her hands hard against the table. 'Well, follow me,' she said. 'He won't take just anybody,' and then, over her shoulder, 'But you'll do, I can see you're the sporty type, Herr?' and Victor, who could not help smiling at the ingratiating slant she gave her insolence, said 'Genscher' and followed her into a room which seemed vast by contrast.

Children; the place was awash with them. The entire floor was covered by a white mat on which two rows of little boys were sitting cross-legged watching one of their number being held in a stranglehold by a slightly older lad. Nearby, half a dozen bigger boys tussled and tumbled about in pairs, uttering loud shrieks as they hit the floor, cries which were satisfyingly melodramatic and theatrical. The old woman threaded her way through them towards a group of adults in the far corner, who sat watching two men circling each other.

'Da ist er,' she said. 'Herr Levison! Ein Moment mal,' and in the same breath, 'Off in here, shoes off,' and indeed she had kicked off her sagging specimens, but Victor had not noticed. His eyes were on the smaller of the two men, the one whose skinny legs seemed lost in the baggy trousers who, while they watched, darted forwards, whirled his hefty opponent through the air and in the work of a second had him spread-eagled on the mat, with one arm locked behind and the other thumping away for mercy. Only then did Meister Judo look up. As the dark eyes fixed upon Victor's face, the mouth slowly opened in a ghastly rictus of a smile. The teeth were jagged, uneven and of varied colours; one was even black against a long canine, the pointy yellow fang of a dog, and the man displayed his broken mouth to Victor in umistakable pleasure and did not take his eyes from his face, not even when he rose, executed a sideways bow of the head at the fellow gasping on the mat and walked towards his new pupil.

# Chapter 2

Tuesday, December 2, 1971

I was seventeen and madly in love with Victor. I'd loved him all my life but had never imagined anything would come of it. It was an unreciprocated grand passion, a folie de jeunesse. I was torn between appearing frail and consumptive, the pale young maiden nurturing a secret sorrow, and the often stronger urge to tell Oma, who irritatingly never noticed anything amiss. Linda knew, but she was the most unsatisfactory confidante and would mock my tragic passion whenever I was stupid enough to confide in her. I was literally struck dumb when Victor asked me to become his wife.

Opa had been dead four days and Victor was helping us with all the formalities. He had gone out with Oma to help her choose a granite slab. It would be very simple, he said, with three rows cleanly chiselled. 'Eduard Luther Rommer' above and beneath 'Geb. 11.4.1893', below that 'Gest. 10.3.1967'. No encomiums, no Latin tags, merely the facts in his mother tongue, precisely the sort of simple directness Opa would have approved of. In fact this bleakness would appear romantic and mysterious, later, in St Luke's churchyard.

Victor came to tell me about it and then he moved in for the kill. He took my hand and said, rather quickly, for Oma and Susannah were rattling about with plates in the kitchen and could return at any moment, that it pained him to speak at such a moment, when I was naturally upset, but that he couldn't leave England without knowing something. He loved me, he wanted to marry me, was there any hope for him?

I was completely taken aback. Dreams were one thing; the physical reality quite another, coming as it did in a wave of lemon scent and in a soft, special voice I'd not heard before. I gawped. My cheeks went beetroot.

'Do you think I'm too old?' he said. His charming smile appeared and, I suspect, a certain amusement in his eyes. I finally muttered something or other, enough for him to deduce that there was indeed hope, and very wisely he left the room and left me to my amazement. How I longed for an action replay, so I could acquit myself more creditably. But the deed was done and we seemed to have made some sort of promise to each other which, because of my youth, was to be kept secret. For seventeen I was staggeringly mature; beneath the schoolgirl exterior lay a throbbing, passionate and witty woman of the world and so I took it for granted that Victor had seen through that shame-faced façade to the glorious creature underneath.

What, indeed, did Victor want? What could he have thought? I didn't exercise my brain on the problem at all, for it was fully occupied with dreams of future glory. I failed to address the issue, as Prof. Schiller would say, for years to come. In my essays I do the same, rambling instead obliquely round the subject in the hope of hitting by chance upon some telling point which will let me off the manifest absurdity of the subject. Victor and matrimony was a preposterous theme, particularly with J. Rommer as child-bride heroine, that much was obvious to anyone but me. I had cherished this notion secretly for so many years that it seemed neither ridiculous nor unachievable.

I address the problem now. Not because I have even the faintest hope of resuscitating those dreams, but because the question remains, hanging in my head, getting in the way. I would like to acquit him of actual malice in order to acquit myself of dumb credulity, of being such a nerd. He made a fool of me; am I therefore a fool? How could I have made such a fundamental mistake? Something was clearly very wrong with said Rommer's perceptions, but are they any different now? The proposition: to analyse events, dispassionately, naturally, and acquit self.

First question: was the whole romance a farce? The evidence for the prosecution is plentiful, for Herr Genscher and I go back a long way. When he first started coming to England to report to Opa on the business, he brought toys for my five-year-old self. The first was a tiny raggedy hedgehog doll, a parcel which appeared magically in his hand. He explained that this was the Steiff trademark toy. All the little animals had the Knopf im Ohr, the button in the ear. It didn't hurt them, they were proud of it, it meant that they came from a great house, as I did. I accepted that compliment with the innocent awareness of the very young, who think they know their place and like it. Every subsequent visit brought a little friend until I had a whole gallery of the charming furry creatures to remember him by. Sentimental fool that I was, I brought that first one to Hamburg with me. It sits on my desk now with its beaming smile between apple-red round plastic cheeks. The German gargoyle equivalent of the madeleine, but quite inedible, and I don't need an aide-mémoire. First of all I have an appallingly exact memory and secondly a numbing tendency to replay events, making them unforgettable.

How, in any case, could I ever forget Victor? For a start he was always striking among my grandparents' friends for his youth, his charm and elegance. Their friends came to play canasta and to eat huge, old-fashioned dinners at which Susannah officiated in a black frock with white collar and cuffs, having moaned over the job of buffing up the best silver all afternoon. This was for the benefit of the bank manager, lawyer, accountant and sundry professional neighbours, all very proper and English. They frightened me until I was old enough to participate and discover that all they did was drone on about golf, or gossip about matters in the city, which they pretended to know intimately from the safe distance of quiet

Hampstead offices. Now and then they bored on instead about vintage wines or the shocking cost of private education, one or the other being the socially acceptable method of draining their fat purses as fast as their overpaid exertions filled them up. It was acceptable, just, to talk about money, providing you never told, or asked, what people actually earned.

The real friends, the German-speaking ones who often, confusingly, turned out to be Hungarians or Poles, were much more amusing. Compatriots in exile, they always laughed a lot; but still, they were shockingly, dreadfully old. For all their elegance, the ladies generally sported a little wave over the ears to conceal the tuck marks; the red-faced gentlemen would flirt outrageously over glasses of Russian vodka, but clearly hoped they would never be called upon to act out their extravagant promises. Some lucky girls at school had parents still in their thirties, who moved in the heady worlds of PR and the garment business, get-rich-quick commodities and property deals. In their fox fur coats, the ladies generally in couture leather suits, they had unspeakable glamour. Alas, they never were invited to the house; no competition for Victor at all, who was even younger than they were. When Victor proposed, he was exactly twice my age.

An interruption: a telephone call from Tante Mausi, who says she's bringing Ingrid to visit me as they're coming to Hamburg for the weekend. Obviously Oma has written. Poor Tante Mausi, she's so transparent. She'll eat too much cake, complaining all the while that she must diet, and Ingrid will cast her eyes to heaven in that unpleasant way she has and correct my grammar. She's like a paler replica of her mother, with added spite: dreary flaxen plaits and those large, prominent light-coloured eyes that stare out so arrogantly. Though Ingrid and I have never liked each other, we preserve the convenient family fiction of friendship, cousinship.

Tante Mausi looks older, though she has tinted her fading hair a brilliant yellow, a colour that clashes with the pale greenish strands of Ingrid's hair. Ingrid has had hers cut into a short, neat bob. They merged impeccably into the luxurious quiet of the Alsterpavillon, rose-tinted retreat of well-to-do wives exhausted by the morning's search for the perfect

English cashmere or the adorable little silk scarf. We all touched cheeks and Tante Mausi sank with satisfaction onto her chair, her blue troubled gaze that really meant to look my way sliding instead in the direction of the cake trolley, nose following the rich aroma of Kaffee mit Schlag. The Alster-pavillon even looks like a cake, like a meringue with cream inside. Ingrid was fussing with her camel-hair coat; too good to lie on a chair it had to be taken away and hung up — properly, mind you — by one of the waiters. It was the sort that, like a fur, had a little chain inside, that she said mustn't be used. The Germans have an excellent word for Ingrid: damenhaft.

You look well, she said, eyeing askance my regulation student gear, which suits me better than Ingrid's clothes ever could, her sober, well-cut uniform as sported by the daughters of the bourgeoisie. Ingrid thinks too-short skirts are irredeemably vulgar. And so do you. Ingrid smirked, fiddling with coffee cups in order to parade a diamond ring resting on her long, pale finger. And I flattered myself that this visit was on my behalf. Ingrid has secured a banker and tomorrow night I am to have dinner with the two happy families to celebrate. Worse; he lives in Hamburg and so will she.

I suspect that Tante Mausi, vague behind the poised fork of Sachertorte, is relieved to be rid of bossyboots. Ingrid has always held the Bock household in thrall. With her out of the way, Uncle Hansi will be allowed to belch, eat salami sandwiches and drink beer for supper and Tante Mausi will guiltily slip into the old housecoats her daughter despises. She kept offering cakes, worried that I wasn't eating properly. Her concern reminded me of Oma and made me feel homesick. Without the heavy make-up she diligently applies as her salute to the Bock family fortune, she even looks a little like her. As usual, she brought a whole case of the stuff for me and I feigned pleasure. She is a dear, really, and the little black zip cases are useful. I keep my diaries in them. That's another reason for preferring to meet them in town: the diaries and papers all over the flat. Ingrid would sneer; worse, she's capable of reading them behind my back. She does offer one benefit, though. She has a salutary effect on my student slang and sloppy ways and I didn't mess up a single phrase, not even a pluperfect subjunctive, under the critical gleam of her schoolmarm eye. Her eyes really do protrude; you can almost squint sideways through the pale discs, but that would mean seeing things in Ingrid's steely light.

Coming home in the S-Bahn, something horrible happened. A man exposed himself to me. He was hidden behind the *Bildzeitung* but even above the roar of the train there were rustlings and I saw movements of his woolly, rust-red suit, then he lifted the paper high so I could see what lay beneath. One bleary eye peeped through a round eye in the paper to enjoy my reaction. I got up at once and rushed to the door, trembling with rage, and at Altona looked for the guard. He was kind, but said they could do nothing. He'll be put together again by the next stop, he said in his flat Platt, and that it was best to travel in second-class when the trains aren't full. Hurrying down the narrow winding road home I started, then, to imagine I was being followed, but when I turned there was nothing, just the flicker of the old-fashioned street lamp turning on to light the last tumbling flight of steps.

It's easy to get nervous moving through this schizophrenic city. The elegant lady on the Jungfernstieg and the worldly matron on the Neuer Wall could be St Pauli whores in their day dresses. When it's dark, strange creatures parade along the neon boulevards and backstreets, the Grosse and Kleine Freiheiten. In the iron-gated Herbertstrasse the ladies of the night lounge behind their windowpanes; the less favoured shiver at street corners. Leather-jacketed louts and US marines lurk about everywhere while respectable paters with their ladies stroll past or sip white wine in cafés to admire from a safe distance the shifting cabaret of erotic endeavour. The clubs shrink from nothing; no act too ridiculous or too bestial, and I have seen a man play the violin while he has sex with a grinning, eager puppet of a woman. The audience is often so respectable and so expense account-oriented that it's hard to believe these things are going on on stage. In the less reputable places there are apparently dogs and worse. Oma would be aghast and so would I. She worries about me and sometimes I get scared or lonely and immediately write her a long cheerful letter to reassure us both.

Four thirty and it's already dark. The coffee machine is slowly filtering its black drops which sizzle on the hot glass; the old walls are losing some of their chill. I sit on cushions with my huge fur rug wrapped around my legs and write on the low table. I mean to exorcise Victor, to take him out of my head where he fills too much space and put him down on paper where I can dissect and be done with him in careful, consecutive paragraphs.

The first question to address: which approach? In our literature essays we're always told exactly what line to take, which social influence to analyse, which dialectic. I have been told today to prepare a paper which discusses the poems of Hartmann von Aue as an expression of the lowly troubadour's quest for social advancement. The poems are irrelevant to the theory; it's words we concentrate on, to show the socio-economic forces of the time, picking out those which refer to riches, power or, 'lady', to class, and waving them triumphantly as proof. Our long, dull tracts vindicate the approach endlessly. Lyricism is passé. To talk about poems of love or despair is to excite ridicule, to miss the point. I am severely censured for my old-fashioned, romantic, rambling approach. Too many digressions, as here.

So: Victor as socio-economic force. Perhaps it's not inappropriate. Opa always called him the mainstay of the house of Rommer. He attributed much of our recent affluence to his energy, his uncanny way of anticipating rises and falls in the market, sniffing out deals and cheap cargoes to be picked up and unloaded at a profit, his shrewd purchases of land and stocks and shares. He was a worthy successor; winking at me, Opa would add that he was also the only possible one; that was why, shortly before he died, Opa sold half the shares to him.

He had actually left Hamburg fourteen years before he sold out, when he was sixty. He called it retirement, but it was no such thing. Victor was only twenty-four then and had been with the firm several years; he was very junior, but already beginning to try out a few ideas of his own. These were generally pooh-poohed by Otto Tiedemann, Opa's right-hand man.

Otto was theoretically in charge; but it became clear that he was not the entrepreneur who upped the dividends. Old-fashioned, prim and proper, he's a stickler for tradition and the correct way. I swear he clicks his heels at me. Once I was bold enough to smoke a cigarette in his office, stubbing it out in the hollow brass anchor on his desk which could never have been defiled before. He became quite red in the face, rushing out with the nasty dirty thing as soon as I'd finished. If I weren't Fräulein Rommer and half-heiress, I think he would have thrown me out. He's seventy now and gives no hint of retiring; he believes, quite wrongly, that he doesn't look his age. Opa promised him he could stay on as long as he wants to, so he remains in the big office, the huge desk distressingly clear of papers, for Victor makes all the decisions. Through his glass wall he is the scourge of junior clerks and terroriser of messenger boys, given to appearing suddenly behind the poor woman who operates the telex and making her jump. Nobody is allowed to smoke, except for me, and I only do it to annoy. It's always Herr Tiedemann I see whenever I go to collect my allowance or to sign papers; Victor is never to be seen. Perhaps he's warned to stay in his office; I don't know. I don't ask.

Rommer Import-Export own their dignified old stucco building in the Esplanade, a stone's throw from the Steinway Haus. As ever, in Hamburg, culture and business go hand in hand. It was a blackened ruin after the war. Opa rebuilt it and he and Oma made a flat on the top floor, which Victor ascended to in due course.

In the brilliant, troubled summer of our engagement while in Paris students ripped up the streets to build barricades, I thought I was storming Victor's. He ushered me round the newly-renovated glories of the flat. He had had new cupboards put in for the endless clothes, the summer and winter suits, the piles of monogrammed shirts. He had new glass sliding doors onto the balcony and had opened up the inside to make one large space. It is desperately elegant, modern sleek furniture, leather and chrome, mixed up with exotica, Korean chests, old Chinese scrolls and art deco screens. Every object is carefully placed at the correct angle to its neighbour and the furniture has little cups under the feet, so

19

the carpet won't mark. Expensive hi-fi and a baby Steinway grand near the open hearth, though he can't play, and everywhere mirrors, walls of them and grand gilt ones and one ornate matching pair with a tiny fisherman in a Chinese hat dangling his rod at the top, his wife bowing humbly in its counterpart. They made me nervous; all those reflections and the shiny, perfect surfaces.

It breathes the bachelor of cultivated tastes, as though he'd briefed a fashionable interior designer. No old photographs or souvenirs, no teddy bears, nothing shabby. It's a statement, sotto voce, of culture and taste, a careful, anonymous mingling of the two with money to burn. It wasn't a Hamburger's flat; no ship's models, not a single clipper in oil, no sea captain's dogs or maritime bric-a-brac, none of the things which clutter our house. He could see that it intimidated me. I couldn't see myself elegantly bending over to place the Japanese place mats at the perfect angle on the mahogany dining table. And yet we lay on one of those leather sofas once, while Mahler, poignant and sentimental, surged and swirled in the warm air. I can't hear it now without thinking of him, that lemony smell on his warm, elegant body. Sometimes I sniff it in the street and my heart turns over.

More digressions, how Schiller would scowl. 'To the point! Fräulein Rommer, get to the point!' He saves his most plangent comments for me, striking up obsequious echoes in my co-seminarees. That weedy clever little worm Behring pointedly puts his pencil away, though not his sharper tongue, when I start to read my papers.

Victor's past: where did he acquire those tastes? His was a humble background, I know that (source: E. Rommer) though Victor never spoke of the past. An autodidact, he also went to night school, swallowing up texts, learning late into the night 'wie ein Mann besessen', Opa said. He would be at work on his ledgers by 7 a.m. and always in before Herr Tiedemann, who is a stickler for punctuality. How that must have needled the old man, especially when Opa was seen to admire that restless energy. Victor must have picked up culture somewhere along the way, though it wasn't part of his apprenticeship.

Victor is an orphan, like me. It was an unspoken point of mutual sympathy. I should cross that out. How I keep on creeping in, as though V. Genscher can't exist without J. Rommer putting her grubby thumbprint on the picture.

Victor is an orphan. He survived the Berlin bombings and at the age of twelve was living on the streets, quite alone, when the Red Army launched their final attack. He survived on his wits and, later, on GI handouts. When he left Berlin, it was in order to go to sea. Was he a romantic boy, with visions of tropical islands lapped by blue lagoons? He saw the world through the portholes of greasy galleys in dirty cargo ships or rather, like that silly song, he saw the sea. He was only sixteen but precocious, of course, and tall for his age and strong and nobody asked questions. Finishing school afloat, Opa called it, from which he matriculated at eighteen. A genteel establishment to be sure and it certainly finished off those romantic dreams, because he couldn't wait to get ashore again.

It was 1951 then, the start of the boom years, empires rising from the ashes and J. Rommer in nappies. He chugged in on one of the dozens of cargo ships flowing into the great harbour. They'd cleared away the burnt-out hulls by then and propped up the ruins of the Michaeliskirche. There was lots of money around, the real stuff, American dollars which couldn't be spent on defence. The city fathers were rebuilding their bombed-out city, though in all humility they left some of it, like St Nikolai, 'eine Mahnung für kommende Geschlechte'.

Opa had already restored his façade; he was busy giving the business a new core. My great-grandfather started Rommer's, trading in rubber, jute, tea and tobacco, crops nobody wanted any more grown on plantations that had been abandoned or destroyed. Opa wasn't about to neglect the shipping side, but he saw there was money to be made nearer home, in land, new apartment houses and stores as well as in ships. Rommer's advertised for a junior clerk (trainee) and two dozen young men turned up ready to make their fortunes. Victor, at eighteen, looked like a man. Equipped with a 'knowledge' of merchant shipping and a smattering of half a dozen languages, he crammed those broad shoulders into a borrowed suit and came, cap in hand, to learn. He said he was ready to start that minute. Opa was always proud that he took him on in the teeth of Herr Tiedemann's disapproval and no doubt he enjoyed discomfiting that sober citizen. Ah, but I saw his worth at once, he liked to say.

Victor survived Herr Tiedemann's petty tyranny; he annulled it with his charm. He mastered the work with ease, for he had a naturally good business head and an eye for an opening and he impressed people. An old head on young shoulders, Opa used to say. Is it my fault I fell in love, when we talked about him so often? Opa described him as the sort of man who, lost in the jungle, would be discovered king of the cannibals ten years on. Of course he meant that as a compliment.

Other clever young men came; turnover doubled in a year, then it doubled again. Opa began to talk about retiring. He'd had a hard war and said it was time for a rest. Of course he had no intention of letting go. He had good old Otto to oversee things and he meant to enjoy himself. He moved country, but it didn't stop him interfering and directing matters long-distance, the inevitable dissension ignored, the counter-advice overruled. The sound of my childhood is the chattering telex in Opa's study. It would stop and then there would be the rip of paper being torn off and discarded as, once again, Herr Tiedemann urged caution and was ignored.

I was the ostensible reason for the move. In reality, Opa was a terrific Anglophile as all the old Hamburgers used to be. He relished the snobbery, the men's clubs, the good tailors and the Ritz, cruising in black taxis to get a new pipe at Dunhill's or have tea at Fortnum and Mason's. He claimed the weather was actually better and he didn't mind the bad cooking, for he had Oma. The queen of the Auflauf, he called her. She makes delicious Sauerbraten, inspired dumplings and always, on my birthday, fragrant lemony cheesecake in a rich pastry crust. And of course there was always Uncle Victor, the bearer of goodwill parcels which were always greeted with surprised delight, even though the contents had been telexed through as an order. He brought us Niederegger marzipan and crusty Zwiebelbrot, unsalted butter and a selection of sausages. Opa liked knobbly hard salami, the sort with wine-red mottled skin which Oma sliced into perfect, thin, densely packed circles, each slice exuding the faint tang of garlic, some with that exiguous desirable dot of pale green peppercorn. I pitied English girls for their soggy egg and tomato sandwiches. Oma's sandwiches were a feast, the dark peppery slices laid on cool lettuce over thickly buttered dense bread, which had crisp onions on top, more succulent fleshy pieces inside.

We didn't really go native at all. We settled in Hampstead in a large house which Opa always described as Ris-sen-Vorkrieg, so for ages I thought that was the name of the place. We were in the middle of the European-Jewish com-munity, where in shops people spoke German, where Anna Freud had a children's clinic and cafés had real coffee and understood what Schlag was. Just as important, we were inconveniently placed for my mother's parents in Yorkshire. They were to be granted their wish for an English grand-daughter without having the opportunity to see me often and to influence me in the slightest degree. I always visited them in school holidays. They are kind and slightly incomprehensible and eat salads of fatty, thick ham, lettuce and tomato with half a hard-boiled egg. Once I told Granny you could make a nicer salad with white cabbage and caraway seeds, oil and lemon, and she laughed for fifteen minutes. Grandaddy, who hardly ever opens his mouth, and looks at me with puzzlement and faint pride, sees me as a not unpleasant foreign element, an exotic flower among the prize dahlias. I never could under-stand how they ever produced a child as adventurous as my mother. They don't hold with foreign ways at all. While they were relieved I'd grow up speaking English, they lamented the choice of London, which was almost as bad as abroad. It turned out even worse than they anticipated, for we lived like colonials, always nostalgic for the old country and recreating it in the way we ate and dressed and in our pastimes. We dressed up on Sundays when our neighbours washed cars, went to spa resorts when they headed for beaches and skied when they stayed at home.

There's J. Rommer, centre-stage as usual. It may be Victor's life, but it's mine too. I can't separate him from my childhood and adolescence and just cut him out of my life, though that is exactly what I have pretended to do. We all carry our past around with us, permanent and heavy baggage, even if sometimes it hardly seems to weigh at all, even if we don't always choose to unlock the trunk and forage. I wish I could get inside Victor's box, Louis Vuitton to be sure and covered with first class stickers, and fathom his secrets. Then perhaps I wouldn't have to trail him around with me wrapped up in that horrid black bundle of regrets and sad misunderstandings that weighs so much I feel permanently bowed.

# Chapter 3

They sat in a small room decorated with sporting calendars so long out of date, so oddly placed, that they had, surely, to be covering eyesores on the florid, mosaic-patterned walls. A rust-rimmed filing cabinet disgorged a mess of papers near the door, an office desk was flanked by two leatherette swivelling chairs that tipped alarmingly. A white-painted cupboard let into the wall had doors held together with twisted wire. This room, jutting out at the back of the house, had previously been a kitchen or scullery. A thick, deep old-fashioned stone basin spanned one corner; one tap, from which the chrome had long flaked away, protruded drunkenly from the wall. Above it was nailed a pink plastic rack on which a cup sat and a plate and a delicate porcelain tea pot quite out of tune with its surroundings. A frayed towel hung stiffly above on a string; this and a cake of white soap suggested that Ludwig carried out his toilette here.

From the look of the bundle in the corner lassooed with string, which resembled the sort of sleeping bag explorers were said to prefer in rough terrain, Victor deduced that this miserable room could also be Ludwig's bedroom. He looked all around, observed everything, the chair anticipating his movements while the dark man sat perfectly still and watched him.

It was curiously, oppressively hot. The paper bubbled and crept away from the walls and rivulets streaked down onto the dirty window-sill; a damp, crumbling place below showed where these tributaries combined and had eroded a route to the spongy lino strip. The heat did not even seem to have a source, for there was no radiator, not even a gas fire in front of the boarded-up fireplace. Sweat was beading on Victor's forehead, but he remained encased in his coat, reluctant to make any gesture which might indicate a willingness to be there. He spoke with a certain amused nonchalance. 'Interesting,' he said at last, 'that it should be you. I should have guessed it. Still hiding in dark corners, I see,' and he let a contemptuous glance stray around the room. 'Well, what do you want? I'm a busy man, I have no time to waste.'

The other frowned slightly. He sat perfectly motionless, seemingly oblivious to the sounds that resonated through the door and quite at his ease, his palms turned up on thin thighs. He drank in the face opposite greedily, with the air of one who had waited a long time for this.

'My dear Victor, this is a pleasure I hardly dared hope for. Let me savour it.' His Berlin accent was strong; his was the sharp and mocking tone of the old Ku'damm bully-boys. 'You, such a busy man, here in my little office,' and he smiled jaggedly. 'How many years is it? And look how smoothly they've flowed past you, for you've not changed a bit. But so very smart. How well you look in your fine coat. Ein teueres Fädchen,' and he made as though to touch it. Victor, who could not return the compliment, sat rigidly and suffered the approach of a dirty fingernail. There was a tingling sensation at the base of his spine which made his buttocks clench involuntarily and the chair lurch a little. He could not keep his gaze from the mouth, any more than a motorist could help staring at a gruesome roadside accident. He knew that smile from earlier days, from unblemished times, when it used to flash out for pleasure, not in this sly, knowing way. This smile was an ugly accusation waiting to be made. There was altogether a knowing look on Ludwig's face, a consciousness of the effect he was having and Victor saw now that he must have rehearsed this encounter often. For all his calmness, the small body held its upright position with a certain effort.

'Don't play games with me,' Victor said. 'What do you want?'

'How suspicious you are,' said the sly voice. 'I remember as a boy you had that look; knowing you'd been caught out, waiting for punishment and still hoping to evade it.' He laughed, a mirthless rictus. 'Yes, it's the same expression exactly,' and the dark eyes stared unblinkingly at him. 'And here I am, waiting for you. I knew you'd come. You were curious, weren't you? But I have changed,' he laughed, a strange gulping sound and then spread his thumbs at right angles to the long fingers and framed his face with these bony right angles, like a picture. 'Oh, don't you like it? But it's not the packaging that counts, my dear Victor, even a fine and costly one. Inside we are both the same,' and he beat melodramatically at his bony breast.

Victor's eyes slid, for relief, from the grinning puppet. 'Or is it the room you don't like? My apologies, Herr Genscher, for the disarray. It's not what you're used to, I'm sure. But you were not always so fine,' and he pushed his head forwards on an elongated, endless neck in which the Adam's apple bobbed and danced. 'This is where you started your career, my dear Victor, take a good look at your handiwork.'

Victor controlled a movement of revulsion and impatience. 'You will leave me alone, do you understand?' he said in soft, measured tones. 'Keep away from me, or I shall take action to ensure that you do.'

The little man was silent for a long moment, staring hard at Victor, testing him with his unblinking gaze. He nodded, then, as though satisfied.

'Action,' he said in a level tone. 'Of course, that was always your way, to strike first. But no, I think not. How is the eminent Herr Genscher to take action, let me see, will he perhaps call the police?' and he was mocking again, his face drawn into a long expressive O of disbelief. 'My poor Victor. It's not always pleasant to look back and see your shadow. How it sticks to the heels and won't let go, even on the darkest days it only pretends to disappear. A little ray of light and, hupla, it's back again. How can it leave you?'

'You have heard me, you understand. Be very careful, Ludwig,' and Victor stood up, sickened with the unhealthy atmosphere of the place and Ludwig made a pretence of starting back, as though in fear.

'You mean to wrestle it perhaps, to take a knife and cut it away?' His eyes were alight with some strange pleasure; he curled back his lips like a dog to show his fangs. 'Now we approach the heart of the matter. What are you going to do about me? But you're nervous, Victor, now that surprises me, I can see that you are. But I know that you have it in your power to be — shall we say, accommodating? You can make a choice. Think of the old days, my dear Victor,' he whispered caressingly. 'Think of old times. Why should I mean you harm, unless you will it?'

He caught up with him at the door, he laid his long hand on Victor's sleeve and gripped it with a force that made muscles bunch on his wiry arms.

'You are a worried man, a discontented man,' he said, his fetid breath warm on Victor's face. 'The higher you climb, the further to fall, my dear Victor, yes, I can see you falling, down, down,' and the other hand raised itself high and thumped down on the door with a sudden, loud report. They stared at each other. 'A pity there is no time now when we have so much to discuss,' he went on, briskly, disengaging himself, 'I don't close at six. We're not in the smart quarter here,' and brushing past him he went into the large room, with Victor following. The mob of children hushed as he entered and separated into rows, all faces turned in their direction.

Ludwig stopped, then turned, blocking him into the corner. 'Listen,' he said very quietly. 'What you see here is the curiosity of a child. Are they looking? Are they staring at you?' And, over his head, a procession of eyes, some blank, some curiously alert, were indeed fixed upon them. 'The need to know, to comprehend, is quite involuntary, as automatic as breathing. What has happened to you, to make you lose it? It's the very process of life, the reason for existence. A man is dead when he ceases to learn.'

The head, under its thin fur of hair, was bumpy. A small crater, a space to balance an egg in, lay in the centre of the cranium. Although the boys could not possibly hear the man's whisper, Victor had the bizarre impression that the eyes were absorbing each word, reflecting back the hypnotic murmur. 'You are perfectly inert, do you realise that? A walking, dead mass. I am offering you a voyage into yourself, to comprehend the cause and effect, to see the pattern so that you can free yourself of it. When the nerves are dead, numbed, it hurts to bring them alive again. The realisation of self is painful, but you must perceive yourself to comprehend life. And then, Victor, we shall remake history together.'

The pink-faced boy was sitting there; recognising him, Victor took a step forwards and the boy averted his gaze. He crossed the room, feet sinking into the mat like a man walking on sand, and was conscious that the heads turned; as he reached the door they all, upon an unseen signal, scrambled to their feet.

The lesson was over at eight o'clock and for a quarter of an hour there was a scurrying about as the little boys got dressed again and crumpled their kits into nylon bags; as those who hired their outfits scrimmaged in the corner for coat-hangers, for Herr Levison was most particular about the way everything was left and not a few of them were afraid of him. The adolescents jostled for a view of themselves in the small cracked mirror where they combed back sweat-darkened hair and eyed the unappealing skin eruptions that characterised that age.

Meister Judo did not offer the convenience of showers or a locker room. There was a lavatory two flights up a rickety wooden stair sufficiently unappealing and badly-lit to provide a small boy with a useful schooling in bladder control. It was not generally known at the school, but one or two of the older boys had been permitted to use Herr Levison's private shower under particular circumstances, circumstances which did not generally apply and which were not the sort that got talked about. A certain boy hung back now, a boy with long, fair hair who was tall for his age; but when he received no encouragement he went with the rest, pushing through the crowd of little kids whose mothers crowded the anteroom, pushing their protesting offspring into thick jackets and gloves, pulling thick, woolly hats down over flushed little faces. It was surprising how many smart cars were to be seen pulled up onto the kerb of the Beckerstrasse, chauffeured by doting mothers from as far afield as Hammersbrook, as Bergedorf even, such was the renown of Meister Judo.

Frau Liebmann trudged about, rolling up the little boys' white belts and returning them to their niches in a resigned manner. This, the odd, desultory flick of a feather duster, the replacement of the toilet roll and her public role as receptionist made up the extent of her employment, for which favours the old woman received lodgings, a small salary and the constant company of children, whom she abhorred. Pleased to see the back of them, she thumped the front door shut, drew across a large bolt and, flicking off the lights with a practised gesture as she went, retired to the more congenial company of her television and a pair of knitting needles. She used these both to manufacture a succession of undergarments and to jab at the dials of the set.

Almost everything annoyed Frau Liebmann, most of all the idea that Herr Levison might think he was doing her a favour by employing her, since she was past retirement age. She treated him accordingly with curtness but also, since this looked like being her last possible job, did what he asked of her, never interfered or pried. Neither of them asked for, nor expected, any warmer human contact. She thought herself invaluable and, in a way, she was.

Listening for the thump of her feet pursuing their erratic path up the stairs, for the bang of her door and the noise of the inner bolt being drawn, for Frau Liebmann considered herself safe from no man, Ludwig awaited the moment when he could enter upon his rightful kingdom.

Meister Judo's acute hearing made out the sound of voices, a snatch of music from above and, abandoning the thick white jacket and trousers, he circled the large room, feinting at an imaginary opponent. For twenty minutes he skipped, finally slowing down and lowering himself to the floor where he sat cross-legged and still, a small blur in the faint light coming from under his office door; a dark yogi on a sea of white. Rising, he padded over to the office and carefully undid the loop of wire on the cupboard door, which swung open letting in a wave of moist, warm, pungent air. He breathed in the heady aroma of damp earth and greenery, the sweet scent of flowers mixed with the acrid odour of decomposing leaves.

A large conservatory lay beyond the door, a great glassed-in space which half a dozen heaters kept at tropical temperatures. This was Ludwig's secret garden, surrounded on the outside by high brick walls with sharp fragments of glass embedded in concrete. It left the house at an oblique angle and was almost perfectly concealed behind the brick box that constituted his office. Part of this structure could be seen from the windows directly above, Ludwig's and Frau Liebmann's, but it was impossible to see through the moisture-dewed dirty panels of glass, which were always filthy two days after Ludwig had cleaned them. Frau Liebmann, in any case, never bothered to look. It wasn't any of her business what he got up to in there. Naked but for a jock strap, Ludwig bent over a bank of flowers and crumbled the soft earth with hands that soon acquired a delicate black tracery over the palms. His skin rapidly turned warm and damp. He trod softly, delicately along the duck-boards, feet pointing slightly outwards, toes descending first, like a mannequin's. His ribs were countable, his belly had a concave curve and his knees seemed exceptionally large-jointed because the thighs and calves were so slender, yet strong muscles pulsed on them as he walked. He was conscious of a fine film of sweat on his body as he worked and relished the trickle that occasionally found its path down his narrow back.

As he went, he bent to pick off dead leaves and examined each plant minutely for signs of blight or disease. He sprayed the leaves with a fine mist from a brass can and took earthworms from a tin, laying them gently on the damp soil. His pupils knew that he would pay a good price for a tin of worms and would dig illicitly in the park for their squirming offerings. They speculated behind his back that he ate them live or distilled them into a potent drink to restore his strength: pleasurable horrors, which did nothing to lessen his prestige. He weeded and cleaned and, at last, walked to the central trough with the newest and rarest of specimens, the young,

31

struggling plants, and examined their tender furling leaves. Carefully, he cleared tiny clumps of earth from new, almost invisible, pale seedlings.

Late on summer nights, he liked to stand in the darkness and look up at the stars. But for the absence of secret animal rustlings and strange cries, he could fancy himself in the jungles of Sarawak or Borneo. Now the winter mists swirled and there was nothing to be seen but the distant orange fuzz of a street-lamp, its glow diffused through the blurred glass streaked with brighter stripes where the condensation ran down. In the summer, birds spotting the luxuriant oasis among grey stone tried to fly into the foliage and often broke their necks on the glass. Only Ludwig was permitted to enter the sanctuary; he almost believed he heard a sigh, when the cupboard door closed behind him; the murmur of a thousand leaves turning in the warm air, of blossom heads dipping in salute. He loved this place; for the heat and silence, the simplicity of growth and decay, rot and rebirth. The glass house was a refuge, which also offered an exquisite form of deferred gratification, for nothing was ever finished. It imposed its disciplines and that, too, he loved. In this place he left behind the petty discomforts of the crumbling, chilly house and forgot that rough, barren streets surrounded him. It was his personal miracle, that such flowers blossomed in Altona.

The school was an imperfect counterpart. Though Ludwig was a good teacher, never bored with the constant repetition, always soothed by the familiarity of the timetable, his boys were not as responsive to his careful nurturing. True discipline and order existed only in his private kingdom. His poor means provided an oasis for the poor, the under-privileged, the kids with no one else to turn to as well as those who paid the full price. He gave them all strength and order and rules to live by and the process used him up, tired and exhausted him. He was often frustrated by their stupidity, their resistance, their failure to understand; it was too much for one man, alone.

Tonight, though, he was happy. He knew how to make a particularly shrill sound through one of the gaps in his teeth: a startlingly loud whistle for which he hardly needed to purse his lips, which came in useful when summoning small boys. Now, while he worked, he drew in a breath and let out this steam-kettle of a noise for sheer pleasure at the prosperous turn his affairs were taking.

At ten o'clock he slipped up the stairs and into the first floor rooms he inhabited; Ludwig's bedroom was a severe space equipped with two futons and an adjoining bathroom. For twenty minutes he soaped and scrubbed himself and scraped out the dirt from under his fingernails. He lathered off the sensual film of dampness and the erotic, mossy smell that clung to the hair, as a man might shower after leaving his mistress, for fear that his wife would detect her distinctive, cloying scent.

Emerging naked from the brightness, it took a moment for him to see the figure lying on the bed, which sat up, blond hair bright in the gloom, tucking long curls behind the ears.

'How did you get in?'

'The window's open downstairs. You've been avoiding me, you've been so cold. What did I do? I did everything, just like you said, don't send me away.' The eyes pleaded. 'My father's away, no one will know.'

Wordlessly, Ludwig lay down. Bernd carefully poured oil into his small hand; inexpertely it began to massage his master's body. His flesh, in the chill air, was covered with goose pimples. 'I'll warm you,' the boy whispered. 'Is this right, am I doing what you said?'

'Be quiet, can't you?' but the body was responding. This boy had a small power over him which Ludwig was loth to acknowledge. Through half-shut eyes he could see another face on the young bright head; in a moment, he knew that some trick of the light, some accidental movement of the pale limbs would provoke, with the sweetness of sudden memory, an immediate ejaculation. But for this extraordinary resemblance, this unconscious ability of his, the boy would long since have been banished. He was such a willing lad; so very able and useful that the judo master could not, quite, do without him.

In another moment, with closed eyes, his body was shuddering in rapture. The boy stared at him through the

33

gloom; he did not expect any caresses in return. A moment later Ludwig turned over; soon he would be asleep. Carefully, Bernd slid under the covers and lay still, eyes wide open. Ludwig never spoke, afterwards. He slid into oblivion as quickly as possible; he would feel sickened in the morning, but now he slept, his breathing regular against the faint, familiar rhythms of Frau Liebmann's box of tricks. Upstairs, the old woman's needles were for once quite still as she peered in slight confusion at the baffling succession of dramatic events which made up Francis Durbridge's latest Krimi. The pink baby wool lay loosely round her swollen finger joints as she thought that perhaps, if it had been in colour, she might have understood it.

The boy spoke in the faintest of whispers into the dark. 'Why don't you care for me? Don't you love me a little bit?'

It was an unpleasant night to be out. A dank misty chill turning to frost made an ice-rink of the streets. The white Mercedes purred along the Elbchaussee keeping a few kilometres within the speed limit. Now and then it overtook an empty taxi, cruising slowly back into the centre. Victor was returning from Wedel. He had remembered the Fährhaus Schulau, where ships of every country were greeted with a blast of their national anthem, a place of official welcome, merry, hot and noisy and always crammed with tourists jostling for tables. It had not occurred to him that there was a season for welcomes, as there was for everything else. As he had entered the main room its solitary occupant, an old man, had put down his glass carefully, the better to observe the phenomenon of late entrance and retreat, the grey head swivelling with the mildly speculative curiosity of vacant old age.

It soothed Victor a little to control this big, efficient machine. He had not yet outgrown the pleasure of owning such an expensive toy. He had developed the habit of thinking through problems while on the move. He made better decisions on the ski slopes or the tennis court than in the oppressive seclusion of his office, that dependable yet stultifying environment where paper clips were counted and letters containing even one error retyped. But on this long loop of a joy-ride, as if to mock him, his thoughts circled vacantly.

Since the Reeperbahn was crowded at this hour, he chose the route through Pinnasberg, up and down the hilly little streets to the Landungsbrücke, up past the Bismarckdenkmal and across the Ost-Weststrasse to St Nikolai. He knew all the side streets; he had made this city his own. The motor idled at the traffic lights and a VW drew up alongside. With slow precision, Victor turned his head, but it was only a young couple who profited from the moment to kiss. The boy's eyes, open above the curly head he gripped so fiercely with both hands, looked defiance at the rich man.

Verwöhnt, verstört, verdorben. The spoilt generation. Victor was not alone in finding them incomprehensible, unspeakably alien. And yet they were the ones who claimed alienation and smashed up their parents' cars; they decamped to dirty communes, remembering to take their stereos and colour televisions. They grew their hair, took drugs and would not eat; they let the orthodontic miracles in their mouths decay to spite the years of enforced care. Indulged and full of hatred, children of the bourgeoisie, they studied anarchy and disaffection at their parents' expense and grumbled if lack of money obliged them to take their frightening, almost unrecognisable selves home on a ritual visit.

And, he thought, those parents could consider themselves lucky. He had often spent weekends in the houses, now grown too large, of charming, cultivated friends. Sitting in the rustic Frühstücksecke over a second cup of Kaffee Haag they would confide in him as if he, lacking that experience, were somehow wiser. They would sigh over the names of darling little children, Udo and Peter, or Ingrid's girl, or did he remember Friedrich's boy, Jürgen, children who had grown up to accuse their parents of spiritual poverty. There was a whole generation that was altogether lost, roaming India or Afghanistan barefoot. Now and then they would send home postcards which babbled in broken capitals the name of some guru. The youth of today: the product of affluent, carefully nurtured

35

childhood years. His friends were right; it was a comedy so black and sharp that only the childless could appreciate it.

Many of Victor's friends had been old enough to fight; they all remembered hardships. Of course they could not understand it. The boyhood of Victor Genscher could have been a film, one he would certainly have walked out of. It would, he thought, have been a low-budget jerky thriller for a Geissendörfer or a Fassbinder to make. A tale of low life, violence and betrayal among misfits and outcasts. Ludwig could even play his own part, the Ludwig Levi he was then, but for that dreadful mouth. Not Victor. He was transformed, a success, and he had atoned in his blameless, productive and valuable existence for the sins of that boy. The boy did not even exist; he had been suppressed into blackness, where he would remain.

Ludwig had long since been banished to that oblivion. Victor had not given him a thought for fifteen years or more. Before then, if some chance word brought back his image, he had told himself that he was dead, or as good as, lost forever behind the wall. That long-gone boy had known him well, too well, had feared him and yet they had called themselves friends, for lack of a better word, in those starving, scavenging years.

Ludwig had always been an oddity. His father was a Jew, his mother a committed Catholic, and he carried within him the inheritance of their irreconcilable differences. His was a legacy of clashing superstitions, fuelled by stories on the one hand of heretics and martyrs, saints who severed limbs and practised bloody self-mutilation for the glory of God and, on the other, by tales of centuries of oppression, of pogroms and massacres, of the sufferings of this life meekly borne with no hope of redemption in the next. He had told Victor all these things, had held nothing back. A communion of souls; that was the term Ludwig, the professed atheist, had used to describe these one-sided discussions.

These bitter parents had vied for supremacy in suffering, had countered each other's afflictions with a worse tale of God-given fury and had brought up a boy who could believe in nothing and in nobody; who readily denied them both. A

36

twisted, complex devil of a boy had sprung from these two, a boy who burned on this fuel and forged in these flames a religion of his own, a cosmology with Ludwig at its fiery heart. He had believed in himself as a saviour of souls. He had set himself up in a little 'mission' and gathered about himself a little tribe of lost children over whom he ruled.

He used to scour the bombed-out streets and half-ruined houses to gather in the abandoned children of Berlin, those who ran wild. There was no one to care whether they lived or died; the more fortunate had long been evacuated to relatives in the countryside. The pinched, white faces of those who remained could be seen among the rubble, digging for an oven which, cleaned up, could be bartered for food. Or, sharp-eyed Kippensammler, they knew how to make a cigarette with seven butts, enough to set up a juvenile entrepreneur in business. For cigarettes, it was possible to get potatoes or even the odd scrap of pork fat. The winters, bitter and long, brought Ludwig the best harvest, for his human merchandise was half-frozen, only too happy to exchange the constant insecurity of the streets for the promise of warmth and shelter. They had survivors' skills: hunger had honed brains under hair crawling with nits. They were portable assets and Ludwig claimed ration cards for the keep of each one.

Victor could still conjure up the humble, triumphant, seemingly self-sacrificing manner in which Ludwig had brought each new inmate home, as though he did not profit from them. And yet this was not the most sinister aspect; worse was the way in which he had exacted tribute from them, in body and soul.

Ludwig had cast off his parents; he knew allegiance to no gods and made himself instead the god of those boys. He ruled them sternly: he demanded from his small followers the physical courage of the martyrs, the patience and endurance of the oppressed. He expected gratitude, he expected love, because he fed them and kept them safe, and yet no parent could have imposed stricter discipline. They used to huddle together in the deep cellar as the earth rocked around them. When the sirens ceased their shrieking wail, which they could imitate to perfection, he would send them out to pick through the rubble. They brought him their daily offerings, a clearing-out of pockets which should have contained marbles, or conkers, or schoolboy treasures. A small god of chaos, what would he not achieve when the world established a new order? How he used to talk and boast and tell them that they needed him, that without him they would all be dead and gone.

Victor had been a favourite, a disciple bound by the needs of survival and unquestioning in his acceptance of the young man's authority. The boy depended upon him and feared him. Yet there had also been a kind of affection, moments of humour and simple kindness. Victor had been bound up in him in the way that a child chooses to remain with a cruel parent, any attachment being better than none. After a year in the streets he had forgotten what his parents had looked like, for there had been no memento to salvage from the blazing flat; he had thought, with a stab of fear, that he would not have recognised them in the street. What would he have done without Ludwig, whose rude caresses offered affection, of a sort? Victor remembered sitting at a campfire in the ruins, one of a small crew of ragamuffins, and the sudden warmth of Ludwig's arm around his shoulders. He had gone home with him, that night; Ludwig had gone out again to get clothes for him. He remembered that he had sobbed with gratitude, for he had thought that he was saved.

It was a miracle, in the final stages of the war, that they had survived at all; one for which Ludwig drew all the credit. Survivors, against the odds, in cold-hearted Berlin, grown prematurely wise, they had developed a pride in their parentless existence. Ludwig, who described himself as a father to all these boys, encouraged them to believe that they were indeed happier and better off with him than with those half-remembered parental ghosts.

Peace, when it came, had not changed the order of things. The devastated city, ruled from sector to sector by a different, yet always summary form of justice, obeyed above all the laws of survival. There were rules, which they had learnt to flout. They were invisible: a ragged tribe of abandoned kids who hopped between sectors in juvenile disregard of authority, at one in despising the poor tricks of the adults who froze on the starvation diet and still queued, dispirited and bitter, for half a loaf of bread. They, who knew better, stole GI petrol, coal and spam; with goods scavenged, looted and bartered, they fed and warmed this monstrous household. Later, Ludwig extracted whole cartons of foodstuffs from the soft-hearted Americans for the unfortunate orphan children. He, who had no schooling of his own, would be found presiding over 'lessons' when such goods arrived.

Herr Genscher drove his splendid car around the city centre, encircling the scene of his triumphs, and saw, in acid counterpoint, the scenes of all his failures. These ugly images would keep coming back; they crept out of some dark recess and forced themselves upon him. Ludwig had cast out a line and Victor could feel it twisting tight around his neck; a little string that connected him to his past.

He set himself, with an effort, to see the Ludwig of today. In every sense a little man. A poor man. A creature who still scavenged in back streets; who still tyrannised little boys. The boy Victor might have feared such a creature, but the man could not. He told himself that the boy was truly dead and could not be resuscitated. He would not permit this past to divert the clear course of his successful life. The monster shrank down to its true proportions and, there, it was only a hobgoblin that played his tricks on him, no devil for a child to fear.

What was it that Ludwig wanted from him? Why come to haunt him now? Seeing, now, that he had come full circle, he turned off and traversed the narrow streets and the car slid underground, lighting up the grey concrete walls. The garage was, as usual, quite empty but for Herr Wachtel's car. It was absurd that Victor should even think to look.

# Chapter 4

Wednesday, December 3, 1971

I overslept again this morning, having stayed up too late writing. It's a long way from Blankenese to the university and sometimes, when Kröger's Treppe is iced up or I stand and wait for the little bus, I regret choosing to live here, despite the beauty of the little villas, ochre and pink and beige blending as they climb up the hill over each other's gardens to the Süllberg. Oma wanted me to live in Pöseldorf, the 'snob' English quarter, and precisely because it is that and because of its touristy preciousness, I was put off, though I could have walked from there to lectures. But I do love the Elbe and all my windows look onto the river, so I can watch the huge container ships slide from the kitchen into the sitting room and on into the bedroom. I am right opposite the rocky little beach. It will be charming in the summer, but it's melancholy now. The wind howls and the foghorns boom across the icy water.

For such an affluent suburb, Blankenese has its oddities. A tall, thin, pimply youth in a raincoat with enormously flapping bell-bottoms, who didn't even have gloves and must have been freezing, sat behind me in the bus. He was just in front of me in the train and lurked all the way from Dammtor to the university, his red-chapped face bobbing along the Rothenbaumchaussee. He was unmistakable, with orangey-red hair that stuck up in whorls. He couldn't possibly have been a student, his weirdness being a different sort altogether, but he followed me right into the building. He didn't venture into Aula II when, horribly late for Dr Heinrich's lecture on phonemes, I tiptoed in. That at least was understandable. Now, in the natural German academic response to excruciating boredom, I hear they've made his course obligatory. Normally it's Turks who follow me, scenting the foreignness, and offering drinks in bars in their funny accents spiced with rich colloquialisms.

I feel happy today and of course Victor is at the back of it. I had news of him unexpectedly at dinner in the Ratsweinkeller. Tante Mausi thought that was a suitable place for her little celebration of Ingrid's engagement as it's so traditional. The fiancé is called Peter Schwantz, which is a bit of a joke as it generally means prick. Poor Ingrid. She's always despised the beery connotations of her name and hoped for a von. Despite this drawback, he's perfect for her: tall, Teutonic, precise, worthy, well-to-do and incredibly dull. They will have three blond children for her to dragoon. I expect they'll give proper dinner parties with fine displays of their wedding present silver and Ingrid will keep a little book recording what she wore and what they ate. Ingrid was a middle-aged baby and her young years weigh heavily on her; she can't wait to become a respectable matron.

It was the best-man-to-be who knew Victor, a youngish banking colleague whose ears pricked up when he heard the name Rommer. He drifted over to ask half-heartedly whether I was related to 'the' Rommers. With my 'wild hippie hair' to quote Ingrid's endearingly frank words – ah, Ingrid's charm! – and the English accent I never quite disguise, he clearly expected me to say no. He's called Uwe Schenck and had on a desperately sober dark grey suit, his stripy tie regimented by a horse's head pin; a laughing nag with a nagging laugh. Now if he'd really known Ingrid, he'd have been fully informed about us. He wasn't the sort, though, to know anyone, not

41

even Peter, whose depths could easily be plumbed with a shortish bit of string. I saw it all; they must have gone together to the baby banker training school and, being Schs, sat together, and Peter will have noted Uwe's thin old silver cuff links with a crest on them and known he was okay. Then real intimacy developed; they will have shared sandwiches and had a beer together and borrowed each other's slide-rules and furled black umbrellas.

Uwe had, however, the redeeming virtue of being most interested in Victor. He has been meeting with him, in some junior capacity, over a vast loan Victor's getting from his bank. He said he had a 'verblüffende Intelligenz' and laughed, as though that was a joke; very disconcerting until it became clear that he laughs at everything he says. He throws back his head to let out his mirth presenting a fine expanse of double chin, beautifully smooth pink skin it was too. He told me all about Victor's interesting mind, his interesting travels and how interesting it was that he was also a good sportsman. I, of course, agreed. By contrast, in fact simply by failing to smile much, the prick appeared very erudite. A solemn young man and just the thing for Ingrid. I stuck by Uwe for a bit, even this crumb being a feast to me. Old Tiedemann tells me nothing; he's under Oma's thumb.

Peter, Ingrid and Uwe suit each other. They are kindred souls. They have neatly ordered lives in which everything happens according to plan; perfect banker material and Ingrid a tailor-made wife. She always wanted to marry young and next year when she's twenty-two it will be high time to start the baby programme, at a correct and decent interval after the wedding, naturally. Poor Uncle Hansi. She'll have him in tails and a top hat in which he'll look ridiculous. She will ask me to be maid of honour, in pink or yellow shiny material, and take care to throw her bouquet at me in a conscious, pitying way after the ceremony with a kind smile.

The evening had its moments. The clear oxtail soup was horrible, but the pheasant delicious, Ingrid's full of shot which she bit upon to her outrage, for her perfect front teeth are all capped. It was a study to see her fiancé's face while she gave the waiter a drubbing. The poor old man explained courteously that this was inevitable with game, provoking an imagined loss of face which made her all the more viperish. She turned up her nose, insofar as that is possible, at the bombe with flambé'd cherries. Too cold for the delicate dentures I suppose; not appropriate for a winter's dessert, she said snottily.

Peter's parents, an unassuming couple, pretended not to hear any of this while Tante Mausi blushed and twittered. Uncle Hansi with his strong Rhineland accent hardly dared utter a word the whole evening. We agreed to meet secretly for a beer before they go home. I know a little Kneipe near the university which is just right and Linda'll be here by then. He'll like her. The archetypal English rose, plump and pink and accommodating and underneath quite savagely determined to get her own way. Uncle Hansi likes to like everyone; he loves to be comfortable and wants everyone to be happy. Nothing daunts him, only misery makes him miserable, particularly the tight-lipped martyrish sort Ingrid has in such abundance.

I still call him Uncle, it sounds natural, though he says with a great sigh that it makes him feel old and since Mausi's a half-aunt he's only half an uncle and that the other half feels so much younger. Incredibly, I called Victor Uncle until Opa died. Uncle, Uncle, Uncle, his title hops across the round childish script and the later, italic affectations of my childhood diaries. I still have them, dozens of exercise books, half of them elegant hard-back ones with swirly pink and blue marbled end-sheets. I used to beg him to bring me those from Germany. I wonder if he knew why I wanted them so badly? I credit him with sufficient prescience. There's the word at the back, in a long list of vocabulary with definitions. I used to try and learn grown-up words to impress him, chanting the definitions until I knew them by heart. Pabulum, excoriate, hegemony, what fascinating conversations I must have offered.

My bouts of intensive self-improvement coincided, naturally, with Victor's visits; then there were our trips abroad, which often seemed to go through Hamburg. He never would stay with us, despite Oma's insistent, kind invitations, preferring independence in grubby little hotels. Later he graduated to first-class establishments. We all looked forward to Victor; Oma for the gossip and women's magazines she, ever frugal, would never have bought for herself; Opa for the long lunches in expensive, men-only places. He marked these occasions by taking his best pipe and putting on his heavy gold cufflinks. I would see Victor at least twice; once when he came and paid his respects to Oma and then at the family dinner in town. Victor would ask politely after school and listen attentively to my inane, vague replies, for I could never think of anything at all witty or interesting to say, for all the hours of rehearsals beforehand. They all conspired to keep me a schoolgirl. I longed to wear stockings instead of the socks Oma considered proper. The dinners were rendered tasteless and joyless in advance because of the awfulness of the little tartan dresses with white collars and cuffs and the socks and flat shoes. In Linda's bedroom we would try on her mother's outfits with nylons, applying thick twigs of eyeliner and pale lipstick, our hair dampened into straightness, so we looked like middle-aged Cathy McGowans. We were always staggered by our sophistication and elegance, though the suspender belts hurt and we couldn't walk in heels without twisting an ankle. How I longed for Victor to see this transformed, adult me.

As each unsatisfactory visit ended, undaunted I started to tick off the days until the next. I learnt to ski at the resorts Victor recommended and sometimes at St Moritz or Ulm I would see him. I have the entry for the appalling Christmas when I bumped drearily down the moguls behind him and an elegant woman whose thick, fashionable Norwegian sweaters emphasised her large breasts. Despite her natural imbalance, she never fell down, as I so often did. A gawky, underdeveloped thirteen-year-old, thin and spindly, I loitered and pretended my sulks related to scrapes and bruises.

'Today Uncle Victor did the Olympic run twice with Inge. They are going dancing tonight. He said he would call in for hot grog but never came.'

'Today I saw Uncle Victor on the toboggans. Opa says they are too dangerous for me. Uncle Victor agreed but he said we would go skating together.'

44

'Today Uncle Victor came to say good-bye. He has to go back to the office early. He said he was sorry about the skating and another time, but it will be a year before we come back here. Oma said I was rude and should try to be more polished. Look at Inge, she said, she's smiling yet her holiday is ruined.'

That page is blotted with passionate, selfish tears. My diary entries were kept carefully neutral, for fear of spies, but they are as transparent as I was. Not only did I anticipate his visits with joy, lapsing into sorrows and sulks when he left, I also forced myself upon him. I would sit right in the centre of the back seat of the Mercedes when he drove, staring at his blue eyes in the driving mirror for long, rapturous moments. It never occurred to me that the mirror worked both ways, a realisation that at the time of my first driving lessons drew waves of inexplicable blushes.

Uncle Victor never embarrassed me; he showed no aware-ness of this smouldering, schoolgirl crush. While I longed for some sign, I was also relieved. There was a kind of a rapport, though, a hint of a look, suggesting friendly complicity, that told me he was aware of me in a way that seemed both adult and safe. He knew, of course, that I was ready to fall into his arms. Humiliatingly willing and ready. I never questioned that he loved me; it was enough that he said he did. I would no more have doubted the laws of gravity.

At seventeen I was quite corrupted by love. Not physically, but mentally. I was ready to practise deceit, not to tell Oma, knowing that much as she liked and depended upon Victor, she would never approve of him for me. I assumed that she would always carry on looking after me and wanting the best for me and meanwhile I mentally shuffled her off to the wings in order for Victor to occupy centre-stage. In fact he needed Oma far more than he needed me; I am the interlude in Victor's story that turned out to be dispensable.

At seventeen, I saw nothing. I had my eyes screwed tightly shut. Love, in my case, was not just blind, but deaf and dumb and stupid to boot. I had decided that we were two souls pre-destined for each other, it was Kismet, fate, all that crap. In that last A-level year I was repellent, day-dreaming, wander-ing around with a sickening smile in love's young dream. In

Victor's absence, I cast around for an acceptable bit of literature to moon over and thought I'd got it in *Wahlverwandt-schaften*. The theory was made for me: that people, like chemical elements, are irresistibly attracted to new partners when they touch, as though it were pre-ordained. Elective affinities when bound pairs of elements interchange: Johanna/grandparents + Victor = Johanna/Victor + grandparents.

The theory was laid out in the book with simple illustrations which we schoolgirl chemists tittered at patronisingly. Calcium oxide + sulphuric acid = calcium sulphate + oxides – though Goethe poetically called them tragic, abandoned vapours. How our hands shot up in class. He's forgotten about $H_2O$, we said, little clever-clogses, as though that put us one up on genius. The story ended badly, but I ignored the bits that didn't fit. Goethe was gospel for my German love; proof, as though I needed it, that literature and life skipped along hand in hand. I was going to have the happy ending, even though I was old enough to realise that the best books, unlike Mills and Boon, went miles out of their way to avoid that.

At that time, I not only believed practically everything I read, but preferred books by far to any actual experience. Who would want to snog with some pimply youth, his breath reeking of beer, to suffer his unpleasant fumblings as the penalty for boasting of a boyfriend, when there was real love and life right there on the library shelves? Linda would drag me out, but I preferred to spend Saturday nights at home, in Rome with Daisy Miller or in Paris wearing a white gardenia. Undiscriminating, but always trying to be literary, with Lorca and Lawrence, Mailer and Molière, the whole mixed-up stew of pretentious adolescence, set books and secret ones sweetened with furtive, saccharine drops: Jean Plaidy and Georgette Heyer. There was nothing in my North London reality to compare with those books; nobody in the juvenile mob, so proud of their first cars, notching up the number of times, they'd got off with somebody or furtively losing their virginity in their parents' bedroom on a Saturday night, who could attract me. I was, instead, defiantly intellectual. A swot with all the answers. Above all, I considered myself a German. It was at my insistence that we spoke only German at home, for I was preparing myself for Victor. My intended was the very stuff from which great German heroes were made.

It couldn't possibly go wrong; not when I had all those authors crammed into my head, not to mention the lists of words, the conjugating and declining, the strong and weak verbs and the pluperfect subjunctive. He, clearly, had not been able to resist all those concentrated hours of yearning, dreams and fantasies beamed at his unprotected head. I had willed Victor to happen; the shock of it having, miraculously, worked, was soon succeeded by blasé acceptance of my powers. Years of effort went into Victor and me, ce couple inouï. I got quite an education courtesy of Victor. Never in the sense of being prepared for life, but book-learning; I owe Messrs Schiller, Burger, Heinrich et al to my Uncle Victor. A dubious heritage.

The strangest thing has just happened. I am going to write it down very calmly. It's just an odd little incident, one of those bizarre things that happen abroad and never in England.

It is very late, nearly three in the morning. The melancholy mourning of a foghorn on the river just drew me to the curtains. I leave them open to let in the night lights and to hell with the draughts. That pimply boy was in the road, standing under the street lamp opposite and looking straight up at my window, as though he was waiting for me. He gave a tremendous jump when he saw me and darted across the street. He might not have gone away. He might just have taken cover where I can't see him.

I saw him distinctly, it gave me such a shock. He is unmistakable. I pulled the curtains to at once and ran to the door, which is double locked, and then I checked the window locks, as though he were a monkey who could climb up to the second floor to frighten me. With the curtains drawn, I'm frightened to look out, which I know is stupid of me. There's something horrible about the idea of leaning out and seeing him looking up just below.

There, I've written the number of the police station in the margin here. It would take them two minutes to get here at this time of night, probably less. I'm quite safe, the door is bolted on the inside and it has a chain, so there's no need for

47

my heart to go on thumping so fast in this pathetic way. He must be some kind of loony. Adolescents are always freaking out and doing weird things, especially German kids who are affluent and snotty and hate everyone and know everything. It's just that at night everything seems sinister when you're alone. I'm going to look out now. It's stupid to be frightened and sit here in a panic when he's probably gone away.

# Chapter 5

The boy had been running and was still panting. His loose trouser bottoms were wet and trailed damp threads on the mat. He bent and a drop fell from the pink nose as he laboriously untied his shoelaces.

'She saw me,' he said. 'Yesterday I thought she had and then early this morning she looked out of the fucking window. Stayed too long, didn't I,' and pulling off the shoes and damp, black-toed socks, he seated himself heavily and rested his head in giant's hands. 'I'm done in,' he said and still dared not meet Ludwig's eye. 'Got any booze?'

It was five o'clock in the morning. Rocking on the smooth soles of his feet, Ludwig looked at this poor speciment with pity and distaste. There were curling tufts of red hair on each of the grubby big toes. He was barely seventeen, but it was hard to find any trace of the interesting pallor of three years ago under the stubble on the raw cheeks.

'Jasmine tea,' Ludwig said. Georg knew he didn't drink; that was his poor piece of self-assertiveness. 'I'll make it while you tell me about it. She saw you twice? A beacon, that's what you are, with that hair,' and he clapped him on the back and led him off into the back room, as the trainer leads the tamed beast twice his size. He extracted the meagre details while the great red hands warmed themselves on the tiny porcelain cup.

The lad breathed in the steam like an asthmatic.

The tart sat up late, Georg said, and how was he to know she'd look out and catch him there? He expressed scorn for the fancy suburb. Yes, he knew he'd fucked it up and he darted another glance at Ludwig and started to tell it all over again with emphasis on the misdemeanours of the fucking tart. He had an adult, swaggering vocabulary, an obscene set of phrases whereby each woman was a cunt, each man a prick, every person reduced to their reproductive element, though he of course had no experience of that form of conjugation. What self-respecting girl would waste her time with a creature like this? He did not have the money for the other kind. Ludwig was the only person who had ever squandered a little kindness on the poor brute and that was why, for all his vehemence, he kept looking anxiously at his protector, conscious of another little failure to add to the huge catalogue of errors that made up his short life.

Ludwig was kind to him. He gave him money; he pointed him towards the mat. 'You have to go at eight,' he said, 'before the old woman comes down,' and the boy curled up like a dog and thought himself lucky. Georg had not dared let on about the police and anyway the fucking pigs didn't get him, did they? Soon he slept; Ludwig lay upstairs and thought that they were right, the people who said that nothing could be done with Georg. He did not blame him for inadequacies he could not help; boys with possibilities were treated far more severely. This one was a hopeless case, who passed his days in amusement arcades when he had money. Drop-out from a special school which had defined him as unreachable, off-spring of a mother who, despite her age, still plied her trade down in the docks, he was not welcome home at night. He had been taught by his mother to drink for pleasure, as another might have encouraged reading or chess, and he sniffed around for alcohol. He was happiest in the late-night dock-side Kneipen where he joined in the laughter. There regulars sometimes bought him a drink for the amusement of seeing him gulp at it so eagerly and of bursting into laughter when they did.

Ludwig lay on his back. He tensed and then relaxed one

muscle after another until his body lay heavy and inert, as though a great weight were pressing on it. Still sleep did not come. A car door slammed; footsteps then laughter and a scuffling, running noise. He heard them all with exceptional acuity. Georg was snoring; an occasional grunting inhalation rumbled up the stairs. He wished him gone. Then he could have gone downstairs to meditate. He had no other way to release himself from the ceaseless ticking away of his thoughts.

Why could he not meditate in this room? He wanted to try, now, but the heavy body refused to move. It wanted the space, the familiar faint smell of sweat in the big room; it wanted the mat. Denied these, it would oblige him to wait for the grey morning light. What power this sack of flesh had over him and yet he never let it alone. He worked it and starved it; he would not have treated an animal so badly. He wondered whether other people, who pampered and over-fed themselves, found their flesh so stubborn. He could labour all day without tiring, could sit for hours in perfect stillness, but his body was a beast, well-trained but secretly rebellious. He ached, now, for release from it and it asserted itself with a cramping of muscles which contorted his cold feet into sharp, painful arcs. He did not move; he would not pander to it.

The old judoka who had taught him about zen had had the ability to master men of half his age and twice his strength. As frail-looking and bleached as brittle driftwood, he used to stand and wait for his opponent to make a move. They, approaching him, seemed to propel themselves onto the mat; his motions were so effortless, so spry and swift, that it was almost impossible to see how he had thrown them. He had explained to Ludwig that he released his mind; that dull-witted thing that thought too slowly and made mistakes, thus liberating his body. The body knew what to do. Its movements, trained by hundreds of thousands of repetitions, were perfect, quite automatic; the body responded faster than the brain could tell it to. He had grinned at Ludwig from his clever old face in which a scarcity of teeth bore witness to a childhood of malnutrition. The old man liked himself; he was pleased with himself in a simple, naïve way and, as he bowed in the correct manner, showing humility in victory, the slitted eyes gleamed with secret happiness. His had seemed to Ludwig a life enviably simple and satisfying: a life concentrated down to the purest possible elements. The body was trained and hardy and the mind released, to soar.

Ludwig, who had thought then that he would be a champion, now knew that he lacked the simplicity which he strove so hard to attain. He was too Western, too complicated; he was a disappointed man. When he explained the notion of zen to the advanced pupils, they thought he was initiating them into a secret how-to-win technique. They would listen very hard, the effort of understanding visible in strained faces. He felt sympathy for them then; pity and understanding of them, so rooted in their coarse-boned bodies and adolescent minds. How could they comprehend? They did not even have conventional religious beliefs; they did not even realise that they had nothing and laboured in a void.

The art could only be mastered in a perfect environment. It had to be a school where the boys lived, where the harmony of surroundings and their simplicity gave the lesson more vividly than any amount of talking. A home for the needy and lost, for the abandoned children of the city, an oasis of rigorous, yet elegant schooling. He could see its white-washed walls and a garden in which nature gathered its most exquisite creations and he tended the young, growing things.

The first steely light shone upon a rigid body and dry-eyed, calculating face. He could not rest when there were so many matters still to be resolved. He cursed his own slowness in failing to find a simple solution to the problem of this girl, and he refused himself the hot tea which made the early mornings pleasant.

He was sharp that day, alarmingly alert, and he terrorised the little boys in the ten o'clock class with his cunning feints and appalling swiftness. Georg had left a dirty mark upon the mat which a grudging Frau Liebmann was set upon to scrub, for it was expensive and not to be replaced in a hurry. She stared accusingly into each face looking for the perpetrator of this filth and her cry of 'Schuhe abziehen!' grew particularly shrill as a result.

Small heads bowed solemnly before each session of Randori; little bodies thumped down. Ludwig thought about the piece to fit this jig-saw. Bit by bit, he had assembled the outline of a worthless, self-seeking life, a picture by numbers which took on tone and shade as the little blobs were coloured in. He did not know how large an expanse of white space Fräulein Rommer occupied.

Ludwig had found his golden boy by chance. By the merest fluke, he had glanced at a copy of *Der Abend* which Frau Liebmann, clucking angrily, had worked out from behind two pipes on the first floor landing. He thought it remarkable that Victor should be enmeshed in the very fabric of his house. Ludwig, who always discarded such trash and never wasted his money on a newspaper, was destined to open it, idly, as he did. He was intended to see the photograph now taped to the drawer inside his desk.

'Prominenten am Spiel', the column was called, with pictures of pop singers and politicians, captains of industry and patrons of the arts, all smirking and drinking too much at parties and nightclubs; caught out with the wrong company or the wrong expression on their stupid faces. And there, where he had no place to be, not possessing a famous name, had stood Victor, edge to edge with the heir to a tobacco fortune and a playboy millionaire turned racing-driver. Victor, unmistakable, with a fatuous smile on his face and one arm round a ripe teetering blonde. Steering a new course? it said. Victor Genscher of Rommer Reederei escorts Miss Nordrhein-Westphalen at the seamen's charity ball.

The shock had set a loud pulse drumming at his temple; then drained blood from his head and sent the excess throbbing round his body. It had never occurred to him that Victor might have survived; he was so clearly the sort to come to a bad end. That he could have prospered was staggering, inconceivable. Ludwig had thought about him every day of his life with sadness, with regret, with the poignancy of desire for lost beauty and youth. It was not lost at all; the handsome face fulfilled that promise at least.

He had known at once that something would happen, but for a long time did nothing. For months the cutting lay in his drawer to be fingered and re-read until the words took on a new and cryptic significance. He was not a man to undertake anything rashly; he would never have embarked upon such a protracted and difficult exercise had he not first convinced himself of its righteousness. He saw, then, that Victor was his purpose. Ludwig had been ripe for a cause and this one was irresistible.

Ludwig's golden age, his time of plenty and benevolent exercise of power, had come to an abrupt end because of Victor. They had formed an invisible and self-sufficient community; now the punitive boot of the Allied Occupation stamped down hard on them. The entire nation bartered to survive, GIs made fortunes from their sufferings and ex-Nazis, denied employment, were growing fat on the black market. Ludwig, who had succoured the needy, was selected for punishment. They had requisitioned his house, taken away the children and imprisoned him. Youths over fourteen were set to salvaging the rubble, brick by brick; the German nation was collectively guilty and should suffer, that was the penalty imposed by the peace-loving nations which had conquered them. Ludwig, who had lost all that he possessed, was a marked man, a criminal. All this was the result of Victor's violence, and for years Ludwig had blamed and regretted him and asked himself where he had gone wrong. Necessity had obliged him to create a living from his hobby and he who, however depressed, was never a defeatist, had made the best of it. He had never ceased to mourn Victor. He had yearned, often, for the impossible: to have that time again.

In due course Ludwig had achieved an uneasy compromise with himself. He had accepted his way of life with its insecurities; he had a constant, irrepressible fear that this, too, could be taken away from him. He was not a happy man, that capacity mislaid alongside his sense of purpose. The unexpected, the sudden advent of Victor, so confident and unrepentant that he had not even bothered to change his name, had brought a small measure of joy into Ludwig's life. He had abruptly ceased to regret any of it; the past had retreated to its proper place as a necessary preamble for the events to follow.

As all this clarified, he had set himself to the work of

discovering what he could about Victor Genscher. It had been easy to find the imposing office building; no trouble to discover where the great man lived, nor to locate the garage where he parked his expensive cars. He had found out what he could about the business, seemingly successful and typical of its type. He had watched old Tiedemann all the way to his leafy suburb; accompanied the prim, tight-arsed secretary with her bag of crochet to Barmbek; tracked the Jewish one to his basement flat in Eimsbüttel. He had struck up a conversation once with the other man in a Kneipe, a halting desultory sort of a conversation over a Berliner Weisse, to do with the weather and the shocking state of football. The man was ill-at-ease, unwilling to be talked to, stiff-necked and taciturn and unfriendly to strangers as Hamburgers often were. Ludwig went back another night, and another, but did not see the man again. He knew better than to try the spinster living with her old mother, knew the effect of his pleasant smile upon impressionable females.

Exhausting these avenues, he had pursued a more fruitful course: a foray into the past. Writing did not come easily to Ludwig and he laboured for many nights on his document, his record of the Prominenten's not-so-respectable past. It was quite a work of art, tied up in green ribbon, one copy safely deposited with a solicitor.

Ludwig did not think or speak in long words. When it came to writing something down, he fell into a curious style. This mixed the sort of words he remembered from the wooden benches of Sunday school all those years ago with what he felt was a legal touch; there was something in it of the Volksschule schoolmaster he might, in other circumstances, have become. He wrote with tremendous effort and very slowly, weighing each word and putting it down with heavy pressure on the paper. Later, typing it out on the old machine, he had found his words strangely impressive.

It was a long piece of work which ran to fifty typewritten pages, executed with the utmost care by two of his bony fingers. He had typed so late into the night that Frau Liebmann had accused him, at one point, of writing a book. This idea, so worthy of derision in her mind, had given rise to her choking snort of a laugh.

Herr Meister Judo had produced a detailed, cunning document. His memory was excellent and he had spun out of it a web of intricate detail. As triumphant dénouement, he had added an appendix. This was the damning testimony, as it were – for Ludwig saw this document as a trial which simultaneously examined, judged and sentenced the accused – of a certain Frau Meyer. She was a very old lady now and he had had the good fortune to find her in Berlin. The truth itself was harsh; he had not shrunk from it, nor had he completely exonerated himself. To achieve his aims he needed a strong weapon. Frau Meyer's words gave him a blunt, hard club to beat a man into a new form.

The trip had been expensive. He came close to cancelling it a dozen times and put it off almost half as often, for he was close with money and hated unnecessary expense. He had gone, grudgingly, certain it would be futile, six months before. He had chosen a time when a great number of children were on summer holidays and when classes had shrunk to the die-hards, local kids who paid a reduced rate and were so often absent from school that holidays made practically no difference to their small calendar of events. So he had closed the school for three days for the first time; it could not be longer for he did not trust Frau Liebmann in the conservatory, indeed access was strictly denied her, and who was to water his leafy jungle?

The old street still stood. There, by a miracle, sat the old lady in the same apartment, ancient and arthritic, half-blind, willing to talk to anyone who said he remembered her boy and still able to squeeze tears out of her rheumy eyes. She could not quite make out Ludwig's face but half-thought she remembered what she saw of it. Certainly, she recognised her son from his description of a young life, needlessly wasted, a flower snapped in full bloom. She thought, without knowing exactly why, for Ludwig had put the idea into her head, that he came in some official capacity. She thought that the state would, at last, be erecting some suitable memorial or, at the very least, rewarding her for years of suffering with a handsome pension. He did not disillusion her; no doubt she waited still for the fat manila envelope bearing the glad tidings to come through the door.

Ludwig had asked Frau Meyer a good number of searching questions. Discovering that she knew very little of the truth, he evolved a story by degrees, one not far distant from the reality of events that were, after all, over twenty years ago. She smiled as he refreshed her memory; he listened while she brought out old tales of the clever little boy, born to delight her in early middle age, stories of his many talents and promise. And, in the end, over a bottle of cognac he had had the foresight to provide, he had got her to dictate these details to her neighbour, for she could not write with her shaky old hand. He had thought, too, to get another neighbour in to append her round signature to the whole. It had been quite an event in the neighbourhood and for many months to come these three would recall the visit of the pleasant official and wonder when the pension would come and say a hundred times that these things took time, for hadn't it taken years for the case to be looked at at all? The old lady was soon convinced that she had initiated the whole thing herself and would congratulate herself on her persistence in never giving up the memory of her Wilfried, no, never, not while there was a breath to draw in her old body.

Perhaps it was an act of charity that Ludwig had carried out. His visit had quite cleared away from her mind any lingering memories she had that her boy had not always been so good; that he had fallen into evil ways and indeed that she had told him he would go to the devil a thousand times. She remembered, now, a young man so good, so noble and generous that he'd have been driving her around in a big car, had he lived, for he loved his old mother so, and feasting her just as she intended to treat her kind neighbours the day her boat came in.

Ludwig had had this document safe for some time and yet held back, waiting for his moment. Meanwhile Victor grew a number of dark shadows, who followed him in expensive taxis around his evening haunts and hung around outside for a glimpse of the well-dressed gentleman with his latest inamorata on his arm.

A time had come when Ludwig detected change. Victor began absenting himself from the office, paying frequent visits to the bank and neglecting his expensive, fancy women. Ludwig, sensing disarray, obliged him into the long-awaited meeting. It had disturbed him that the man proved so fortified, so hidden and unmoved, that he could not gauge his reaction. He, who knew everything, had counted on the effect of shock to reveal yet more. Because he could not afford a rejection, he found himself growing anxious. Here was a man without close friends, with women in abundance whom he took to hotels, like whores; a man who believed himself secure. That was what made the Rommer girl important. Her position had to make her a lever to move him; a chink in the façade. What young girl was not malleable, susceptible, gossipy? He would find a way to use her.

It was a pity that his special boys were so young. Ludwig had raised these urchins from the gutter and taught them to master pain and endure setbacks, to be modest in their occasional triumphs. He gave talks in local schools on the character-forming aspects of the sport and never failed to attract new pupils, drawn initially by the attractive notion of a small expert easily defeating a larger foe. When the bullies had been weeded out, a gratifying percentage remained. The more intelligent of these formed an inner circle, a small, trained battalion that he could deploy.

Bernd, who aspired to leadership, who had an unquench-able enthusiasm for taking the initiative, had taken it upon himself to follow the girl home, returning triumphant with the revelation that this occasional visitor to the office was J. Rommer. He wished it had been anybody but Bernd. He could not help feeling aversion for the boy for besmirching him, for his evident incomprehension and pale, silently accusing face, for his never ceasing to try and attach him.

Ludwig reviewed the young men of his acquaintance. He did this while, mechanically, taking a group of twelve-year-olds through Osoto-gari. A simple throw, unusual in sending the opponent backwards onto the mat. He kept advancing, right leg forwards, towards young Piepe, who failed each time to use the opening.

'Use your head, Piepe, if you have that ability.' The other boys smiled; Piepe kept on hooking feebly, ineffectually, with his chubby right leg.

'Clearly not,' he said. 'As a child could see, my dear Piepe, you also need to use your right arm. Watch,' and he beckoned forwards Schultz. Teacher's pet.

Schultz, with his bullet-headed obstinacy, would never join the inner circle, but he had a natural talent for the sport. Ludwig knew that a good teacher had to dazzle a little, when the kids began to lose interest, when they were starting to get tired and frustrated. There was no horseplay in the Becker-strasse, no boisterous larking about, none of the neck-lock strangleholds that could be observed in supposedly better establishments.

Schultz neatly went over backwards for the second time and came up smiling. The mechanics of judo were simple enough. The opponent had to be caught off balance, so he could be thrown along his weak direction of posture, force used against itself. As Piepe tried again, Ludwig said to himself that, yes, Victor was indeed off balance. Roughly, for he would not learn, he threw the boy, who was clutching ineffectually at his jacket.

The lesson was ending and the roomful of boys lined up in the approved manner, sitting on their heels in order of rank.

'Sensei ni Rei!' A gruff shout from Kiechle, the senior student present, who for some moments now had been clearing his throat in anticipation of the honour and in dread of that post-pubescent squeak that sometimes betrayed him and made the little boys snigger. They all bowed; Ludwig bowed back.

The rabble of little boys scurried around, throwing off jackets, scuffling around for shoes and socks and breaking into an enervating chatter. A tall, dark youth standing in the doorway was watching the scene with a faint sneer. Seeing Ludwig observing him, he nodded at him, as one man to another, and leant back against the wall, crossing bony legs with studied nonchalance to show off high-heeled Cuban boots, an object of aspiration for every passing boy.

Now that he was fifteen, Wolfgang Schmidt considered

himself a man, that maturity signalled by the acquisition of such badges of manhood as boots and a short black jacket with an elasticated waist. This had a leather grain imprinted on its shiny surface and evidently he believed that it could pass for the real thing. Though not a pupil, he spent much of his time hanging around the school waiting for Bernd and his other friend, Heini. Ludwig looked at him and, suddenly, remembering, he smiled.

Wolf's brother was in his entirety an object of the deepest envy for the small fry, who dispersed, however, too soon to glimpse the paragon's arrival. Tall, well-built, in an expensive black leather jacket, he had a face so Italian, so patrician, that nobody would have taken him for the Hanseatic he undoubtedly was. He had, too, that Mediterranean self-assurance and air of grooming. An angular bump in the polo-neck sweater showed where some pendant, a medallion or tribal token dangled. This had to be assumed to be gold, such was the expense of his appearance.

'Incredible,' he said, dark eyes swivelling in slow derision. 'It's all the same. It's like a time warp in here.' Change was clearly a highly desirable phenomenon in his eyes. Unbidden, he threw himself onto a chair, nearly toppling it.

Ludwig, still wearing his thick white jacket and trousers, sat cross-legged on the narrow chair in delicate balance and smiled affably at the renegade.

'I preserve everything,' he said. 'What's this but continuity, of a kind, a museum to a thousand boyhoods? Why should I change it? It's only the young who must have everything new all the time. Now, don't you feel nostalgia, sitting here?' and he smiled at the expression on Sigi's face. 'How much more difficult life is outside, eh, Sigi?' and he went on, flippant and accusing, 'Your brother tells me you're still out of a job and when I think – oh I do think about you dear boy – of your poor old mother still slaving away – what a very nice jacket you have. What a fine skin,' and he reached out a hand and laughed when the young man drew away.

'Lay off,' Sigi said unpleasantly and extracted a packet of cigarettes from an inner pocket, puffing out the smoke in Ludwig's direction. 'Wolf said you had an interesting proposition to make. That's the only reason for my coming.'

How blunt he was, direct and confident. Sigi was not just typical of his kind, he was the very archetype. That was what made him such an inspired choice.

'Let me think now,' he said slowly, as though he was considering it. 'A proposal, yes. You see me here in an unusual role, my dear boy. So very unusual that I can hardly believe it myself. Can you see me as a matchmaker? But that's what I am, just for you. I have a delightful proposition, a young, rich girl, living alone in a most select neighbourhood. The girl of your dreams, the sort you, dear boy, would never meet. And I am going to introduce you to this marvel, no – don't thank me yet – ' the young man, who had not opened his mouth, was staring at him with the most curious expression – 'later you can express your gratitude. When you have, how shall I put it, examined the merchandise.'

'You're a cold-blooded swine, do you know that Ludwig?' Sigi was stung, defensive. 'I know your merchandise, it's not the kind I like,' and a speck of ash dropped onto one gleaming black shoe, a loafer with a gilt chain, and was flicked away irritably.

'Not so hasty dear boy,' and Ludwig made a show of locating, after some rifling through the bottom drawer of the desk, a small rag which he offered solicitously and which was refused. 'There's even money in it – now leave that shoe alone, won't you? Oh, does it mar your beauty? A lot of money. In return for which I expect only information, of a particular kind, the sort of little details you young people tell each other when you're like that,' and he held up two crossed fingers and stroked them, leering, with the digit of the other hand. 'Five thousand, Sigi, what do you say to that?'

'Five thousand?' The young man's tone was incredulous. 'There's something very – ' and he searched in vain for the word.

'I see. Nice of you to come, my dear boy. I've got a business to run. If you're not interested, you can go,' and Ludwig picked a paper out of the pile on the desk and scanned it. He waved a hand at the young man. 'Shoo, go away, can't you see I'm busy?'

Sigi ground his cigarette out on the floor with an unnecessarily vicious twist of the foot.

'What are you after? What's it all about? Come on, Ludwig, you've got to explain.'

Clearly, the bait was so large that the little fish had trouble swallowing it. Ludwig sat back, watching the hot brown eyes which cupidity had sharpened.

'Shall I tell you a little story? Once upon a time, my dear Sigi, when I was young and foolish – no, never that, but shall we say more credulous, I lent a large sum to a man who never repaid it. Who disappeared. Now you mustn't cry too much for me, for I've come across him again. He's wealthy now, he can easily afford it, but he refuses. He acknowledges his debt, but he doesn't want to pay. I'm a poor man and he thinks he can play with me. Now if I were rich and had influential friends, he'd have paid up at once, so you see what a sham morality his is. Now of course he won't be let off so easily.' Sigi was twisting about in his chair; now he took his jacket off and folded it carefully over his knees.

'Oh, am I boring you?' he asked solicitously. 'Another moment and I'm done, do you think you can manage that?'

The brown eyes expressed resentment, but Sigi smiled, an easy, winning smile. He was extraordinarily handsome.

'The girl, my dear Sigi, is a kind of relation of his. She doesn't know about this debt, but she knows him, she's involved in his business. I want information on that, on his private life, anything. I shall make use of it merely to approach him. Do you begin to understand? Are you following? Good.' The young man listened intently; he had, at least, the wit not to interrupt. 'A spy in the enemy camp, that is your part. You have nothing more arduous to do than to take her out and ask questions in your artless way. Your legendary charm, my dear Sigi, is what I require, for I think even you can see that the young lady will be more, shall we say, accessible, to you than to me.'

Sigi was silent for a few minutes, then, speaking slowly, he said, 'I won't help you blackmail anybody.'

Ludwig laughed; he made a show of wiping tears from his eyes. 'How crude you are. It's not illegal, talking to a girl. I don't expect you to find anything disreputable, quite the reverse. You will snoop, my friend, in a good cause, remember that. Not just for my benefit, my dear Sigi. If a man doesn't pay his debts to society, he's locked up, isn't he? This man has imprisoned himself; he is the victim of his misdeeds. To pay a price – a very small price – will release him.' He gazed at the uncomprehending face. 'I will pay all your expenses in taking her out, you will collect your money when I do. And if I don't get my money, well, neither do you. You will have to content yourself with having had a charming experience. You must take a small risk, my dear Sigi, for the greater gain, as I do. That will be a little incentive for you to do well.'

The young man, frowning slightly, was now contemplating his polished shoes.

'Here, she's not deformed is she?'

Ludwig's mirth, now, was scarcely containable. 'No, no, what a strange fellow you are, Sigi. Nothing wrong with her. Not bad-looking at all. She might think there's something wrong with you, of course. Have you thought of that? No, I suppose not, you are so very – successful in the field, aren't you, my dear boy?'

'Very well,' Sigi said. 'I know what you want. It's a very – no, never mind. I could do with the money, but not enough to do anything illegal, do you understand? If you've lied to me, I'll make sure you get dropped in it, not me,' and he put on his little show of bravado, his small display of self-respect in a hard voice. 'What's her name? What's the man's name, the one that owes you?'

'No details yet, my dear boy. I'll tell you what you need to know later. When I've found a way for you to meet her, by chance, I think. And I'll simply have to rely on you to do your best, won't I, Sigi?' and he smiled to himself, the smile of a man relishing a private joke too good to share.

Otto Tiedemann glanced at his watch as Victor sauntered into the office, an irritating habit he had which was inappropriate when connected to the arrivals and exits of his employer, who scarcely glanced in his direction. He knew he shouldn't do it; he knew it did him no good and was not a gesture inspired to win the confidences he so fervently desired, but there, it had happened again. His mouth tightened for a moment before relapsing into its customary bleak look.

Herr Tiedemann did himself far too much credit in imagining that Herr Genscher had noticed this gesture of his. Indeed that general self-importance of his, a fault he altogether failed to perceive, did him more harm than any of his old gentleman's tics. Victor had not seen him. He had other matters on his mind and proceeded into his office with no thought in his head beyond his personal affairs.

The post had brought him no card yesterday; no card today; nothing in fact but a missive from Heidi bemoaning the days that would intervene before she had the pleasure of seeing him again. He, too, was counting the days, but not for that young woman's benefit. Walther wanted to wait a month before presenting his fait accompli to the newspaper's staff, would not be budged from this decision and insisted that nothing could be done before Christmas, even less when staff were away on holiday and that January, when their pockets were emptiest, was the most telling moment to strike. It irked Victor and yet there was not a thing he could do to move the man. He saw that he would have to abide by this decision. He hated to wait; he liked to move things along at a brisk trot. Trivia bored him; the kind of pernickety examination of detail which appealed to conscientious Otto irritated him. A hundred, no a thousand, times, he had suppressed the urge to tell the old man to get on with it, or to shoo him away as he stepped purposefully into the inner office with yet another folder full of carefully docketed slips of paper.

Otto Tiedemann, over years of careful economy, had formed the habit of writing on odd scraps of paper or the backs of envelopes which he first cut into neat rectangles, attaching these crabbed annotations to the documents in question with a special, removable tape. He went out to buy this himself, an operation which necessitated the creation of another careful little note for Fräulein Schmidt to put in her petty cash box. These pieces of paper were as irritating to Victor as an itch. He had often wished him retired, gone, anywhere; he would have despatched him to look after the firm's business in South America or Africa if there had been the slightest chance of his being useful there. Instead he kept him here. It was not so much because of Eduard Rommer's promise to the old boy, but because he was so very finicky, so very conscious of the past glory and present honour of Rommer's that he did have some small usefulness at times, even if it was only as a walking memory bank or as a thorough checker of figures. There was a further reason Victor did not so readily admit to himself. Tiedemann had always been a fixture in the office. He represented all that Victor once aspired to; the solidity of position. He needed him there to prove daily that he had indeed surpassed his wildest ambitions; as witness to the reality of the present.

His distinctive knock at the door, a rat-a-tat-tat, purposeful in a military way, now roused Victor from his reverie. He made himself smile; he had been irritated, too, all that day and all the previous one with the need to do something about Ludwig.

Curiously enough, Herr Tiedemann looked almost apologetic. 'Störe ich?' he said and for once did not glance at the empty desk in innocent sarcasm. He had something on his mind, just a small affair (what else?) and wished to impart this (of course) to Herr Genscher. The sort of unpleasant little incident that was so regrettably a feature of present-day life (get to the point, old fool). He was an old man, he knew, and old-fashioned in his ways and it disturbed him to think of a young girl, alone and unprotected in the city, being subjected to that sort of thing. Oh, Herr Genscher need not alarm himself, it was nothing more sinister than one youth – loitering with intent, he believed was the expression – and with no more circumlocutions the old man finally got to the point and discovered that he had an unusually attentive audience.

# Chapter 6

Thursday, December 4, 1971

The policeman's gone now and old Frau Beckmann is fussing around, clicking her tongue, making her panacea for all evils, a good strong cup of coffee. She vouched for my good character to the police detective, unsolicited and in her usual shout, and he treated me with the utmost suspicion. Later I have to go and make another report, a written one, at the police station. His attitude made it quite clear that this was a formality, a necessity for their files, and not because he thought for an instant that there was any point to it. I think Frau Beckmann has a soft spot for me. She called me a young girl 'aus gutem Haus' and an exemplary lodger; she is convinced that the loiterer must be a would-be rapist.

She is muttering to herself about the wickedness of the Lumpen who hold up cars in broad daylight, lifting up the side of a huge, heavy Mercedes until the terrified woman driver hands over her fat Gucci purse or, she whispers – that being anybody else's normal volume of speech – worse. She reads the *Bildzeitung* daily from cover to cover, devouring the muggings, sex scandals, the occasional murder and the incestuous crimes from the dull flatlands of Schleswig-

Holstein. She admires my composure, which is entirely due to her reassuring presence, the comforting shelf of bosom encased in the dark suit she must have had made thirty years ago, the prim little white collar and short bootees.

She believed me, but the policeman evidently thought I was neurotic and had invented the incident to make myself interesting. He eyed my Hasselblad enviously, asked about jewellery and suggested finally in a quarter-hearted way that it might have been a burglar on the look-out. A boy, he said, and smiled sardonically and spouted statistics on youthful crime. 'You'd be surprised how often they come from good families round here,' he said and gave me a look as though I had at least a dozen skeletons in my closets. I suspect the reason for this second visit, in broad daylight, was to have a better look at me, for there could be nothing to add to what I told them last night. It's probably a crime to waste police time and they'll whisk me off to jail if I'm not careful. The fact that the youth beat such a hasty retreat when the police car showed up makes him guilty to me, but invisible and probably imaginary as far as the Polizei are concerned.

For a reason I can't begin to defend, in the small hope that news of this would percolate to Victor and disturb him, I called Herr Tiedemann. He, predictably, hummed and ha'ed at first, then got very excited and concerned and told me I should come and stay with them, that the driver would collect me in forty minutes, he and his wife would be honoured and so on. I suppose it serves me right. I could dissuade him only by letting him know that Linda is coming to stay, so I shan't be alone. It's true; she arrives from Harwich tomorrow at the St Pauli Landungsbrücke and no doubt she'll have some young man in tow who thinks carrying her baggage will advance his cause. I'll be well repaid for that piece of stupidity if the old man writes to Oma and worries her unnecessarily.

Monday, December 8, 1971

Linda is asleep, exhausted by her evening's exertions. Victor's letter has been in my pocket for half an hour, waiting for her to conclude her post mortem on the charms of Sigi. Herr Tiedemann clearly panicked sufficiently to tell him, for all the good that does. Epistolary Victor is a disappointment. Worse. He doesn't rate analysis.

My dear Johanna,
Please do not concern yourself too much about this unpleasant incident. Such things, regrettably, can happen in our city [as though I came from a cottage and had straw in my hair]. It is good to hear that you have your girlfriend to stay with you. Please contact me immediately if you require my assistance. With my best wishes for the festive season – your Victor.

And happy Christmas to you. As bland as butter, an old man's short dull letter. No breath of interest in my adventure; no hint of passion. No hint of anything. He can't remember Linda if he thinks she'll protect me.

The writing slopes downhill a little on the creamy paper; sign of a dilatory, melancholy character. Miserable, uncaring Victor who has not called me. There's no stamp, but he can't have come here. I expect I was another errand in the driver's busy day; I expect he complained at having to come so far. I have read it five, six, ten times, uncomprehending, as though a real message lay behind the round vowels, the n's that look like u's, the w that looks like an m, the over-sized capitals. How my little heart pounded when I recognised the writing. Victor's letters were never like that, they were pacy and charming and full of fun, not this old uncle's tract. I would get them out now but Linda's asleep in the sitting room and the desk drawer creaks. Perhaps we will hold a post mortem on Victor tomorrow. The sympathy in those big round eyes will be tempered by her not very well-hidden antipathy to my 'uncle'; now she believes that she was prescient, if anybody was.

Linda will hint that it's all to the good and ask me if I liked whatshisname. Linda has already acquired her throng of admirers: three including Uncle Hansi. Before meeting him we went to an afternoon's labour on *Ulysses* in Aula I. An English lecture seemed a good idea as her German is so rusty, and besides it's fun: two hundred heads bowed by the symbolic significance of the text, dissecting Bloom's Dublin day on neat charts. Plotting a cyclops on cellophane, siting sirens on street-maps. The English department likes to dissect and draw graphs: their perfect analysis of a work of literature would come on long paper readouts, in a mountain range of different inks. Blue blocks for the most-used words: green waves for the rhythm of the text; red crests when a character rises up, to fall back again. In short, all the characteristics of a madman's encephalogram. Linda stifled her laughter in the back row while the note-takers ruled lines and carefully placed their little red dots.

Uncle Hansi was conspicuous in the little pub as the only non-student, his silly hat with the feather on the bench beside him. He was drinking one of those huge glasses of Berliner Weisse which he insisted on us trying; raspberry cordial and beer in foaming, diuretic masses. He warmed at once to Linda's noble attempts with the language, admiring her pink cheeks and what he called her English rose charm. What he meant was her voluptuousness, the long blonde curls and blue eyes rimmed with flaky mascara. I could see him making a mental note to send her a trunk of Bock products. She won't disappoint him; she scorns no aid to beauty and travels with a heavy bag of lotions and potions, two hairdryers just in case, heated rollers and an outfit for every occasion.

I do love Linda; she's a clever girl with no respect for anything intellectual. She wants to have as much fun as possible, to live life in the fast lane. Underneath the giggling and the batting eyelids, she's a dreadful tease, an inspired mimic and ruthless at getting her own way. She never mopes, not ever, and she always enjoys herself hugely. She arrived with a tiny suede bag swinging and behind her a young monk balancing her vast case on his shaven pate. The handle broke, she said blithely, and he leapt to the rescue. She was artlessly giving wrong telephone numbers to a middle-aged man in a mac when I caught up with her, the monk bobbing and bowing in front and waiting his turn. He must have been absolutely freezing; a woolly sweater half-covered his saffron robes and his bare legs were goose-pimply. She says he's going to take her to visit his temple.

I suppose she picked Sigi up too, but it was one of her subtler manoeuvres. She bumped into him in the doorway of the Kneipe; apologised – 'Ent-schul-dy-gung' – and he not surprisingly said was she English? and she gave him her most bewitching smile and hey presto he was at the next table sending over a gin and tonic for die nette kleine Engländerin, and what would I like? It took a further half a minute for him to join us at our table.

He is called Sigismund Schmidt, known as Sigi and quite good-looking if you care for dark men. Linda does; she was doing her best to transfix him with her killer orbs. I suppose it will be a flaming romance. He seemed quite amazed, indeed flabbergasted, that I was English too and paid me all sorts of fulsome compliments on my command of the language but I wasn't fooled one bit. He's young, I think our age, and I suppose he is rather handsome. Well-dressed in a flashy way with one of those awful gold chains nestling on his hairy chest, the shirt buttons undone to reveal it, which always makes me want to shriek. He's muscly, or, to use Linda's phrase, a hunk. Not a student; too flash and brash for that. I don't know what he does, but he's a smooth operator and winkled our number out of Linda in five minutes, volunteering to show us round Hamburg. When I said I could do that, she kicked me quite sharply, under the table.

I could see Hansi was having a good time. Out came the old jokes about 'Noch ein Bock für Herrn Bock' and he ate Bratwurst and chips in outright defiance of the dinner date with the fiancé's sober family and sighed for his lost youth and the student freedoms he never had and suspects me of – free love being wasted on the young and so on. Linda said crossly when I got home that I sat there like a prune, radiating pale waves of superiority. I suppose she is right. I don't like the picture of myself as a martyred, superior little madam. Tomorrow I shall be outrageous and flirt.

Linda is not a girl to languish by the phone. Just in case Sigi was thinking of changing his mind, she had the outing organised ten minutes after he'd moved to our table. A walk on the frozen Alster and down the Reeperbahn to see the sights. What a shame, he said, falsely, that Herr Bock wouldn't be able to come, for they're off home tomorrow.

Yesterday Linda insisted upon a trip to the Hare Krishna temple, which is just like a Girl Guides hut, one of those cheerless barracks which has one large room and a small adjoining one, the whole covered by an icy, corrugated iron roof with rusting pipes fighting to get away from the brickwork. You can't see in for the multi-coloured pictures of inscrutable goddesses and pugnacious gods waving their hundreds of arms in the window, their brightness dimmed by a matt layer of dirt. There was a faint humming noise, the sound of the acolytes at their prayers. One of them let us in with a broad beaming smile and hurried us into the big room, hot and noisy, a swaying mass of saffron in front under the pall of incense hanging in the rafters.

The streets are pervaded by these monks and monkesses, chanting and hopping around and thrusting their begging bowls at scandalised matrons. The burgers don't understand at all and certainly don't approve. Looking closer, they can see these aren't starving Indians at all, but European kids, their shaven heads, strange clothing and bare legs epitomising everything they don't want their sons and daughters to become. They cross the road when they see them coming; hide their hands behind their backs rather than accept one of their pamphlets. I don't know how the monks survive, but they are here in strength. They all smile so charmingly when anybody gives them anything or shows the slightest interest.

The girls have long hair and wear saris in the same orangey fabric and they too smile and smile; they seem as happy as it is possible to be, the most convinced religious fruitcakes ever, untiring in their efforts to explain their beliefs. Linda says they live together as brother and sister; that they never sleep together unless the master ordains and that then it is for procreation only and with the partner the master selects. If there was a master there, we didn't see him.

The room was draped with all sorts of hangings and sheets

dyed in shades of red, even the incense sticks are red. It looked as though we were worshipping another set of gaudy pictures, at any rate the frothy wave of real believers at the front were, lifting up their arms and swaying while they chanted. Behind them the hoi polloi, the cynical student body, mumbled along. Hare Krishna, hare Krishna, it's hypnotic and rhythmic and we knew the words in a second and a half. The reason for the packed house on Sundays is not that the kids have heard the word. The monks produce a lunch, the most delicious vegetarian food, for only DM5.– and half an hour's prayer. There are various messes, also delicious rice things and puddings that are small sweet balls, cream and pink and pistachio green with a nutty, tangy flavour. Linda cornered a plateful of those and the monk of her voyage, engaging both in serious investigation. He's a beautiful blue-eyed boy, an American, his blond hair razored to reveal all sorts of interesting little bumps and craters with a long tuft à la Mohican at the back. Linda claims that it is to pull them up to heaven. After the sweetness, the sell: plates replaced by leaflets and the monks close in to harvest souls among the well-fed unbelievers, who all started doing a backwards shuffle towards the exit.

I went in search of the loo, but there wasn't one. What do the monks do? I was looking at the back of the big room and had the feeling there was somebody behind me and turned around, but it was quite empty. There were no doors there so I collected Linda and we started for Altona Station and I had the same feeling, that we were being followed, and spun round. I got the merest glimpse of a man, a shortish man in an overcoat, ducking into a doorway. We went on, faster, and stopped round the corner and waited, but nobody came apart from a bunch of kids who'd been in the temple, laughing and singing the tune. It was getting dark by then; that awkward time on a Sunday when anyone with any sense is home in the warm, the streets practically empty, so we hurried on and I could just hear from behind the click of somebody walking at the same speed as us and when we stopped, he stopped. It made my blood run cold; an expression which is very exact anatomically and not figurative at all. We ran, then, for the station and hurtled across the large gloomy forecourt and straight into the ladies' loo which nobody can possibly have thought welcoming before, as it is glacial and stinks of piss. We stayed in there a good twenty minutes and then got our tickets and saw nobody, or at any rate nobody who paid us any attention. We chose the fullest compartment in the train, stuffed with at least fifty schoolchildren going home to Rissen from some excursion and were glad to be obliged to listen to their puerile shrieks. We were both unnerved. We even took a taxi from the S-Bahn, remembering the boy on the bus.


Wednesday, December 10, 1971

No doubt about it, Linda's in a huff. Sigi kept making advances to me, leaving poor Linda in the unusual position of lemon of the party. It was mystifying to both of us; we're under no illusions when it comes to her feminine charms and how they rate against mine. I must say there's never exactly been a competition before, indeed there isn't now, as he's not at all my type. He didn't precisely ignore her, but seemed strangely unconscious of her charms; if it's a cunning ploy to gain her attention, he's certainly succeeding.

The Alster was beautiful, full of little groups of walkers and skaters all bundled up like Breughel figures, black on the scoured ice, which the setting sun turned gold. We walked and slithered round the edges and Sigi pointed out various landmarks, most of which he got wrong. I skated a bit and Sigi kept slipping on his thin leather soles and shivering in his showy leather jacket, but we were merciless and walked for an hour.

He offered hot grog in one of those little wooden huts at the far end of the lake. It was sweet and alcoholic and we had three glasses each. While Linda delicately nipped the peel from our lemon slices, he raised his glass to mine in the silliest way, as though we were drinking Brüderschaft, except of course everybody says 'du' straight away. It's universal among students and always makes me want to 'siezen' them. Germany always makes me feel very proper and English, it's definition by contrast.

73

He asked me about Rommer's as the third round came; I denied the connection. I thought he looked at me rather strangely, but Linda, ever quick on the uptake, chipped in with her execrable accent that I'm sick of being asked that. Getting her own back. 'Es ist dur Zu-vall,' she said, that I have the same name, for she knows I hate that kind of categorisation. Is he in our business, I wonder? He doesn't look the part.

At his insistence we got a cab to the top of the Reeperbahn. He's at home there and no mistake; he knows every corner. I bet he's right in the middle of an enjoyable misspent youth. At the second set of traffic lights he suddenly grabbed my arm and pulled me into a phone box, flicking through a dog-eared directory and finally showing me a page with Greek symbols marked next to a name: gamma, alpha, Levison L. It didn't mean a think to me. He gave me a long stare then moved on. 'Guck mal,' he said and there at the next phone box were other symbols under that name and a page number. The next kiosk would continue the message, he said; this was how spies communicated with each other and he laughed hugely when I asked what happened if somebody tore a page out and would that ruin the whole thing? I suppose he was joking. I had the bizarre notion that he'd prepared those pages specially for me. He was most odd. He took my arm, again, and whispered don't tell your friend and then led me back to Linda. I kept having to unwind that arm, which went on snaking round my shoulders as though it had a life of its own.

We were outside a discotheque and Linda perked up somewhat. He got a great roll of money out of his pocket and pointed out another phone box, nodding seriously as if to say, you know. I had a vision of a latticework of phone booths lurking at street corners, absorbing the city with their electronic ears and linking up illicitly to transmit their messages out while the good burgers snore. Either he's not quite right in the head – nicht alle Tassen im Schrank, as Oma would say, or he's got an arcane sense of humour. I wouldn't let him pay as I loathe feeling beholden and that really bugged him, as it were, heaven knows why.

It was the usual place. Dark, dirty, loud, with flashing lights and a wooden floor throbbing to the bass notes of heavy rock.

German youth adores Frank Zappa, King Crimson and Led Zeppelin. All the Abitur failures who couldn't buy a train ticket to Ramsgate to save their lives know the words of 'Twenty-first Century Schizoid Man' and offer their moaning accompaniment to 'Blood rack/Barbed wire/Politicians' funeral pyre' while they conduct their drug deals at the back. Hamburg's musical tastes divide neatly between rock freaks; fans of the city's own golden boy, James Last, the bearded purveyor of folk songs-a-gogo; and the opera buffs. German students being what they are, rock lyrics have reputedly been subjected to Marxist analysis, though I've never found that mythical avant-garde seminar where they take the scalpel to Zappa. I'd like to offer them my new Jefferson Airplane L.P. It has an amusing gobbledy-gook German number called 'Never argue with a German if you're tired'.

There was not much in the way of pleasure in the disco. People clustered round the back eyeing each other and a few exhibitionists strutted on a wooden platform like a boxing ring a couple of metres high. I wouldn't dance, for I hate it, but Linda soon joined them, her bottom gyrating expertly opposite some man's large clenched buttocks as he jiggled from one foot to the other and shouted inaudible pleasantries. He was soon ousted by an audacious and extremely handsome Turk, a Che Guevara with hair-oil, who twitched his bulging pelvis suggestively.

I winkled Linda out at one in the morning, disappointing both the Levantine and the other wretched man, who had by then spent ages nursing a beer and staring gloomily up at her while Sigi and I shrieked meaningless remarks over the din and he kept trying to make me dance, and I kept refusing, and very dull it was too, for he wouldn't dance with anybody else. I amused myself by imagining I recognised fellow phoneme-sufferers frozen in contorted poses, grimacing faces painted pink and blue by the harsh lights.

The Turk followed Linda out and slobbered over her in the street, to be repulsed with some brutality. Sigi got us a cab and looked as if he had half a mind to jump in himself, but wasn't invited. Linda fell asleep at once, only waking up when we got home to remark, while scrubbing her face, that Sigi was probably a bad lot. Look at the funny way he stuck to you, she said as proof positive. False modesty was never one of her attributes.

Linda's presence is very reassuring somehow, even still asleep in her black pyjamas. Comforting in a naughty sort of way, for she's just the girl to lead someone astray. There's room for a great deal more of that joie de vivre in the person of J. Rommer, swot and superior little madam. When I think of our long association, I have the mournful impression that one of us has consistently and enjoyably been up to no good and the other, ever a non-combatant, has been content to observe and get on with something worthy, like an essay or cleaning shoes. It's not much of an epitaph.

> Here lies J. Rommer, a dreadful swot,
> Who polished shoes and mooned around a lot.
> She gave but little pleasure,
> And as she gave, she got.

Linda and I chose each other from the very first day at school. We were wealthy, but it was fashionable to be highbrow; it was mutual adversity which attracted us. I remember that we all had to say what our parents did, a piece of snooping disguised as general interest, and there among the doctors and lawyers and bankers, the architects and authors and MPs, were my parents, dead, and Linda's father a builder-developer, which was arguably worse. Ours was the attraction of compatible but differing characteristics, more of those elective affinities. She would never swot, producing the briefest and skimpiest of misspelt essays in the back of the car on the way to school. She applied herself fully to the composition of elaborate, inventive excuse notes, which deserved As for imagination and calligraphy. She acquired an intimate knowledge of the library's shelves from the dreary hours spent in detention after school, supposedly writing lines or doing prep, but mostly spent staring vacantly ahead among the sniffling, remorseful juniors. Eventually she was spared this humiliation by virtue only of her age.

Linda's love life was always thrilling. While I brooded hopelessly over my secret passion, Linda commanded the vanguard of juvenile romance. At morning break we would sit enthralled, a circle of knees quivering under our box-pleated skirts, breathless under our green-striped blouses, while Linda munched a biscuit and gave us the highlights of her amorous adventurings, one sweet mouthful after another. And then he – and then I – and then I took my top off. Oh Linda, you didn't. Yes I did. And my bra. She would smile enigmatically through bulging cheeks as the bell went and savour her cliffhanger.

When we got into the sixth form, her large audience for episodic romance was banished and I became sole confidante. Let them read Kinsey for their sexual field-work, she said dismissively. We were all virgins except for Linda, her initiation an event she planned with much care and which nevertheless so disappointed her that for a long time she forswore a repetition. She dragged me to parties and chose clothes for me, which I then concealed from Oma; I did her French proses, subtly altering my version to elude discovery. We did the same A-levels. It's the only practical choice, Linda said, blithely abandoning history, at which she could have excelled, in favour of my fluency in German. Her reports stock-piled the clichés of the non-achiever in tautological columns. Could try harder. Linda does not do justice to her intelligence. Linda must work much harder to develop her natural abilities if she is to succeed. Once again Linda's laziness has betrayed her talents. Their urgings never had the slightest effect. Linda's natural abilities are exactly that: they are manifest as a degree could never have been.

My diary for our A-level year records Linda's driving lessons and the instructor who tried to lure her into the back seat; her triumphant gravel-scattering occupation of the headmistress's parking space in her new MG and consequent disgrace; Linda ironing her hair and singeing it; Linda getting an A for her mock orals because the external examiner fell for her madly and she promised to meet him in the pub afterwards and did. There was the shocking episode when 'one of our girls' brought shame upon the school by smuggling two boys into the Sixth Form Common Room during the school dance, the culprits escaping by vertiginous flight over the rooftops. The PE mistress refused adamantly to climb up and catch them, pleading fear of heights, and thus precipitated open rebellion from gym among lower-school minxes, already deflowered, debauched and despicable. The times they were a-changing and Linda led the vanguard.

They couldn't expel the whole lower school so she, conspicuous in the timid sixth form, bore the brunt. She was caught both smoking and snogging at the school gates, grounds for expulsion in those innocent days. Miss Dalrymple was loth to know which crime appalled more; her lean spinster's soul revolted at such escapades while her canny Lowlands brain computed their possible worth. 'After prayers, Dullrumple announced the most generous contribution to the New Sciences Wing by Mr Davenport. Her moustache twitched at Linda in a grimace. It's now going to be called the Davenport Sciences Block, she said and there was a definite gargling noise as the old bat spat the words out. Linda bent her head modestly, she nearly choked. Dullrumple looked quite approvingly for once. I do believe she thought she was blushing for shame, for what she likes to call proper, maidenly modesty.'

And yet, for all her perspicacity, Linda never liked Victor and did not approve of him. Foreigners were in then. Everybody was conducting a long-distance romance in parroted French or garbled Spanish with a holiday fling. The common room was a morning Tower of Babel as we puzzled out each other's love letters, passing the best bits round, and scanning our A-level texts for flowery bits to incorporate in our replies. Linda combined her more earthy English amours with undying passion for a romantic Frenchman who sent her beautiful poems which turned out to be straight lifts from Verlaine. There was a Spanish beach boy who also wrote to her, sending countless pictures of himself in bronzed, muscly poses for two devoted years after their brief Minorcan romance. He was a waiter and eventually, much to her horror, turned up on her doorstep, pallid but still passionate, shivering in his uniform of thin black trousers and white shirt and fully expecting her to elope with him. When Mr Davenport packed him off, he sent her as his parting shot a particularly unflattering photo of her pulling a face and bulging out of her bikini with 'Muy gorda, muy gorda' written on the back. It joined a collage of his rampant struttings which we used as a dartsboard for a while.

Out of all these nonsensically unsuitable paramours, Victor alone – he the only serious, professional, mature lover – met with her disapproval. I treasured his letters too much to profane them by handing them around, but would condescend to read her the wittier bits. She set her face stubbornly against him. A smoothie, she said, and too old, too sure of himself and she didn't believe in marriage anyway. Had they but known it, she and Oma were for once in perfect accord. I introduced her to him and she refused to be charmed, conducting an uncharacteristically stilted drawing-room conversation about the weather, resonant with unspoken dislike. She found fault with all the unarguable points, such as his advanced age. Victor unappreciated: it was an unpleasant, incomprehensible novelty.

And he liked her, it was obvious that he admired her good looks. He kept on saying flattering things which she ignored. Lush blondes, as Oma has hinted more than once, are Victor's preferred type. Victor's blondes: a subject to consider at length, but one I have always avoided. Because the next subject would have to be why did he propose to me? I remember saying to Linda at the time that she could be more graceful, since she benefited after all from my passion for German and ceaseless strivings to master it, all to make me worthy of him. You were always a swot, she said baldly. He focusses it, that's all. It was the swot in me she disliked, though she deigned to copy my notes whenever necessary. She made it clear that I was her friend in spite of an over-studious bent and that she did me the favour of overlooking it.

I think she saw Victor as another character fault, an aberration she put up with. She's never been in love. Plenty of flings, crushes and mad yearnings, but never for an instant the desire to tie herself down. She approaches men with the sort of clinical detachment they are reputed to use when pursuing us, the same profound disrespect for the softer emotions, the same scorn of soppiness and tears. All the characteristics that I suppose Victor showed. I hope some of her rubs off on me. I could do with a good, thick layer of indifference right now. I must wake her soon. Today we are going to town to collect my allowance: another session outside the inviolable closed door of Victor's room, the place where he sits to write his horrid little notes.

# Chapter 7

A neat little man was following two girls in the street as they proceeded from Dammtor Station up the Rothenbaumchaussee and into the modern part of the University complex. He loitered in the chilly spaces, rocking on the cobbles, each hillock making its personal impress upon the balls of his feet. They didn't spare him a glance when they emerged, warmly wrapped, the pretty one's bright blue jacket and mane of blonde hair unmissable. Back they went and down the bridge under Dammtor and on into the Stefansplatz. At Esplanade they crossed to the right-hand side and he slowed down, loitering, even indulging in the contemplation of his dapper self in the shining windows of the gentleman's outfitters, for he reckoned he knew where they were going.

He toiled up the grey-painted back stairs, panting a little, meeting an emaciated woman swooshing the upper landing with her wet mop, the shiny aluminium bucket of hot suds leaving rings on the vinyl tiles. They exchanged a ritual 'Tag', her suspicious little sharp-nosed face peering at him as he laboured on and up, the tip-tap of his ascent echoing into the upper regions, and then the woman let out an angry 'Huch'. He had stepped in dog shit and was carrying up with him a soft little lump of turd, neatly stamping the same malodorous brown fleck on each alternate riser.

Poor Frau Meier; she listened and heard he was going right up to Herr Genscher's apartment. She would have to lift the heavy bucket again and drag it up another three flights, taking care not to slop it for that would again double her work. She had mopped the whole lot once already, in loving servitude to Herr Genscher who tripped so lightly up and down her shiny floors with his friendly greeting and pleasant smile, never too proud to say hello or remark how immaculately kept his 'escape stairs' were. She then thought the man might trek that filthy lump, wedged between that pretentious Cuban heel and sole, over the beautiful cream carpet upstairs, which she shampooed only last week. Clenching her pink rubber glove, Frau Meier shook it silently at the ceiling and decided that, since it was nearly eleven, she would go down now for her second breakfast in the snug caretaker's room and leave the floor until he had done his worst. Shaking her head, she went down to bemoan her lot to Herr Frisch, who thought for the hundredth time that she was a decent woman and, were it not from the two teeth missing at the front, almost attractive.

Upstairs the man knocked three times at the kitchen door and was admitted at once.

'I know, they're here,' Victor said mildly before he could open his mouth. The man raised his shoulders in assent and watched his boss. It wasn't much of a job, the shoulders implied, if this was all it amounted to, but he didn't complain. He sat stoically, looking around.

'Uni then here,' he finally said, laconic.

'And nobody followed them? No boys or children?'

He shook his head without curiosity, for what business was it of his?

'All right,' Victor said after a long silence spent looking into his vacant face. 'Keep with them, Herr Bruch. Report back to me tomorrow evening about seven.'

He nodded, rising, and left without another word, his footsteps echoing down to Frau Meier. She bit into her Rollmopsbrötchen with the left side of her mouth, that being the preferred cutting edge, and, mumbling through her herring, told Herr Frisch to help himself, go on, take one, while he could not stop staring at the silvery grey morsel of fish winking at him through its white enamel net.

Downstairs behind the sanctity of the glass wall, the girls watched Herr Tiedemann count out notes, which he then placed in an envelope to render them invisible for the delicate transaction of handing them over to Fräulein Rommer. He accompanied them to the door. Pressing their reluctant hands in farewell, he insisted that they must come to tea with him and his wife, her damp seedcake the punishment concomitant with the introduction of the charming Engländerin.

Herr Tiedemann longed for greater intimacy, for more confidences. He wrote regularly to Frau Rommer, addressing her with the utmost respect. He managed to convey through the expression of his vorzüglichste Hochachtung that he, her least worthy and ergebenster Diener, was also her most reliable and faithful. Punctiliously he imparted those scraps of news he had managed to acquire, receiving in due course replies which began Mein lieber Otto and which thanked him politely for taking the trouble to let her know how her granddaughter was. Old busybody, Frau Rommer always thought, as she addressed the envelope in her best hand, as though Johanna couldn't and didn't write herself; she would, however, have been alarmed, had his letters ceased.

Herr Tiedemann always spoke fondly of Frau Rommer. The days of her participation had been his most glorious. There were few people still alive who could recall that they used to call him Hamburg's jute king, der Jutekönig. Frau Rommer remembered the halcyon days of the old world, when the lowliest worker in the Calcutta gunny works knew him and bowed to the glistening face, then pink and round, under its sola topi.

'Sunday, then, at three o'clock?' he said and bowed stiffly, heels drumming a faint staccato tattoo. 'My wife and I are looking forward to it very much.'

It was one of the many small tragedies of Herr Tiedemann's life that he, Herr Rommer's right-hand man, retained this position with Rommer's successor only by a humbling reversal of his former self. Herr Genscher required not initiative, but unquestioning obedience; not authority, but subservience.

The messenger boy probably knew more than he did. He was a doorman guarding the inner sanctum, an occasional teller of small sums, a document-checker. In return, he received an excellent salary at an age when many of his contemporaries were miserably touring the world in the company of their gaudily bedecked wives. Die Greisen reisen! Herr Tiedemann thought of the vulgar brochures that came through the door and shuddered. He had no intention of joining the band of cheerful, geriatric wanderers; that was as odious to him as the prospect of empty days at home with his quiet spouse. He could not risk any loss of dignity by ever complaining of his lot and thus it was only his wife who was obliged to hear his daily account of petty humiliation. In company he played his part well, every centimetre the venerable partner, and Lotte watched and nodded and dreaded his eventual retirement day far, far more than he could begin to imagine.

Upstairs Victor, half-wondering whether he had not over-reacted to a trifling event, was passing a half-hour in recalling one episode of his life; that brief and unfruitful romance with Johanna Rommer. He had not given her a thought for many months. He was skilled at the game of selective memory, for he had the ability to apply himself fully to the matter in hand and exclude irrelevancies. Victor had rigorously suppressed all the men he might have been, eradicating weaknesses and irrelevancies in order to create the perfect version: an artful, clever assemblage of the attributes which assured success in business and worldly terms. He could not understand contemporaries who let their failures rule their lives, who sat in the box created by a series of poor decisions and allowed the lid to close over their heads.

Victor was his own life's work, the most perfect figure that could be made from his chunk of marble. He had cut out the flaws, rubbed away the dark streaks, honed the whole to perfection and polished it up with years of study and application. Victor had learnt to please when it was necessary; to be ruthless, albeit charmingly so, when it was not. He was not cold-hearted, though some women accused him of that. Simply, he had never found pleasure or satisfaction in the abandonment of self, the morass of self-pitying emotions which they called love. His experiences had taught him that these raw emotions brought nothing but grief and he had suppressed them, alongside such unproductive feelings as envy and malice, and knew that he was now immune. He could not imagine why a sane man would want to place his happiness so entirely in another's hands.

Thus, when he had contemplated marriage, it was for logical and sensible reasons. He had decided to secure a young wife who could be moulded, who neatly rounded off his assets, who could bear him heirs. Johanna Rommer had possessed, in addition to an ingénue's charm, the advantage of one day inheriting the family fortune. He considered it his own long before he took the steps to secure it.

Victor flattered himself that he could have wooed her successfully had she been indifferent, but that was far from being the case. Her liking for him had been a deciding factor; she had long had a schoolgirl crush and nothing could have been easier than gratifying it. She was too young for his tastes, but he saw the importance of securing his due before some chance intervened. The arrangement had been as neat and orderly as he could have hoped for, in the circumstances. He had been obliged to use caution, for he knew Frau Rommer well enough to be sure that she would take a little persuading. It was to have been a fait accompli.

He remembered Johanna, not so much with regret, as with faint pride. In his dealings with her he had exhibited exceptional selflessness. He had put her interests before his: that was the precise phrase he had used, some time after his first declaration, to Frau Rommer during their first and only discussion of the event.

For Johanna, clearly out of her depth, had expected from him – well, he didn't quite know what; a schoolboy's feelings perhaps. He had soon discovered that it was more than a crush. She had a genuine passion for him. How she used to hang on his every word; how quietly she would sit with his friends to please him. It had been touching to watch her look round with those soft brown eyes and listen and learn and copy. It had been flattering and a little alarming to observe her quick intelligence as she perfected her language skills and used that immense, that endless adaptability of hers. Watching her, he had grown wary. She wasn't interested in possessions or clothes like normal girls. She wanted something more. She wanted to own and be owned by him and to get inside his head. That of course had been out of the question.

Observing this, he had withdrawn little by little and found her puzzled naïvety a little painful. Her anxiety had made him nervous, for there had been no way to explain to her that he neither wanted, nor was able to offer, the sort of intimacy she aspired to. He was not capable of such loss of control. Even physical intimacy had become a problem. He had forborne taking her to bed, a piece of self-denial altogether necessary, for if she felt these things about him now, what would happen then? No, there had been no risking it, and that had made matters worse. He had found her troubled, pale face beginning to disturb him. He had discovered in himself a little worm of affection, a desire to spare her a painful awakening. A pity, but he was in any case already rich enough for most men. And so, with some regrets for himself, he had done the unselfish, the honourable thing and cut short an idyll which was destined to be messy. He thought it a pity that Johanna had never understood the rules.

All of Victor's successful amours had been conducted along better-regulated principles, clearly understood by both parties. He prided himself on being scrupulously fair with the women of his choice, selecting independently-minded and soignée ladies who knew how to appreciate all the luxuries of such a liaison. Never promising love, he had waltzed them happily along the little milestones of romance. He never forgot a birthday or anniversary, as husbands did, never failed to produce charming gifts and trinkets on the slightest pretence. His accounts with the discreet jeweller on the Jungfernstieg, with Parfümerie Douglas and the Atlantic Hotel flower shop bore witness to a reckless generosity.

Victor's lovers enjoyed memorable weekends in magnificent luxury in Europe's cultured capitals (it was his rule that his elegant flat was never to be violated by a woman's messy accoutrements). He enjoyed particularly the dual pleasure of

85

taking a pretty woman to La Scala or the Opéra, Glynde-
bourne or Bayreuth, for the bourgeois arts had become his
sole enduring love. This connoisseur's passion was all the
more precious for having been laboured at, for Victor had
forced himself to listen to scratchy records in his bachelor's
garret and had peered at the mysteries of modern dance from
the cheapest seat in the gods. It was his stated opinion that the
finest pleasures in life, whether gourmet feasts or an evening
with a Diva, not omitting athletic pursuits both amatory and
sporting, were to be bought. The auditors of this revelation,
old pals whose smart dark blue Yacht Club blazers could not
conceal bulging beer bellies, who couldn't even go out with
the lads and get pissed without getting hell for it in the
morning, were frankly, openly envious.

Victor held these truths with all the more certainty for
having made mistakes: mistakes which had female names.
Cherchez la femme, he thought ruefully; surely Ludwig could
not possibly know of Johanna?

He was uneasy with good reason, for there had been a time
when he would have sworn that Ludwig could not possibly
know of Charlotte Bamberg. The first of his mistakes. Eyes
closed, searching in the blackness of an image of her, he found
that he could not, after all, remember her face. Yet she was an
error for which he might be called to pay a price, though what
price remained to be seen.

He recalled instead, vividly, the velvet texture of her pliant
white thights against a brown over-stuffed sofa. The butcher's
daughter. He conjured up the cold white shop with its stone
flagged floor and saw again the red butcher hands wielding
Krupp steel, eternally raised in a gesture of denial against
hungry faces while fat pigs' carcasses lay piled in the cellar. He
saw the white enamel scales which Herr Bamberg daily
balanced minutely in his favour and the pale stains on his
floor-length apron which no amount of bleach would remove.
It was strange, this selective memory of Victor's which had
blotted out his beloved's face. It was lost in a welter of bright
blood.

Victor had been in love. He had known that Ludwig would
have raged, that it would have seemed to him a strange and

abhorrent aberration in his fourteen-year-old self, a bizarre and unhealthy association with plump flesh. For Victor had been so very ready to deny that part of himself, had been almost touchingly eager to remake himself in his master's image. Orphaned, abandoned child, he had cast off his past as his childish revenge upon his parents for deserting him. Asked about them he used to reply, quite simply, 'A bomb,' and would shrug his shoulders, alarmingly composed. He had followed Ludwig as a clever mongrel dog clung to the master who rescued it, who fed it and gave it shelter. And Ludwig had loved him, the brightest, most promising child. He had been Lucifer, the shining angel, the one who had farthest to fall.

There had been no sign in the eleven-year-old of a possible betrayal to come. At twelve he had used his quick intelligence to learn scraps of Russian, of English, of French and, winsome child, to smile at a soldier for chocolate or cigarettes. He brought Ludwig his gifts as a dog would carry a bone and wag its tail. His small body could creep unnoticed through the ruins. He had learnt how to locate scarce goods; by judicious eavesdropping to plot the movements of lorry-loads of valuables. Eggs, boots, cigarettes for the illicit army to plunder.

With the onset of puberty he shot up suddenly and grew too tall for a child's role. At fourteen he had the height of a man; old enough to want a woman, the butcher's daughter with her butter-blonde hair, her soft palpitating bosom under the dark dress and cotton apron, the white cotton stockings rolled up over plump knees. She had smiled at him, cut an extra hundred grams of horseflesh and not charged. She was fifteen and already experienced in taking advantage of the lunchtime break when, stuffed with pork crackling, the butcher lay with his wife, animal grunts turning to regular snores.

Young, precocious Victor had not felt he was taking advantage of her when he felt the exquisite pleasure of resting his head against the round, white body. Their couplings took place on the horse-hair sofa in the parlour, which the parents only entered on Sundays, its dim light filtered through white lace curtains and a green, thorny hedge of Mother-in-law's Tongue. He had become a lunchtime absentee for the forty minutes of Herr Bamberg's nap, his loud rhythmic noises guaranteeing safety and covering theirs. Charlotte: a soft, giving blonde. A type that could only be described as maternal. He, who loved her, knew enough to conceal the liaison from Ludwig. Blue eyes, long plaits curled over her ears which she could sometimes be persuaded to undo, even though this greatly increased the danger, for it took Charlotte at least ten minutes to recreate her prim, matutinal self. He remembered, but still could not see her face. Her image was overlaid with one of Ludwig's creating, with his words spoken nearly twenty-five years ago. A china doll, he had said, with round blue eyes that shut and legs that open when she lies down. A toy.

Victor had thought the liaison perfectly concealed. Certainly the butcher had no time to notice anything. He had tramped home from the war, footsore and ragged, and had fallen onto his great creaking knees and blessed the good lord when he saw his shop intact, his womenfolk spared the Russian atrocities. He had had the further good fortune of discovering a distant American cousin among the GIs based in Dahlem; his brother in the distant countryside was raising chickens. He rapidly set about becoming a rich man, a process which drew from the man of peace feats of cunning and bravery the former soldier would never have contemplated. Herr Bamberg's daring, night-time expeditions in defiance of the curfew made his fat legs tremble; his daytime negotiations with the less favoured sharpened his wits. The effort of putting an expression of sympathetic, albeit unyielding commiseration over his big bleary face gave the soft-hearted butcher nervous headaches and stomach pains.

Nobody saw the thin boy creeping along the back alley, knocking softly at the back door. Sometimes Charlotte gave him chitterlings, which he carried away in damp, soft parcels. Because he loved her, because he feared discovery, he would press these love tokens into the hands of the nearest urchin, the beatings of his tender heart stronger than the rumblings of his stomach. He had feared that Ludwig, unnaturally sharp-eyed, would read a message in the blood stains in his pocket, not realising that Ludwig had already decoded the oracle. For months in that balmy summer, Ludwig had chosen to ignore this aberration in his golden boy, waiting for it to pass.

For Ludwig too was preoccupied; everyone was bustling, hustling, scraping and, thanks to the black market, surviving. The shrewd, the lucky and the well-connected did rather better than that. The Allies with their punitive rationing and their bursting depots provided the defeated nation with the fundamental requirements of entrepreneurship: plentiful supply, separated by a hazardous, lucrative obstacle course from desperate demand. The grey acres of rubble proved to be a fertile training ground for Ludwig's private army. They had survived; now they were determined to flourish. Victor knew just where he had acquired his nose for a bargain, his gift for smelling out a deal; he knew the source of his remarkable single-mindedness in achieving his aims. He had learnt these things, not just from his mentor, but from the heroic conquerors, those masters of the expedient, who trafficked in the streets under the signboards forbidding fraternisation. Victor had learnt their particular brand of callousness, which talked portentously about punishing the guilty nation even while setting about making a handsome profit out of their sufferings.

He used to push his way through the mob in the Tiergarten, threading a route past the Allied uniforms and the clusters of Berliners, each with their pitiful bundle. Victor was pitiless. What did he care, if this object was the last family heirloom? He could not take into account the painful thinness of the old man here, the gnarled, arthritic hands of that one, or let the cry of a child affect his calculations, any more than the Amis did. If he began to waver, the sight of a GI would sustain him, reminding him that only a few years back he'd been ready to risk his pitiful life for a half-smoked butt thrown from a lorry by one of these gods. He and four other kids had been happy to throw themselves under the wheels if there was a chance of getting it. No, there was no going back to that.

Ludwig's boys all despised the workers, who laboured for a day for less than a cigarette would bring and thought themselves lucky to get a hot meal. They thought men stupid, to queue all day for a job with a 'future'. They knew the future was something that had to be manufactured, not in some factory but piece by piece, with cigarettes and pieces of soap. They used to sneer at the gaunt, middle-aged men who stood with cardboard notices round their necks: 'Ich suche Arbeit. Ich nehme jede Arbeit an.' Victor had known that they were defeated, finished, the abandoned relics of a collapsed empire. The future belonged to him and to the others riding out of town on the Silk Stocking Express, taking their flimsy valuables to the country folk in the fertile paradise outside. For stockings, chocolate, cigarettes, anything could be bought. Bartering could give a man a new Persil Certificate identity, whiter than white, or a fine set of professional qualifications. Sometimes, if he had a seat on the train, out of a mad, uncaring bravado Victor would light up a cigarette and consume the whole thing, that unheard-of luxury earning him the open-mouthed respect of all around.

That bright summer was darkened by a new fear, that was lay behind the propaganda front, the cultural competition and the Allies' failure to agree on anything. In London, they had failed to secure a joint German settlement and the city was nervous, electric with rumours. Half the country was still on the move, the displaced with their cardboard suitcases, the scavengers and barterers going about their business. Allegiances shifted; people were afraid. It was a strange time of unholy alliances, of profiteers and black-marketeers and men who said they were idealists and yet were all three. Even Ludwig was nervous, amassing property and at the same time fearful that an eventual return to pre-war stability, which none of them remembered too clearly, would throw up lures to seduce his boys away. Ludwig, by then, had bartered his way to a whole house and lived, as his status demanded, in the whole of the first floor. His rambling flat lay behind a grey façade with tall windows looking onto the flattened remains of a once-elegant boulevard. Miraculously, the house was virtually untouched. Ludwig had seen a new opportunity in it and, in an attempt at respectability, had let a few rooms to lodgers. These were young men with an apprenticeship or some other form of steady work, priggish young men, whom the others avoided.

It was a beautiful day, a brilliantly hot day. Victor had gone to the station early through the summery haze and had heard the rare and precious warbling of a bird singing, somewhere in the rubble. He had passed the walls plastered with hand-lettered posters: 'Looking for Brandt, Heinrich, reward', or 'Schmidt, Alfried, missing Dresden 1940' or 'Flat Wanted'. In that morning clarity he saw them, not as messages of despair, but proclamations of the inextinguishable optimism of the ordinary man. It was too early for the good-time girls, who asked a packet of Lucky Strike for their favours, and who were already plump and affluent in short fox capes and American nylons. The women at the station were those who never gave up, who wore round their necks placards with the name of a missing husband or lover above a tiny passport picture or blurred holiday snap. Rocking on their wooden wedge heels, they used to stare into all the faces that passed, awaiting their personal miracle. It was a good day, a special day. Victor found a seat on the train and by midday he was back, his knapsack bulging, one pocket still stuffed with Allied currency. Running to Dahlem, to his love, he felt the heavy weight of good fortune knocking against his thin shoulder-blades.

There was a crowd outside the shop. People were milling about, ducking, snatching and two policemen tried ineffectually to move them on. Pushing through with violent, desperate motions, Victor saw blood, everywhere, shocking him who had seen so much already without being moved or angered. The fat carcass lay across the door of the cold room, blue eyes gazing at the ceiling in perpetual surprise, the little pink mouth open in an O of shock. The stains on the apron seemed so innocent; pig's blood or human, they both looked the same. And now, horribly, the body began to move, to twitch, as the door was pushed open, as though the creatures inside were coming out, at last, to see the act committed in their name, to avenge their slaughter. Blubbering, her thin body shaking uncontrollably from cold, shock or both, Frau Bamberg pointed towards the parlour. Charlotte lay on the couch, face-down, and could have been asleep, but for the hand, the twisted hand pointing the wrong way, the white skin still gripping the chop with a frenzy that even death had not diminished.

'They said it was a Polish refugee, a madman. That he shot the butcher dead when he refused him meat and then went after – her.' Victor, who had run across the city howling, now sat perfectly motionless in Ludwig's apartment, his hair metallic in the brilliant light.

A long moment passed and then he had held up his hands to Ludwig, showing him the rust-red dried streaks.

'Why should he shoot her?' he had asked, stupidly. 'She gave the meat away.'

Ludwig had stood at the elegant windows, casting his shade over the deep red Persian carpet, which he had bought for 100 pounds of potatoes.

'A casualty. People get killed all the time,' and he had shrugged his shoulders. That was their attitude; that others suffered but it did not matter, as long as the 'family' was all right. Victor would not retreat into this callous safety; like a dog sniffing at its master's clothes for the sausage hidden in a pocket, he whined and pawed.

'He followed her into the parlour to shoot her,' he said and drew from a pocket the Russian army-issue gun. 'The mother said a second man was there who watched and smiled and didn't see her, hiding in the cold room. Dark and thin, your height, Ludwig. In a black shirt like yours.'

He waited for a reply.

'Who doesn't have a shirt like this? Look at yours? And who's fat in these lean times, apart from your butcher friend?' and it was said softly, as though Ludwig had sympathy for his boy, for his adult body which had outstripped the soft mind. 'There was nothing you could do,' he said. 'These things happen every day. Forget her. What was she, a china doll with round blue eyes that shut and legs that open when she lies down. Don't you think you can do better than that?' And Victor saw that Ludwig had given himself away; the older man nevertheless still smiled at him, as though he were offering forgiveness. He had a particularly attractive smile; he had a way of carrying his smallness as though it were an asset. It took Victor a moment to comprehend that Ludwig thought this crime a just punishment for his betrayal; that he expected everything to carry on as before.

It had been a weakness in Victor, one that he had always regretted, that he did not shoot then. He remembered his arm lifting the gun, deciding instead to arch forwards, and the jarring hammer-hit of the blow that knocked his master down.

'You smiled,' he had said at the figure lying stunned, and heard the sound, like china smashing, his front teeth made, audible even through Ludwig's piercing, bubbling cry as the handle came down again, this time rupturing soft lips. He had lifted the gun again, but it was aimed, not at Ludwig, but at the young scared face that appeared at the doorway and was blasted backwards into red, howling pulp. Victor had never known what his name was; he had been new, a worker, an unknown.

It had been clear to Victor, scrambling his way through the American sector to safety, that to love meant to lose. His short life had punched home that lesson, if no other. He had made a consequent and more catastrophic error; he had left behind a mutilated and vengeful Ludwig instead of a corpse. At first he had shivered at every step behind him in a dark street. In mortal terror of his bogeyman, he had not felt safe in Germany and did not experience security until he was on a ship, where every face soon became hatefully familiar. In a world of hard men and hardships and humiliations, Victor became a man. He had learnt that he was more intelligent than the others; he had determined to remake himself, to succeed. In Hamburg he cultivated the hard northern accent, succeeding only in losing his Berliner's twang. He had chosen Rommer's because he knew about ships; had not Ludwig taught him to be adaptable, to please, to listen and to learn? These skills flowered in the fertile ground he had picked out for himself.

As time went by he decided that Ludwig must, surely, be dead. He forgot about him; forgot that he had killed a man and blacked out the unhappy years. He became all that he pretended to be. Herr Genscher's name commanded respect. Wealthy, astute and generous, he belonged to the best clubs, gave to charities supporting orphans and waifs, appeared at his box at the opera on all opening nights and never failed to celebrate each new, dividend-rich year with a magnificent party at the Vier Jahreszeiten. He sat now in his immaculate eyrie and formed the sudden notion that a temporary abandonment of power or his demise, either improbability, would hoist old Otto into the nub of a business empire he barely comprehended. This notion made him laugh out loud.

Frau Meier, hard at work swabbing the top stairs, parted newly-painted lips in a broad smile to rival Ludwig's for sheer pleasure at the sound of lieber Herr Genscher's happiness, so well deserved.

Descending the back stairs in good time for his lunch appointment, Victor noticed a letter in his postbox which must just have been delivered. It had no Absender, but he did not need that detail to identify its provenance. It was a typed single sheet of foolscap with a large margin, double spaced, which had at first glance the look of a legal document. He stood in the entrance hall, turned at a slight angle, and read it. Fräulein Schmidt, passing with a cheerful greeting on the way to rummage through the Alsterhaus's pre-Christmas bargains, was obliged to repeat it twice before she elicited an automatic response.

' . . . with some of the loose girls of the neighbourhood. I was to discover this later from talking to some of the other boys. I believed that he threatened them, to ensure their silent complicity.

'Victor had survived through petty thievery; now, as he grew, this activity became his small piece of self-assertiveness, his form of independence. It was his way of mocking the system. He was clever in his methods and I would not have discovered them, were it not for the complaint of a small boy whose watch, a much-coveted item, disappeared. He returned it with a good grace and accepted his punishment. This incident taught him to conceal his activities, which were of increasing scope.

'He has, indubitably, the soul and spirit of an entrepreneur, quick to see ways to turn events to his own advantage. It was and is the spirit of our times. There was no disgrace in buying and selling on the black market, but rather the notion that anyone who failed to take advantage of it was a fool. Circumstances had obliged us all to trade, in one manner or another. Victor's intelligence, his adaptability, made him an expert and laid the foundations for his current prosperity. The amassing of property and wealth, the manipulation of money, the quick taking of profit are construed, not just as enviable, but as positive virtues in a society where to be poor implies not just material, but spiritual and mental poverty.

'In our simple lessons, we discussed the concepts of real, spiritual wealth, and I would speak of poverty and humility as virtues, rather than disgraces. I remember the charming smile this graceful boy gave me, his reminder that without more material sustenance, however obtained, the hostel could not continue its mission. I made every allowance for his youth, the circumstances we could not control. Young myself, I was a worse teacher then.

'A serious incident at this time gave me pause. I caught Victor attempting to sodomise one of the younger children with whom he shared a room. I fear this incident was but one of many and the child had been bought with the promise of a reward. I could not decide what to do with him. To set him loose would have been an abandonment of all that we stood for and I still believed that he could be saved. He was severely chastised and given a room of his own, a considerable privilege in our cramped quarters. I myself was obliged to share with several young boys. I spoke with him at some length and tried to explain the difference between right and wrong. The moral teachings of a more ordered age were rendered so unassimilable by the facts of his life, by his evident need for love and human warmth. I believed that his amorality was not intrinsic but a condition of his circumstances and knew that I had failed him.'

Victor's impulse was to crumple this piece of hypocritical fantasy. Reflecting, then, he smoothed it out and again climbed the stairs. He locked it in the safe in his flat.

Ludwig had pawed at him; even in public he had been unable to resist touching his hair or straightening his jacket. He had given Victor a room of his own to facilitate his nightly visits; refusal had been the only way for Victor to exercise any power over him. He had known how to make him miserable, if he chose. After sex, embracing him on the narrow bed, Ludwig always used to talk and talk. He would say that it was not wrong, meaning that he knew it was. He would say that their love was something beautiful and glorious and pure. There were days when, catching him alone in a corridor, he would plead for a kiss. That was the price Victor chose to pay for privilege. Once he had embraced one of the smaller boys, seeking his own comfort and love. He remembered the terror he had felt when discovered by Ludwig and the vicious, jealous beating that had followed. He had learnt caution by the time the miraculous affair with Charlotte happened the following year. She, poor innocent, redeeming him from degradation, had usurped Ludwig in body and soul.

He locked his door; he ran down the stairs. He realised that he would have to kill Ludwig. He was a good twenty minutes late at the restaurant, painted dark green with white shutters keeping the muted interior in pleasantly dim, dappled light on bright days. The Kommissar had made himself comfortable while awaiting his host.

Das Fischerhaus, named in that archly rustic style appreciated by Pöseldorf sophisticates, was a fish restaurant of the type that offered carp and caviar, rather than salt herrings, though the proprietor was happy to cater to any fishy whim given a little notice. Victor often lunched there, finding that even jaded bankers and over-worked newspaper magnates could enjoy a dozen oysters or a fragrant mussel soup. Peter Schwantz had not been immune, nor Herr Kortner. Even the Kommissar was almost rubbing his hands at the prospect of a little pot of Beluga caviar to accompany that second glass of aquavit.

Herr Siemens was an old yachting pal. He knew without ever having put it into words that the pleasures of the *Rommery*, all twenty metres of shining beauty, and those of the table, so happily unlike the police canteen's, could be paid for by the reciprocal compliment of a little harmless information of the type businessmen often sought. Nothing illegal, just a little ferreting around and perhaps a call to an old friend growing fat in charge of an army of files. Everybody in the department did it. Herr Siemens suffered terribly from the fact that he, who took, did not give.

His obligations were all the greater, for he was an epicurean who could not afford to lay down wines; a sailor who would never own a boat. He ate his lunch knowing that he would always refuse to overstep the thin line that differentiated everyday helpfulness from minor, understandable corruption, even though a price had to be paid for such pleasures. This unspoken refusal in turn put him further into his host's obligation; he would then compound his misery by agreeing to a weekend trip on the boat or a splendid dinner. The conflict of puritanical beliefs and sensual appetites had etched melancholy ridges down his narrow face. He longed to be offered a fortune, so that he could give up and luxuriate in the comfort of betrayal. How simple it was to be a rich, bent cop. Known to be incorruptible, he was never approached. Instead he accepted minor, temporal pleasures which paid no bills, he obliged nobody and made himself thoroughly miserable. It was a torment that Herr Genscher never asked for anything; he did not even have the glum satisfaction of turning him down.

'Prost!' Victor said and the fiery liquor dispersed some of the chill he felt. 'So,' he said, grimacing at his poor wit, 'how's a life of crime?'

'Fragen Sie bloss nicht,' said the Kommissar moodily. He had recently been seconded to the police officers' training department. Desk work was inevitable, at his age, but training was both tedious and politically sensitive; there was at the time a witch-hunt in progress for left-wingers and subversives. 'I miss the old days. I spent four years in St Pauli picking up drunks, stopping sailors breaking up bars, finding under-age kids on the streets. Can you believe anybody would miss that? I used to end every shift depressed, feeling dirty. Now I'm nostalgic, even for the cells full of vomiting old men. It was a simple job, the dirt was clean,' and he took a delicate teaspoonful of the caviar and smiled in his melancholy, self-deprecating way.

'You were at least a man of action,' said Victor briskly. 'Now look at us both, handcuffed to bureaucracy. The older I get, the more I think we're trapped in the system. We're not capable of doing things any more.' He thought that this applied, certainly, to the Kommissar, a man who had evidently given up.

The Kommissar nodded agreement at the still-youthful face and thought of his ailing wife, who would be waiting anxiously in bed for him, the pain lines on her face temporarily erased by her welcoming smile. Hating himself for it, he went home later and later; he could not bear to watch her suffer. He never told her about pleasant events, such as today's lunch, not since she had become completely bed-ridden. Instead, he exaggerated all the worst aspects of his life in small, bureau-cratic echoing of her greater suffering. She thought him dreadfully over-worked and sympathised; if she complained at all, it was on his behalf. He envied Victor profoundly for his complete freedom from responsibilities, from the rigours of sickness, for having the money to do anything he wanted. A happy man, he thought, who lived in no one's debt.

'You're not trapped,' he said. 'You can do anything you want. I can't even resign, I have to think about my pension rights. Still,' he said with an attempt at good cheer, 'it's not so bad, we do a good job. If I didn't train new officers, who'd catch our thieves and murderers, who'd sort out the traffic jams? We keep the wheels turning.' One of the mottoes of the training school, which he particularly disliked, was 'Keeping society safe'.

'Do you catch them all?' Victor said ruminatively. He was referring, of course, to a current scandal, a series of inexplic-able attacks on old women living alone, found beaten or clubbed to death for their meagre pensions. The Kommissar, who had installed two new sets of locks on his shabby front door, grimaced.

'Oh, we do pretty well on the percentage of unsolved crimes, considering the sort of city this is.' He had all the figure off pat; it was part of the pep talk he gave at the start of the course. It was important to motivate the new inspectors against the dull grind of paperwork, the average pay, the long and irregular hours. He saw Victor's quizzical face. 'Oh, I know what you're thinking, but we catch a lot of murderers. Some are simple cases, people don't even try to run away.

There are plenty of unpremeditated ones, you know, people who kill out of rage, jealousy, when they're drunk. It's not hard to find the husband who knifes the wife's boyfriend.' He was talking easily, rapidly. A lot of people seemed fascinated by police work, saw it as glamour, all crime and sex. He always tried to recall the details of juicy cases; it was something to offer. The small coin of repayment.

'They always used to teach that there was a pattern to everything; that criminals made mistakes.' The Kommissar smiled at such innocence. 'We still find some arsonists standing around the fire to watch. Firemen are still told to look at the crowd as part of the job. But we live in a different age now, murderers aren't stupid enough to hang around the scene of the crime. Now we get drugs killings, kids who think they're being attacked and defend themselves. People like the "pensions fiend",' and he twisted his mouth over the stupid name, for every policeman in Hamburg was sensitive about it, 'they're hard to find. Psychopaths who do it for fun, who move over a wide area, they're difficult to find. We know what he's looking for, but there are so many possible victims, all living alone. We should have fingerprints of every citizen, but they won't have it, abuse of civil rights. It'll come, though, eventually and the system being what it is, then we'll fail to match them.'

'But there are clever murderers.'

'I wouldn't call them clever,' the Kommissar said. 'People get away with terrible things, yes. By luck perhaps. Sometimes by good planning. A buddy to invent an alibi that stands up in court. I wonder what those pals think afterwards, as the years pass. I wonder what the criminal thinks. Sometimes I feel they probably just feel simple pleasure at having got away with it. No remorse at all.'

The Kommissar, who had experienced all the torments of remorse without ever committing the crime, could envy such simple souls. Victor, who had set up this meeting with a motive beyond the normal routine of keeping in contact during the dry-dock season, was looking at him closely. He had invited him the previous day with the notion of delivering his problem into the hands of the law, or rather these particular, delicate fingers which had often held a fork or pulled a rope at his expense. He had never asked, nor expected any favours. He thought that he could, at the least, expect a sympathetic hearing. He had picked at this idea over the mussels, rolled it round over the unseasonal, unnaturally bright strawberries. He saw that it would never do. He had nothing to incriminate Ludwig, no pasted-up note demanding money with menaces in the bold capitals of the *Bildzeitung*; he had a document which could not be shown to anyone.

'Of course they feel remorse,' Victor said, 'of course they feel guilt, it must eat away at them,' voicing the commonly-held truth to the morose and cynical face. He thought, but could not say, that fear of being caught abated. It gave way to calm. In time a man just forgot about it, as he forgot other incidents in a crowded life. The Kommissar would never understand and Victor knew he could not talk to this man; indeed he could not talk to anyone. He had lacked a person in whom he could confide for so many years that he would have found it distasteful at least, positively embarrassing, to try to talk of himself. He was at ease only when safely locked inside his own head. He would solve his problems by himself, as he always did, and the notion was gone, swallowed as swiftly and irreversibly as a second snifter of cognac down the oesophagus of the melancholy Kommissar. It brought a small measure of warmth to his sad brown eyes.

# Chapter 8

Monday, December 15, 1971

A dozen red roses, the long-stemmed kind, are standing on my desk. They arrived this morning stapled into one of those expensive boxes that attack fingernails. The card inside said 'Dein Sigi'. This courtship of his is the oddest thing, with no expense spared, and yet he doesn't even have a job. On Saturday he bought a single rose in the restaurant, the kind with a rubbery stalk that's dead within half an hour and costs a fortune and he insisted on getting a photograph of us from one of those bright-faced pushy women who come around. The still-damp result was all too revealing, me a smirk of sheer embarrassment, him a practised film-star show of white teeth. He saw my face.

'You think that's common, don't you?' he said. 'I suppose it's not done in Blankenese,' and then, studying it, 'The camera never lies,' and he shoved it in his pocket. He made me feel ungracious; but he was being rude, not me.

Sigi orders the most expensive things, commands absolute service from the head waiter and rewards him accordingly; God forbid that anyone should question his status. It's embarrassing and all the more so for being done in my honour. I bet East End villains are like that when on the spree; throwing money around, enjoying themselves doing corny things and touchy where their pride is concerned.

Linda, advancing with her plate of bacon and eggs, sniffed at the dark perfect blooms, but they are the hot-house kind with no scent. My perfidious Victor used to send me roses; they never smelt real either. These are already wilting under the powerful blast of Frau Beckmann's radiators, formidable, cast iron specimens which, typical of their generation, know no moderation: it's either gurgle, hiss and boiling heat or silence and cold.

'They won't last of course,' Linda said gloomily. 'Just like men.' Hers don't last because she picks them in bunches. I developed this entrancing theory for her benefit: too many alien flora jammed into one receptacle, I said, but she merely severed her bacon rind with precision in order to enjoy it more fully. Far from being offended, I think she's flattered.

Linda is resilient. I would be prostrate after her evening with the Turk, but her appetites are undiminished. He invited us both to dinner, cringing and wheedling, but I cried off to finish my essay on precursors of national socialism in Hugo von Hoffmannsthal, a piece of nonsense for which total abdication of self is required. Then Sigi rang, so I have the awful thing still in front of me.

The wretched Turk didn't take Linda out at all. He cooked himself in a kitchen which she says concentrated the dirt of ages, the nasty fatty mutton bones being assaulted in a black iron pot bearing witness to half a dozen previous culinary attempts. No wonder she couldn't stomach it and became light-headed instead from throwing down several smeary glasses of Turkish fire-water.

The lunge, when it inevitably came, had a certain awful novelty to it. He told her that he actually preferred boys, doing her the honour of considering her voluptuous female bum almost as good. He would accept it, in the circumstances, which were as squalid as they come. He was amazed, baffled, that she shouldn't be flattered, didn't simper and oblige, and he tried to overcome her English reserve with a garlic-flavoured rough and ready attack. She beat him off, of course, after a moment of stunned, alcohol-befuddled bewilderment, delivering what she hopes was an extremely painful kick in the goolies.

What a scene it must have been; the exchange in their garbled German as sole lingua franca and the full horror of his offer not immediately apparent. 'Wie bitte?' she kept saying, politely. Ah, but you could speak in the language of love, I said nastily and, to do her credit, she laughed. She left him writhing on a dirty couch amid a welter of filthy dishes. She's crazy; she must have known what was coming, but she's fatally, insatiably curious. It's extraordinary how Linda exudes and attracts sexual urges, forever getting into dubious situations entirely of her own making. They'll find you in a gutter one day, I told her lugubriously. With your throat cut.

(Now the above, my dear Ingrid, should you chance to rifle through my diaries while innocently looking for a comb, is called BUGGERY. I don't expect you've heard of it.)

The ladies are coming for lunch on Thursday. There was no gainsaying the urge to report to Oma on the state of my living conditions. I am sure that Ingrid's long thin nose will soon detect anything that is not quite ladylike, Linda's lingerie, for example, which I must remember to conceal. I shall indulge in a morning's truancy to make the flat respectable; Linda is to be coached in acceptable small-talk and encouraged not to wear that rather fetching new dress in purple satin which finishes a good ten inches above the knee and is indecent when she sits down. I did think the dress was a trifle provocative for a nation which dresses its women in black floor-length sheets.

She had to be toned down for our afternoon in Aumühle, a select suburb a long way out and not as chic as Blankenese though expensive enough. We were early, for there aren't many trains on a Sunday. The Tiedemanns' house is nearly in the countryside at the end of a long, ill-maintained private road rutted by the frosts, a constant source of rage to Otto, whose perfectly maintained and painted house shames the neighbours, or rather, fails to.

Oma used to take me there on courtesy calls as seldom as was decently possible, for each call entailed a dreaded return visit. They would arrive at the flat; later at the hotel, punctual to the minute, laden with flowers and chocolates, theatre guides and silk scarves, expensive presents which obliged Oma to reciprocate in kind, ever deepening a friendship which must have seemed to them to be beyond price.

True to protocol, they gave me two pearls for a first birthday present. Each year more would arrive with Victor to be viewed with bored incomprehension by my small ungrateful self, always wondering why it couldn't have been a dolly. Last Christmas they were ceremonially returned by Oma for the addition of the final pair, the stringing, the careful choosing of the diamond-set clasp. Herr Tiedemann handed over the long black suede box this summer at my 21st birthday party, thus culminating the ritual which is traditional for godparents. They aren't though, my wayward parents having failed me in that respect; the act of presentation was another of Herr Tiedemann's mutely eloquent reproaches. I should of course be grateful for such an expensive gift, so carefully assembled; just a small token, he said in an interminable speech, of the great affection he has had for me over the years. But I don't like pearls and nobody wears them. They're so old-fashioned. It was deadening, having to express my gratitude, as if I hadn't long known about and dreaded the event. I expect he bought the pearl earrings which are the wedding present; I am sure he is secretly pleased that it hasn't come off. He made another of his long, carefully prepared speeches when our engagement was announced and joked with hollow wit about having held me on his knee first. He expressed his rapture at this union between the two halves of the firm with such wooden enthusiasm that it was only then, watching him mouth his platitudes, that I realised how much he disliked Victor. There he was, once more usurping him, unfairly achieving in one step a closeness to the family which years of flowers and little Andenken and remembering wedding anniversaries haven't brought him. I can't help feeling rather sorry for him. If he only realised how irritating it is to have to feel grateful; the hardening of the heart at another thoughtful little gesture. It's so easy to admire people who are difficult, who must be wooed, whose respect seems unattainable. Any normal person is bound to despise somebody they please without effort. Ergo, my love for unattainable Victor; his rejection of me. Nobody wants the apple that falls at their feet, over-ripe and wormy; everybody wants to have to climb the tree, select and pick for themselves.

However, because I'm such a hypocrite, I wore the pearls to give him pleasure. Lotte got into her usual tizz over us. She's one of those highly nervous, faded thin blondes, carefully manicured to the utmost ridge of her thin and brittle nails. She wears a blue stone signet with the family crest and can't leave it alone, twisting it round and round as though she couldn't get the position quite right. The soft gold has worn, it slips more and more and she adjusts it endlessly. Old Otto stares at her in silent reproof, making her all the more nervous. I bet he puts her through gruesome post mortems on her inadequacies.

Everything came on special doilies, little crocheted ones to anchor the coffee cups, a larger one for the china cake-stand full of home-baked cakes. It's rather an empty house with shiny, polished surfaces with those spiky plants on every window-sill. They have all the fashionable things, English dining-room furniture, modern upholstered sofas, the china sea-captain's dogs, but it's too empty, it's sterile. Of course they never had children to mess things up and make it homely; no grandchildren for Otto to spoil and terrify.

I longed for a cigarette the moment we set foot inside. Linda's bored sighs verged on the audible and after a minute I just had to have one. Lotte darted back and forth emptying each inch of ash and bringing a new ashtray like a manic jack-in-the-box, still maintaining her rigid smile. Otto's welcome wore thinner in the noxious blue haze. Linda, almost totally silent, scoffed and scoffed; poor Lotte couldn't take her eyes off her, gripped by the endless mastication and her hair which is naturally streaky and looks as if somebody has doused it with peroxide. Then there is her make-up, which is evidently excessive for a nice young lady. God knows, Lotte's face has never been polluted with such filth and her crowning glory is lacquered into that awful, straight-back slightly bouffant style, which should make her look younger but just succeeds in emphasising its general sparseness. You can see right through it if there's a light behind.

After the third cup of coffee, Linda's fifth bit of cake, Lotte offered to show Linda round and she, obligingly, stood up at once, scattering a fine shower of crumbs all over the floor, and they left us to our tête à tête. Otto hummed and ha'ed in that way he has, fiddling with his collar. He has to be correct at all times. He'd stoop to tie a shoelace in a fire. He set off in a typical pleasantry about how nice it was to have me there, how he'd like Oma to be there too, what a deep respect he had for her and how she, of course, remembered the old days and so on; what a shame I hadn't seen the office in those days and what good times he and Opa used to have. He calls me Du of course, having known me since I was tiny. When I was seventeen he made a big thing out of my being a young lady now and having to say Sie, obliging me to insist upon Du. He'd have loved to 'duzen' my grandparents, but the offer was never made; a permanent chagrin. I wasn't listening very hard, just nodding sympathetically now and then, when it emerged that he was leading up to something. What it boiled down to from a thousand circumlocutions was that things were not like the good old days, in one particular respect: that Herr Genscher had seen fit to exclude him from his confidence. In other words, Victor was up to something and he wanted to know what it was and, more to the point, he thought that I could help him. Why I can't imagine, for he's been the door-keeper who's made sure I never get near. 'I never see him,' I said unhelpfully and baldly. I had another cigarette then, when matters were getting interesting, and it was a study to see him control himself and even look around for an ashtray in a helpful manner, no doubt gritting his yellow old teeth.

'Ja, ja,' he said, 'die liebe Frau Rommer hat es wie immer gut gemeint, aber die Zeiten ändern sich, nicht wahr?' And he said, smiling ingratiatingly, that he wants me to meet Victor in a sort of semi-official capacity as the other half of the firm and find out what he's doing. And then he added that in these special circumstances he felt it would be quite correct – and he was thinking of my dear grandmother – if he accompanied me to such a meeting. As though I'd want him there, big ears flapping; as though I needed protection from Victor, who is hardly likely to rape me on the carpet. He, who guards Victor as though I had the plague, offers him up now, just because it suits him.

Of course I was furious, but I could hear Lotte's voice dithering on outside about how they'd be redoing the hallway and apologising for its shabbiness, which might be apparent if the wall were examined with a x50 glass. So I said very primly that my grandmother would not approve at all and he winced a little. I even did my best to evoke Oma's robust presence; seeing Linda appear in the doorway with a pleading look, I reminded him that 'ein junges Mädchen geht nie mit leeren Händen aus dem Zimmer', and collected up a heap of china to take out, signalling departure. It reminded me of how I used to tease Oma by carrying quite essential objects, such as her reading glasses, out of the room. I cleared the table, banging Lotte's delicate porcelain down on the shiny draining board where three dirty ashtrays winked reproof. She fluttered about me like a crazed butterfly, nipping at my arm and saying it wasn't necessary, no really not, her anxiety exacerbated by the high probability that I would smash a piece of her irreplaceable set and by Otto's scowling at her as though, as usual, everything was her fault. How can she bear him?

So I have wilfully thrown away an opportunity for an official summit conference with Herr Genscher. We left; Otto was anxious to fumigate me away.

'Herzlichste Grüsse an meine liebe Frau Rommer,' he said. 'Ganz herzliche Grüsse sollst Du von uns bestellen,' as though I didn't know he writes regularly. He couldn't quite bring himself to kiss my nicotine-polluted hand, as he sometimes does, giving me instead his firm Prussian grip while his wife smiled and waved and uttered little choked-off politenesses in between her seigneur's farewells.

I interrupted Linda's description of the antiseptic perfection of the Tiedemann bathrooms with their scrubbed grouting; her little pitcher of scorn lavished on the nattily embroidered guest towels and flower-shaped soap, both of which her own dear mother affects. Lotte showed her everything: the leather volumes in Otto's study alongside the row of pipes, identical to Opa's, which he never smokes, and even the symmetrical pyramids of cans and boxes in the Vorratskeller.

'You know, he may have a point,' she said, and then, 'Oh I see. You only want to see him on your own. Well for God's sake do it, sneak into his flat or something.'

Linda does not appreciate the subtleties of the situation. Even I know that old Otto thinks he is trying to help, in his accursed, nosy way. He always says things like 'I'm ready to serve' or 'I know my duty' with a vaguely military air, though everybody knows he was too young for the first war and evaded the second by staying in the Far East. He thinks girls need protection, as though the one thing a young virgin dreams of in her maidenly bliss is stalwart Otto's crooked arm to lean on. I can't help resenting his assumptions about my purity, even though they're perfectly correct. Does he even know, I wonder, that to be a virgin at my age is an aberration, a shameful anachronism? Sometimes I think there's only me left, and Ingrid naturally.

I think we were the last year at school to leave virgins, with certain exceptions including my precocious friend. The last pure A-level year: another damning epitaph. I have been thinking of it, now that Linda's here, for we were so close then.

That summer was bright and brilliant as exam times always are. We lay in the orchard under snowdrifts of notes until the backs of our legs and forearms were brown, wasps buzzing around the crabapples. The murmur of our strange incantations, German, Spanish and French quotes chanted in unison, rose to the fourth form classrooms where the juniors, poor innocents, hung out enviously and thought us lucky to be outside. Overwrought and slightly hysterical, we played infantile jokes on our mistresses, such as hiding in the locker rooms. We were permanently tired from late-night revision; Linda from her evenings with a student who, more grandly, was to fail his finals for her sake. The night before each exam I sat up until three coaching her, a parade of my knowledge and her abysses of ignorance. I admired her calm, unruffled manner as she sauntered into the sunshine and down to the pub to meet Bobby while we were still scribbling at question two.

We were coldly scornful of the swots who left each exam in tears, swearing they couldn't do a thing, when we'd seen them raise a hand for paper three times. Joyce Highley's pink, mottled face blanched white in horror when the customary cacophonous post mortem on the English Lit paper revealed that she had answered all the questions in one section, throwing away two thirds of the marks; she threw a heel-drumming tantrum and had to be collected by her mother. Joyce it was who went on to find that fairground novelty, a bearded woman, concealed in her French translation. 'Et it entrait une personne barbue, bossue, basanée, qui avançait peu a peu, qui badaudait, qui vacillait . . . ' In came a woman with a beard and hump, wrote Joyce robustly. She mangled that so thoroughly that the ignominy of January re-sits and another term at school became inevitable: Joyce, whose reluctant companion was to be Linda, for this time Mr Davenport put his foot down when three O-level passes joined the eight she already had. It was during the blazing fortnight of our A-levels that we became a little estranged. I found her irresponsible in the face of coming disgrace; she disliked my self-righteous pompousness and we parted a little coolly.

I travelled with two vast trunks full of books and photographs, my sentimental baggage strapped up tight. The night before the ship sailed, I confessed to Oma, who had not failed to notice Victor's characteristic downhill scrawl on Hamburg letters, that a little romance was in progress.

'I know,' she said and shook her head sadly. She spoke of the city's delights and all the young people I would meet and how hard I had to work and how busy I would be; that I should enjoy myself with more of those young people and, on the other hand, not let myself be distracted. She told me the details of Herr Tiedemann funding me and said how pleased she was that I was going out into the world and not a word against Victor. I didn't mention marriage, knowing exactly what her views were; I let her believe it was not serious and callously suppressed the knowledge that she would be lonely without me and worried.

'I am glad that you decided to tell me,' she said and made me feel even more of a heel.

Oma was practical and kind, carefully packing my case, folding layers of tissue paper round dresses and sneaking in bars of chocolate double-wrapped in tin foil and, as her parting gift, a shiny black briefcase. I was in tears, but not she, erect and indomitable on the dusty streets of Harwich. But Oma is nobody's fool and she knows me too well.

'Sei vorsichtig,' she said, at the most vulnerable, parting moment, speaking in her penetrating voice the language that, surely, half the other passengers could understand. 'Enjoy yourself, but do not let Victor take an advantage of you; he is a gentleman and I trust you, but nimm Dich in Acht.'

It cost her an effort to say this and I flushed beetroot at this first-ever mention of sex and gave my word, ambiguously, not to do anything foolish. A promise howling to be broken.

She needn't have worried. Victor behaved impeccably. He was a perfect gentleman, as though he subscribed to the same dated etiquette book as Oma. He installed me in a comfortable, well-guarded hotel near Dammtor station, a place where the chambermaids were motherly types and the manager a personal acquaintance of his. It was full of families of German tourists with scarcely a soul between the ages of twelve and thirty and a wholesome set menu with four kinds of potatoes, to be eaten in a large, immaculately clean dining room where half the tables were always empty. If a bottle of wine was ordered it was a small occasion, the bottle carefully recorked and brought out with a label on it at the next meal. In the evenings, a few old couples would watch television in the faded sitting room where the empty chairs were arranged in neat, sociable circles and nobody under the age of sixty ever intruded. You had to ask for a key if, outrageously, you contemplated a late return.

Victor took me out to dinner a lot, to elegant places where he talked wittily in just the tone he used with my grandparents. At the opera I listened with the right expression, staying awake for love. We frequented smart cafés around the Alster on Sunday afternoons, and a dozen women smiled and waved and weren't always introduced and other tables seemed much jollier than ours. We passed crowded student places and Victor would cock an interrogative eyebrow, as though I was really dying to be there, with the amused look of a parent observing the younger generation at play. We sat once or twice in his flat, chastely apart, with the huge bed throbbing away next door. I never quite knew what to talk about and was silent for long spells, tongue-tied and anxious, my occasional pearls of wisdom coming out as hollow and juvenile as a plastic bead.

Victor's life is studded with formal occasions: black-tie dinners, gala balls, intimate evenings with dressy friends carefully planned around the lobster and asparagus seasons. He sailed away one weekend with his yachting cronies and the water widows invited me to their ladies' evening. Terribly informal, don't dress, they said, so I squirmed in jeans, gauche beside their nautical silk evening sweaters. They jabbered on about their children, who were practically my age, and about the difficulties of looking after parents who were younger than Oma. They ate, drank and laughed a little too much, complimenting me on my cleverness in a way that demonstrated that universities were for ugly blue-stockings and their clever boys. I sat stumm with no meeting ground but Victor, whom they all seemed to know far better than I did; as tense and bored as is mutually compatible. I envied them their womanly elegance, which didn't suit me, while they eyed me over long cigarette holders, clearly wondering what, apart from the Rommer fortune, he saw in me. It was a question I was asking myself.

'Doch keine Schönheit,' I heard one whisper, 'aber sehr liebenswürdig.' An annihilating verdict: sweet, amiable.

These women without a serious idea in their glossy heads, who never read anything more demanding under the hair-dryer than the latest blockbuster by Johannes Mario Simmel, observed, smiled and found me lacking. There was more to Victor, more to me than these brittle ladies thought, but he hid from me behind these ghastly friends, their exquisite flower arrangements and lobster bibs, their pastel tennis skirts and matching balls, their bottles of Sekt and good works.

Meanwhile, as though everything was hunkydory, Victor went on making the right gestures. The roses were delivered each Friday night with a card saying 'See you tonight, greetings Victor', or 'Till Sunday, your Victor' but he never said that he was mine, he never told me that he loved me. He behaved as though everything was arranged.

The engagement was announced privately, to Oma's sad disappointment. There was a half-hearted evening which Otto insisted upon and nobody enjoyed. Oma came for the weekend, looked at me unhappily and insisted on knowing whether I was happy and of course I insisted that I was. We went to an intimidating jeweller's to choose a large sapphire, which he decided should be set with diamonds in an art deco design which I knew was too grand and too adult for my bony fingers. All the time he was watching me, faintly amused, ever charming but remote, kissing me goodnight with respect, without passion. Weak-kneed with silent lust, I told myself that he respected me, unlike my predecessors. His affairs were legion; it could hardly be possible that he didn't believe in sex before marriage. I couldn't bring myself to mention it. I couldn't break through his poised aloofness, the appalling way he kept treating me as though I was an adult and knew the rules. I think he exposed me to the stuffiest of evenings and stiffest business friends in the hope that I would revolt, but I was too biddable, too anxious to please at all costs.

We talked about the future. He said, for example, that he wanted children. I asked myself furiously if it was to be an immaculate conception. I worked very hard at convincing myself that he was truly in love and therefore did not want to take advantage of me. I had all I had dreamed of and felt blank despair. If he loved anything, it was surely our firm and I saw all too clearly how neatly I was an extension of his career, a thought which in England had never entered my head. An ugly suspicion, which nevertheless didn't stop me loving him. As long as he wanted to buy, I was selling, at any price.

That summer I was alone for the first time in my life. I bought a huge lexicon and spent hours looking up words I found in long, solemn books to improve my German; as though the language were at fault; as though in English there would have been no silences. It was a test and I was revising in the only way I knew. I wrote to Oma daily, giving long and, alas, accurate reports on Victor's gentlemanly ways, feeling horribly young, unprepared for everything and out of my depth. He was the same Victor and yet everything was subtly different. In Hamburg he had reverted from lover to uncle, behaving as though they were the same thing. After a while I began to write to Linda, telling her the truth. She was marvellous, encouraging, packing the pages with terse descriptions of her romantic jugglings, so many balls up in the air at once, as it were. She never once said she'd told me so. Go on, seduce him, she said.

I bought new dresses and carefully applied make-up to look older, invested in scent and lace knickers to no effect and made myself sound cheerful and unconcerned while whimpering inside. That Sunday in August I broke the unwritten rules, running to his flat with my A-level results, the telegram stuffed into my pocket. I wanted him to be the first to know how well I'd done.

He was caught unawares in a bathrobe; in a slight, uncharacteristic disorder of Brötchen crumbs and Sunday papers. The rush, the heat, the momentousness of the occasion, my own daring, the aroma of coffee and five flights of hurdled stairs all made my head swim and he looked at me without the mask and with an unfamiliar expression.

Action replay: Victor amorous. The big scene, the one I have watched and criticised hundreds of times. I held out the telegram, but he wasn't looking. He took hold of me (slow motion, first kiss) and he kissed me properly, tasting faintly, deliciously of apricot jam. Heroine, stupid girl, can barely stand. We tumbled onto the sofa in a heap. The cotton dress I wore had at least twenty buttons down the front and he undid every one with care, in between kisses. (Shouldn't he have ripped the dress? Touch of brutality surely de rigueur?) I thought my heartbeat was louder than the Mahler; it should, of course, have been violins. He is beautiful naked, my Victor. He is brown and polished, tiny neat white bum a delicious contrast. Apart from Opa I'd never seen a grown man naked, never realised how huge an erect prick is. Heroine isn't, of course, supposed to look. But then, though I hadn't heard it, somebody shouted, 'Cut!' Inexplicably, without a word, he just got up and put his bathrobe and his face back on and said quite formally I'm sorry, please forgive me. We had all the ingredients for romance: the music, the place, everything, it seemed, but sufficient desire. He had his armour back on but I was half-naked in a crude crumple of clothes and I shut my eyes for a moment and opened them again, as though the scene would change and revert, and had that strange sensation of everything receding you get sometimes when falling asleep. Victor and the room diminished away into the far distance. (Was that the mistake, not keeping my eyes shut the whole time? Would that have helped?) Miles away on the other side of the room he poured a cup of coffee and came back life-size and offered it to me, the cup jangling on the saucer in my shaking hand. Poor heroine, who needed a double brandy at least.

It was bitter. A profound, bitter humiliation. I wanted to vanish or to scream. There was nothing either one of us could find to say. Was that pity in his eyes? I don't know, the camera hasn't recorded it. Suddenly intensely embarrassed, I got up to find one arm was numb and did the buttons up all wrong in my fumbling, shamed haste. I ran away without a word, a blind march back past Sunday strollers, singing the sad Mahler in my head so the thoughts would be driven out until I was safe in my room. I remember thinking, but I have three As, as though they were a talisman to protect me. I didn't realise, until the receptionist handing over the weighty key stared just so, that my dress was all askew.

An hour later the letter came, the first of Victor's special, hand-delivered notes. It was a kind, affectionate letter full of crap, saying how very fond he was of me and how he had realised that I was after all too young and he was taking advantage of my inexperience, though the fact was that he had cruelly quite failed to do that. He regretted, he said, to cause me pain, but I would soon see that he was right. I deserved a far better, younger man than he. It was a horrible letter, the only one of his which I destroyed.

I think I knew the first day in Hamburg that it was already over; knew when he put his bathrobe on that it was hopeless. I knew as I sat in that horrible hotel in the pale green room with its over-stuffed clashing green armchairs with spidery anti-macassars, holding myself together until something happened, until the letter delivered the coup de grâce, that I had failed the test. No amount of revision would have helped. He had found me physically distasteful. Men could screw anybody, I knew, the worst, gaudiest, over-the-hill prostitute, but not Victor, not me. I was helplessly, insuperably inferior.

Poor abject worm that I was, I wanted to see him one more time. Another Victor, yet more remote but politely attentive over lunch in an expensive restaurant with a waiter hovering always too near for intimacy, a place he probably chose for that reason. The smell of fish made me feel sick. My throat ached with keeping back the tears; I couldn't eat. He said all the same meaningless lies again about being too old in a gentle, final voice. We didn't mention Sunday. Too proud to cry there, I listened and tried to make my face look normal, to school my nervous eyelid. Yes, I said, I understand, as though I meant it. We sat on and the coffee came and got cold and we were the very last to leave, because while I stayed there I could still look at him.

I told Oma on the telephone, very carefully, repeating over and over again that I was absolutely fine. Such calls are a mistake. The line magnifies the quavers, accentuates the pauses, conveys a hundred secrets when none is mentioned. She rushed for the next plane and, childish with relief, I sobbed for days and she stroked my hair and soothed me and listened to me insist how kind and considerate Victor had been throughout. A gentleman. She went out one morning to see him and returned without a word.

The next day she took me to a crowded resort in Italy, where from the back every other man had a look of him and where I lay inert, blasted immobile by the sun, feeling my heart thump painfully against sand crests I had no energy to smooth away. Oma told me old family stories to make me smile; she hinted by reference to her first husband that first love was not always the last. One day we got sloshed on schnapps and I told her everything, exactly what had happened and what it felt like. When I had finished and we had bawled our eyes out, she said with restraint that it was all to the good. She said, dear Oma, that she blamed herself for allowing the relationship to develop; she said that she should have known. Much as she liked Victor, he was not suitable husband material for anyone and certainly not for me.

There was something I didn't tell her, could never tell anybody. I had the feeling that I was disfigured, and he knew it; he had seen through the young, unblemished skin to something bad inside. I knew it had nothing to do with age or inexperience. It's almost as though I had always known there was something like that; always expected to be found out one day. The real explanation is hidden behind his courteous, polite phrases and I want that truth, however bad, for my peace of mind. Inscrutable, deceiving Victor: a wicked uncle indeed, not to have told me the truth.

I took my turmoil back to Hamburg and started my course as though nothing had happened. I couldn't face the English university which Oma recommended. It was more alien by far, stuffed with horrible, raucous English youth, with one or two of my immeasurably distant schoolpals from another age. To go back would have been a total defeat; I needed to find myself here and persuaded Oma that I could be safely left alone, putting on a great show of bravado and confidence. Darling Oma; she did her best. If you must stay, she said delicately, it will be less painful if you don't see him at all. I can arrange for Herr Tiedemann to handle all your affairs; nothing would please him more. Selfish in misery, walking wounded with Oma as my crutch, it never occurred to me that I could be putting her in an embarrassing position.

Braves Kind, I agreed to everything. Fine, I wouldn't see Victor; I didn't want to anyway. I needed all my strength to conceal and carry my unhappiness, like a belt of smuggled gold that mustn't be seen to weigh. Oma searched for flats and babied me. She told Opa's best jokes, which she always starts with the punch line. His ghost sauntered around the city. She saw it everywhere, an elegant lounging figure trailing a fragrant plume of smoke from its pipe, while I, heart in my mouth, saw only a blond metallic head: a poltergeist Victor at every street corner. She found the flat, awing Frau Beckmann with the thoroughness of her inspection, and the day I moved in I saw a picture of Victor in the paper. He was at a charity do with a blonde on his arm. I cut it out and later burnt it. How quick he was to console himself.

When Oma left, I determined not to be lonely. I met a few kindred souls in the unlikely environment of Aula II; a few bored window-watchers among the bowed heads. There is a group of Hamburg daughters, smart gossipy young ladies who live at home and snarl the traffic with their little sports cars and summer racing bicycles, whom I avoid. There are dozens of men, hordes of foreign students, glistening-browed giggling Nigerians, young Turks in every sense, bearded radicals plotting in safety at their Stammtisch. There are graduate students with their universal metal-rimmed spectacles and neatly annotated folders; there are the so-called Anglophiles, who dress in Scottish lambswool and tartan scarves, who smoke pipes, drink ice-cold beer at the Queen's Pub in the Gänsemarkt and would love to hone their accents on me. I've tried, but I can't work up the slightest interest in any of them, even those who laugh at my bad puns, tell me I'm pretty and lunge quite effectively – for they all lunge, sooner or later. My type is quite different; regrettably specific, just as Linda is Victor's type. The archetypal female companion: vivacious, a little plump and outrageously blonde.

And now it seems that I am Sigi's type, and yet he's just the sort to go for something flashy. Here is a thought more interesting to consider than my essay, that overdue piece of sleuthing into Prof. Burger's devious little brain cells.

Points about Sigismund Schmidt: No visible means of support, as the bishop said to the actress. No job and yet he spends money lavishly and is carefully put together. His jeans are pressed, shoes polished, and as well as the baubles round the neck there's a thick gold ring. In fact, in a suit he'd look like a ponce. He took us to a dockside Kneipe on Wednesday; we were slumming, but he was clearly in his natural habitat. There was a row of women perched on high stools, exceedingly exposed when it came to cleavage and length of skirt, on the other hand perfectly concealed behind the lavish colouring on the face. Looking at the flounces, sparkly danglers and heels, I thought they might be whores. I realised my mistake when he took us to see the real thing standing next to anchor chains in the docks, bulging bottoms in minis, white plastic boots and black fishnet stockings and surely freezing despite the twee little boleros that never got near covering the upthrust bosoms. They didn't like seeing women in the car; one pointedly turned her back. Linda, gripped, asked thousands of questions and Sigi knew a lot of the answers. He is familiar with their world, though highly disapproving. He was scathing about those girls and when I said I felt sorry for them he laughed and said I was mistaken; a lot of them thought it easy money. They could get waitressing jobs, if they were less greedy, he said, and that in Hamburg prostitution is strictly regulated by the police with compulsory medical check-ups by doctors who issue certificates to show they are free of disease. A cold business indeed. There was no nonsense in him about sympathising with the oppressed exploited proletariat, none of the generosity of feeling you get from student radicals. As far as Sigi was concerned they were slags and deserved what they got. Some were schoolgirls, he said, run away from home to go on the game and enjoy some freedom. He'd have put them all in a strict reformatory.

There is no question of Herr Schmidt being an Autostrich client. I saw them, fat middle-aged men in big cars who drive slowly past with their ugly heads hanging out of the windows. Greedy-eyed men, who park at the end where the street lamps peter out and screw the girls in the back of their cars. Sigi is much too handsome to ever have to pay.

His car: a bright red baby Alfa which he drives much too fast. Expensive, like the rest of his tastes.

Sigi and women: his attitude to 'decent' women is very protective, downright old-fashioned. He wants to pay for every drink, was offended that I insisted and certainly wouldn't let me collect a round from the bar, that haunt of vice. A drunken old man reeled by and made some stupid remark about him being with two girls and one to spare, eh? and Sigi was beside himself, He got up, took off his jacket and was ready to fight him, sleeves rolled up and fists clenched. The old guy got quite a shock and slunk away, saying no offence, mein Jung. We went on to a transvestites' cabaret, at Linda's request, and he loathed it. I can't say I liked it much myself, as the audience sits jammed together inches from a small central space where the 'girls' sing and prance, staring offensively at any woman in the audience and making rude comments, meanwhile showing off their silicon bosoms. Linda, who didn't understand half of what they said, was smiling, but Sigi wouldn't stay; it was an affront and he shooed us out, though not before making a few cracks of his own in incomprehensible Platt.

That protectiveness does not, however, exclude the arm around the shoulders. He wasn't pushy; no lunge, though that wretch Linda zapped out of the car into the flat like a rocket, leaving us idling at the kerb. He gave me a small ironic smile, which recognised that he wasn't going to be invited in, said might he see me alone some time? and held out his hand, for heaven's sake.

Saturday night was a demonstration that he knows how to live; that he can crack a crab and not drink the water in the finger-bowl. His treat and it cost a bomb; after the way he'd outfaced the waiter I didn't dare offer to pay. I have the usual middle-class guilt about upsetting the servants and always smarmy up to waiters and over-tip if they show the slightest willingness to serve. Not Sigi. 'You think I'm bad-mannered,' he said. 'But they're paid to serve. They laugh at you behind your back for paying so much, they outstare you at the end for a big tip and in the meanwhile they'd spit on your food if they could. Me they understand; they respect me. You watch,' and he was right, 'we'll get the best service in the place.'

It was easier to talk without Linda there, leaning back as if to say go on, enjoy yourselves, don't mind me. He questioned me all about family and friends; even suggested that I had relations I wasn't admitting to as though I hadn't got enough. There was, of course, always Ingrid so I treated him to a few episodes of her unblemished career, and then he started an interrogation about boyfriends. Fine, he said, when I was starting to get cross, now I'll tell you about myself. Fair's fair.

He told me the facts without, somehow, conveying at all what it felt like being him. Widowed, hard-working mother; one brother, a childhood in Altona. He was clever enough to have done his Abitur, but refused to change school and leave his friends. There are some fierce, misplaced loyalties in there. He's sporty and goes to a gym, even thought at one time of

119

becoming a boxer, but decided not to spoil his pretty face, and raised his eyebrows when he said that in self-mockery.

In fact I don't think he's vain. Like pretty girls who stamp their feet and insist it's brains that count, he cares not about looks but status, or presence. What matters to him is being treated with respect. Nobody's going to push Sigi around. He may be, mortifyingly, prettier than me, but educationally he's got pimples. Lots of break-outs. He went to a technical school to be a draughtsman and left because it was boring; started an apprenticeship as a mechanic but hated being bound in that way and the pay was lousy, so left that too. He shrugged his shoulders. Good at drawing, at machines, a man of all parts but no stamina.

Swot Rommer immediately said he could go back to school, get an Abitur, start again, etc., and offended him. In Altona we don't go to University and become doctors and professors and then, disconcertingly, no, don't get me wrong, I don't usually talk to girls like this, I'm not used to it. But don't get me wrong, I think I'm as good as you are, but I do things my way. I sat there thinking what am I doing with this failed mechanic bully-boy and he smiled then (he has a very sweet smile) and said okay, now we're going to the Dom. I'm a hell of a shot, you'll see.

He must have won every prize in the fair ground and hit every bull's eye. He made the coconut man's night a misery. I was laden with blue nylon teddy bears and stale gingerbread hearts and sticky with candy floss. It's terrific at night, icy and brilliantly lit, and we went on every ride and he was admired by every girl who passed and I felt rather proud of him. He cracked jokes with the stallkeepers and bought me junk until I hadn't a spare finger left for another thing.

On the way home we talked about England. It's a mystery to him, a mythical land of pop singers and mini-skirts, tea-drinking and Carnaby Street and an anachronistic Queen, for he is a Republican naturally. We have serious faults, such as warm beer and driving on the wrong side of the road, but much can be forgiven a nation which has given the world the E-Type Jaguar and the Mini-Cooper. Why Hamburg? he said, so I told him about Rommer's and was ashamed of having lied;

and, to expiate, told him about my sort of uncle who wasn't a real relative and that I'd come here to be near him and he said Aha, as if he'd known all along there must have been a romance in it somewhere. I was shrieking over the roar of the nearly exhaustless car; the speed must have loosened my tongue. In the sudden silence outside my front door, quite unnerved, I heard myself asking him in for coffee.

Linda hadn't yet returned from skirmishing with her Gastarbeiter. He wandered around looking at things while I put coffee on and he didn't make a single move. We lay companionably on the fur rug and ate nuts. He said, predictably, have you actually read all those books? and I lied, to impress him. He rolled over then in a nonchalant sort of way to kiss me and instead of leaping to my feet to get more milk I sort of leant towards him and at that precise instant we heard the key in the door and leapt apart like criminals; that fact not unnoticed by Linda, even in her disarray. He didn't stay; he went off saying I'll call you in a casual tone but instead, today, the roses came.


Tuesday, December 16, 1971


I can't believe this. I went to the post office to despatch my long-overdue letter to Oma and when I got back Linda let me ramble on for twenty minutes before throwing in Guess who phoned? in far too mysterious a tone. Victor has asked her out to dinner. I loathed her for an instant and she saw it. For Christ's sake, Johanna, he's probably being polite. Look, I don't have to go. She shook me rather hard. Look, goddamit, have I ever done anything to hurt you.

She's going. I want her to. I have to have confidence in her. We spent the evening avoiding the subject, since it was settled after all, drinking a lot of wine and chattering as though it hadn't happened. I kept waking up in the night and thinking about it, about how neatly she corresponds to his feminine ideal, and then hating myself. Wisely, she's gone out and left me to my own devices. That bloody essay sits here and mocks me with two paragraphs written, both of them lousy. She's seeing him on Thursday. I feel slightly sick all the time, guts churning away. The head sends out messages saying don't be so stupid, but the stomach is deaf.

I want so badly to see him. There are a hundred scenarios: the street-corner encounter, the knock at the door of the flat, the accidental meeting in the great glass foyer of the opera.

'Who is that beautiful girl in the blue dress, Herr Genscher?'

'Why it's little Johanna, grown up at last.'

Surge of violins as hands touch; soft-focus as eyes sink deeply into another pair. But then I remember that Sunday and my courage fails me. What could be more pitiful than raking over the ashes of an old affair, than being seen to care? It's Anne Elliot, I think, who says that women have the dubious privilege of loving longest, when hope is lost. But the tone in which she says it gives the Captain hope. These things happen only in books.

Linda, naturally, subscribes to the realist school, the kitchen-sink drama. She believes in pleasure, not romance. Men are 'tasty' or 'delicious', to be gobbled up; she'd make an excellent female spider, the predatory kind who make love and then crunch up the male, discarding the husk. She, too, had a few night thoughts. Her little pressure-cooker of a head finally blew this morning, venting a lot of hot air. Linda's advice: see him, demystify him, there's nothing more off-putting than an old flame in the flesh. You'll look at him and think how could I, she said, with a wry grimace, that awful retrospective self-disgust. Lay the ghost. Dear Linda, it is not the ghost I want to lay.

The sight of my misery decided her to give me some advice for once and she settled herself in the way people do when preparing to say something unpleasant; arranging her feet, smoothing her skirt, looking me in the eye with friendly concern.

'Now I expect you don't want to hear this,' she said by way of a preamble and I steeled myself, lit a cigarette and said, 'No I don't,' but she carried on as people always do when the proselytising urge overcomes common sense. I have an obsession. An unhealthy fixation; it's awful for a friend to watch me suffer, and so on. Earnest and unstoppable, she zapped me with her nasty mixed metaphors.

'Thank God he doesn't want to know, because you'd run off to be his doormat at the drop of a hat, he only has to raise his little finger.' Or something in that style.

People who pride themselves on never meddling think that when they do, for once, open their mouths, what comes out is Gospel truth. The more unpleasant the revelations, the more honestly and frankly they are delivered.

'This whole business of being in love is a fallacy,' she says. 'All that passion goes away and you'll be stranded in some house with dishes and screaming brats. You don't want that, do you? It's never going to happen to me.' I have got to rely on myself and not the props of romance or the myth of the perfect marriage; unhappiness ever after.

She made out quite a convincing case against Victor. She remembers all the bad things I've ever, stupidly, told her and even my old letters became evidence for the prosecution's accusing finger. I was unhappy when I was with him, I felt completely alone and abandoned, did I remember that? I am, in short, ruining my life and making a mockery of my independence, wasting my time on a shit. This is called being cruel to be kind. She generated as much heat and rage as if she'd been the offended party. I could feel myself harden, not against Victor, but against Linda. For offending the basic rules of friendship.

There is never any defence against this sort of thing. The accused, poor deranged soul, can only plead temporary (or in my case permanent) insanity and hope for leniency. She sailed on to her grand finale, while I muttered, 'I know,' every now and then, ending with her pious hope that I would come to my senses. She tailed off then and became faintly apologetic in a slightly defiant, you'll thank me one day, manner. 'Oh Christ,' she said as I sat mute, 'shall I pack my bags?'

How could I say yes? We made a truce, peace of a sort. I said she was right, as I suppose she is, to console her; I saw her off with a smile. Why do people always need comforting when they've been horrible? The most irritating thing about people meaning well is that you're not allowed to hold their home truths against them; you are expected to be grateful. There seemed no point in explaining that the thing is unfinished; that I mean to let go of Victor the instant I have explained the whole thing to my satisfaction. I can't just proceed with my life as though it hadn't all been turned topsy-turvy.

I must stop and do this essay, I'm supposed to give it in tomorrow. I'm almost relieved at something to fill the great void. I've skipped four lectures since last week, one supposedly obligatory, and must atone. The ladies are coming the day after tomorrow; Ingrid seems a suitably thorny stick to beat myself with.

# Chapter 9

Victor was dismissing Heinz Bruch. For nearly two weeks he had trailed Fräulein Rommer and found it dull work. On the day of composing his little signe de vie to Johanna, Victor had recruited the ex-steward, a dapper little man who had slithered expertly and silently out of upper and lower deck cabins for so long that his whole demeanour was that of a servant: unobtrusive, unnoticeable, laconic and sly. Bruch, infinitely purchaseable, had seemed an excellent choice. His merchant navy career having long since come to a dishonourable end, his happy spell on luxury liners having been abridged by a congenital weakness for gambling which had obliged him to dip without prior permission into the purser's pockets, he had settled happily for lucrative employment with Victor. The windfall had discharged a small, necessary number of debts and enabled him to swagger into the tailor's of his choice with a fistful of the ready. Now, after a fortnight of assiduous work and a good many evenings spent shivering at street corners, he found himself turned off. This was merely, it seemed, because he had not seen any hooligans menacing the young lady. Looking sullenly at his employer, he wished him ill.

Victor paid him no attention at all; Bruch left his mind as abruptly as he left the room. He felt only relief at one thing less to concern him.

Another letter had found its way into Herr Genscher's postbox. Herr Frisch could consider his honour intact; this letter was delivered quite unremarkably by the normal agency of the Bundespost. And yet, if the yellow hunting horn that adorned that worthy system had let out a blast, he could not have received a greater tremor upon discovering it that morning.

This second, anonymous yet perfectly identifiable document was more difficult to decipher than the first. It was not typed but hand-written in a female script. The tone, in other circumstances, would have made Victor laugh.

'My son, Wilfried Ferdinand Meyer, was a handsome, upright young fellow, the pride of my heart. He was struck down, cruelly, before his prime by a wicked murderer who has never been brought to justice. He was seventeen and had just left home. We didn't want him to go, but boys will be boys and he wanted to go into the world. He had been offered a job training as a machine-tool maker, a skilled trade, for Wilfried was always good with his hands. There were few such opportunities in 1947. The factory was on the outskirts of Berlin so he had to travel a great distance every day, for we lived at the other end of the city. It seemed only sensible for the boy to live nearer his workplace and so he found himself a place in a hostel run by a young man looking after boys who had no homes. It was central and clean and decent. We packed up his things and off he went and I remember my dear boy shed a few tears in his mother's arms, old as he was, and my eyes were not dry.

'My poor Wilfried was an industrious and hard-working lad who never got into any trouble. He was gentle and easily influenced. He had sometimes become involved in the sort of childish pranks high-spirited boys think up. In this place, he came under an evil influence. There was a boy there called Victor Genscher, a rough street boy who envied him his earnings and his place. A trouble-maker and violent too. I believe he had run away from home and later I heard that he terrorised some of the small boys in that place. I often think that if only my brave boy had come home, this terrible tragedy would never have happened, but he –'

There it stopped; there Victor stopped, staring out over the quiet street. The boy was at his usual place on the street corner opposite. Victor's alter ego, his blond youthful counterpart, lounged under the street lamp and stared blankly into the thin, cold air, unnerving him with the meaninglessness of his vigil. Was Ludwig expecting him to run away?

For Ludwig had issued a challenge, in his own sly way. The second post had brought a note, quite innocuous to other eyes, informing Herr Genscher that his private tuition with Meister Judo was to commence the following week on Monday at 8 p.m. An invoice enclosed demanded the sum of DM200.– for eight lessons, payable upon receipt. There were several typographical errors on these pieces of paper; they would never have been permitted to depart from Herr Tiedemann's august out-tray.

Victor had re-read the letter several times, for there was a wealth of instructions xeroxed onto the rear; to the effect that a traditional Judo suit must be worn (available on a rental basis), that a doctor's check-up was advisable if the pupil had ever experienced back or knee problems; that children under the age of seven could not be admitted; that finger and toe nails should be cut short and rings or other metallic objects should not be worn; that pupils starting a course of instruction did so entirely at their own risk and the school could not be responsible for any injuries sustained. Meister Judo, the bottom line proclaimed, was affiliated to the International Judo Federation. This was, though Victor could not know it, no longer the case. The association with authority had long since lapsed, Ludwig's premises having been rejected on the grounds of insufficient hygiene and notably the absence of the foot baths recommended to practitioners of the sport.

Victor scanned the letter again, seeking the code that made sense of such trivia. He read the documents alternately until he knew them by heart, meanwhile pacing backwards and forwards past the elegant coffee table in a circuit that just stopped short of the windows. Earlier in the day, two little lads with satchels, whom Victor could not acquit of complicity, had amused themselves by drawing faces in the frosty glass of the tradesman's entrance until Herr Frisch shooed

127

them away. No innocent, playful children these: he had seen a certain ancient watchfulness in their eyes. The boy had been there from early that morning. Victor had seen him when he drew back the sitting-room curtains and had suppressed the unreasonable urge to flatten himself against the wall. Didn't he go to school? When did he eat, piss, sleep? These questions revolved tiresomely in Victor's head. He suppressed an urge to go up to him and say something; that would certainly be a defeat of some kind.

He noticed them and gave no sign of so doing. He counted the days. He believed that in another few weeks, when he had the newspaper, he would be invincible. After a while he searched for a match and watched the Meyer paper blacken in his kitchen sink.

Four floors below, Herr Tiedemann worked in utter silence. He had rung Lotte at seven to inform her, with a great degree of satisfaction, that once more he would not be home for dinner; that he would be very late indeed and she was not to wait up for him. With a little smile trembling on her lips she put down the telephone carefully and gathered the artifacts for a minor crime. Carefully, she placed not a doily, but a plate of crackers and cheese, a tumbler and, from the back of the freezer, a bottle of vodka on a little tray. Vodka, she knew, could not be smelt on the breath. The whole was to be consumed with hedonistic abandon in front of the television set, but not before she had carefully set the breakfast table for tomorrow.

The office was dark, apart from the lamp on Herr Tiedemann's desk. Everything was left properly, the typewriters covered, each chair pushed under its desk and the waste paper baskets neatly lined up to make life easier for Frau Meier. Once or twice the telex machine broke into startling, chattering life and the long curl of paper it was pushing out grew by ten or twenty centimetres. Herr Tiedemann's slim gold pen, a gift from Herr Genscher to mark his seventieth birthday, scarcely paused in its task. He was preparing a methodical transcription, line after line, of all of Herr Genscher's assets: the current value of Rommer shares, estimates of profits to be made from transactions in hand, not forgetting current liabilities, the interest on outstanding loans, bad debts and outstanding credits. Nothing was to be omitted. He had before him in a neat pile Herr Genscher's bank statements, his private portfolio of investments, current valuations for the property and, even, for the car. He noted that a great many shares had been sold recently to raise cash.

Herr Tiedemann was in seventh heaven. He quite forgave dem Chef for neglecting to inform him about the land purchase in Bayern made some years ago, for the forthcoming Olympics had sent prices rocketing. He examined with care the risky, speculative stock dealings of five years ago and noted the gains, nodding his head as the figures were totted up. A tribute indeed to his boss's acumen, as was this hush-hush special job: a laborious and exact piece of work which only you, my dear Herr Tiedemann, always so efficient, can be entrusted with. He had devoted a separate sheet, with double underlinings, to Rommer's current and largest yet venture, a risky, difficult undertaking which had elicited a great number of head-shakings and tuts from the old man.

Herr Tiedemann was the first to know about these secret negotiations. Foolhardy, frightening and yet, Otto thought, an interesting proposition: *Der Abend*, no less. The city's ailing evening paper, in constant and unsuccessful competition with the flourishing *Abendblatt*, was known to be a bed of radicals, peepers and priers who feathered their nest while they raked over the doings of Hamburg's eminent citizens, pretending sanctimonious shock. A paper known to be a mere scandal sheet, which had never passed through Aumühle's shiny front door. A fat manila folder at Otto's elbow contained a jumbled set of documents that had occupied him for an evening: the balance sheet of the flagging concern, whose proprietor was eager to unload to the right party; photocopies of an article in an equally scurrilous, satirical weekly listing the prospective purchasers. These ranged, incredibly enough, from Axel Springer (an asterisk pointed to a footnote: unlikely) down to a half-forgotten 60s radical student turned lawyer who had formed a consortium with a group of left-wing friends (yet more dubious, the footnote said: journalists reject overt political inteference). Herr Genscher was not mentioned. He was a surprise candidate and likely, it seemed, to be favoured, for the publishers wanted a non-political proprietor, the sort of respectable money-man who could put the paper back in the black while honouring the views of an independent editorial board.

Herr Tiedemann had read through a document produced by the circulation department which purported to prove that although three hundred thousand people bought the paper each day, it was actually read by a further 4.8 persons per copy. There was a 'readership profile' listing the assets of these supposed readers, each with their Eigentumswohnung and Opel Kadett, their annual holiday in Gran Canaria with 1.8 children and subscriptions to 1.4 weekly magazines, their Krankenkasse contributions and passion for football. There was, it seemed, an identikit *Abend* man, an imaginary low-to-middle grade manager, small garage owner or lesser official, whose every thought and expense were known.

There was, too, an analysis of advertising, explaining the downward curve in evasive terms and always in reference to such factors as 'across-the-board agency cuts', to socio-economic trends and, above all, to other newspapers which were doing even less well.

Herr Tiedemann had turned almost with relief to a separate, crisper document outlining plans for improving all these figures in a hundred different ways: reader competitions with holiday prizes, Lotto, advertising supplements, special feature issues, sporting spin-offs and television personality columns. Every idea, it seemed, had been rejected by the editorial policy committee. *Der Abend* regularly offended its major advertisers by publishing articles finding fault with their products, their sales methods or the private lives of their directors, articles 'without fear or favour'. Herr Tiedemann had smiled at the suggestions from the journalists on how to improve their paper. More money for them, new management, more money for contacts, budgets for 'feature exclusives', for travel, for research, for exclusive photographs of film stars and royalty; a special fund for paying the wives and girlfriends of murderers, rapists and bank robbers for their exclusive stories. They wanted a tabloid format, more staff, a weekly magazine in colour. He had glanced with distaste at a piece of paper setting out the current annual wage claim of these excitable, opinionated journalists: more money, shorter hours, paternity and maternity leave, time off for educational activities, more staff and fewer duties. He had turned with relative relief to a list of printing costs; appended to it were lists of printing firms and estimates from all over Europe and even from Singapore and Hong Kong for printing the *Abend*'s projected magazine.

Amongst all these papers, Herr Tiedemann had come across a small set of clippings: references to Rommer's. There was a photograph of Herr Genscher with a beauty queen at a charity ball, a three-line reference to his winning a yacht race five years previously and one to Rommer's undertaking a large lease-back venture with a major Reederei; nothing, naturally of a more scurrilous nature. He had been pleased to note that his firm offered little of interest to *Abend* readers. From the half a dozen copies of the paper attached, he had learnt that the Opel Kadett driver enjoyed shocking revelations about the private lives of Hamburg's worthies; their messy divorces; 'The night I had to say no'; the secret life of the 'Beast of Binnefeld'; the police officers' porno party; the local councillors' hidden SS past. All was revealed under the banner of truth and decency. SPD or CDU, FDP or NPD, none was exempt; it was noticeable, however, that the paper, broadly speaking, backed the SPD on major policy issues and took particular pleasure in mocking the activities of the CSU and Herr Franz Josef Strauss, a man whom Otto Tiedemann held in the highest esteem, even though he was a Bavarian.

And, right at the bottom, lay a letter from the editor-in-chief, Herr Franz Walther, a confidential letter advising Herr Genscher that his offer was being favourably received and that, in view of his unblemished standing, impeccable credentials and non-political stance, it was likely that he would prove more acceptable to the staff than a proprietor 'of the old school'. Herr Tiedemann had sighed over this letter. 'We all believe that the time is right for a liberal proprietor, a man of sound standing, who can finance the *Abend* towards a healthy future, providing new confidence and a vigorous outlook, while wisely leaving the editorial policy to those old hands who understand it best.'

He had no idea why Herr Genscher wanted this newspaper. He could not believe that he would wish to stand back from his ailing, expensive toy and feed these rapacious people. He smiled at the erroneous notion that Herr Genscher would leave matters in wise old hands. Then Otto reflected that the bank would not advance such a large sum if they did not have good cause to believe a success could be made of it and look, he thought, at the profits being mopped up in Bayern. A newspaper, he mused, would occupy Herr Genscher a great deal; he would barely have time for the day to day affairs of Rommer's. This thought had prompted a small pencil note in the margin, a cheery little 'Sehr interessant! Hals und Bein-bruch Herr Genscher!', an expression he considered suitably sporting. He wrote this a couple of centimetres from the bottom line figure: a projected loss, for the next half-year, of at least three quarters of a million, conservatively speaking.

Tonight, the fourth night of Lotte's liberty, Otto began listing Herr Genscher's personal assets. A prudent man, Victor had recently chosen to triple his life-insurance, the premium tax-deductible. Otto made a faint pencil asterisk beside the sum which estimated annual maintenance and running costs for that expensive boat. Such pale stars repre-sented Herr Tiedemann's humble personal contribution to his master's affairs, for he meant to repay this exceptional expression of confidence with one or two astute suggestions. These were modest enough but, he liked to think, nevertheless rewarding. The *Rommery*, for instance, which ate up so much money, should be sold to the firm and run as a chargeable business expense for official entertaining.

Drifting in and out of Herr Tiedemann's mind was the notion that Herr Genscher could again be contemplating matrimony. What other reason could there be for a man in the prime of life wanting to draw up a balance sheet of everything that he possessed? A trifle old-fashioned, perhaps, but that was a virtue in Otto's eyes. There were one or two ladies he could think of, charming young ladies of good family and well-connected. Herr Genscher of course, ever the individualist, would find someone a little unusual. He hoped that the lady would be a worthier – no, a more suitable choice than dear little Johanna. He respected the young lady's modern, independent mind but then there were her odd friends and her, well there was no other word for it, her ingratitude. A small scenario formed quietly at the back of his mind in which he and Lotte befriended an older, a charming and yet modest Frau Genscher, a girl who appreciated the finer things in life. There would be Sunday afternoon trips to Aumühle and, yes, small blond children tottering on the lawn with genial Uncle Otto to lend a hand with their first steps. It had not escaped his notice that there was no beneficiary named in Herr Genscher's will, a document still unsigned that lay near the bottom of the pile.

Marriage was a stable, a sensible choice. He kept returning to this notion as an escape from the sea of paper. It was curious: much as he had wanted to know, much as he had ferreted and probed and worried about being left out, knowledge did not really satisfy Herr Tiedemann. These undertakings fell outside his normal orbit and he foresaw dangers and difficulties in these supposed opportunities. Herr Tiedemann tended to worry about things. He needed to have all his problems solved, to have everything neatly docketed as Disposed Of. He hated things that ran away with him, hated the unpredictable, the unsafe. For all his new self-importance and the not by any means negligible pleasure of letting Lotte know how indispensable he had become, a little bit of him kept thinking that he had been easier in his mind when he had had only his own position to worry about. Now he was worrying about Herr Genscher's as well. Now he had real issues to think about and they upset him.

One floor below, in the caretaker's flat, Herr Frisch delicately inserted his fleshy tongue into Frau Meier's mouth, avoiding the gleaming new bridge at the front which so remarkably altered her face, making it, as he had assured her, positively youthful and plump. He tasted of the Römertopf she'd brought, carefully wedged with towels into her shopping bag. Now it lay nearly empty on the table. She, relaxing in this long-awaited embrace, uncomfortably aware however of the grinding against her narrow pelvis of the hard buckle of his leather belt, a truss to support his overhanging, well-nourished belly, resolved inwardly that when they were married he would be put on a diet. One eye half-open, she again examined the furnishings. They would have to be replaced. The caretaker, lost in the rapturous enjoyment of sensual pleasures, all unaware of her busy little notions, wouldn't have changed places with anybody in the world. Not even with rich Herr Genscher who, for all his wealth, sat alone, again, tonight.

Something was going on. Even Frau Meier sniffed it through the carbolic. Herr Genscher had cancelled his week-end at La Scala, pleading overwork, but his desk was empty. He had put off seeing Heidi, as rosy and flaxen-haired as her name suggested, for the fourth time and she, offended, was turning a little snappish. It would take more than the sapphire pendant to placate her; that she considered her due and already overdue. His mind was not on her and that had been noted with a certain degree of sharpness, of disappointed sulking. The flesh did not fail him, it never did, but the spirit had been absent and Heidi had sat up with a flounce, saying that she could be a puppet for all he cared. He had marvelled at this, her first perceptive remark, happening just at the moment when he had mentally abandoned her. He would, as his florist suggested, 'Sag'es mit Blumen!', a most apologetic and florid arrangement with a small farewell card, a 'Leb wohl' tucked into the fragile, hypocritical blossoms.

Victor had lost his sense of well-being. That ease of his, an invisible but vital garment, had slithered from his shoulders; now his skin felt as though it no longer fitted. Other people, behaving as though everything was normal, seemed to him shockingly callous. He could hardly bring himself to thank Fräulein Schmidt when she placed that first, best cup of coffee of the day on its little place mat. He touched the pile of papers on his desk as gingerly and reluctantly as though they had been metamorphosed into cuneiform slabs. To append his signature to a letter or memo had become so meaningless that he felt a weight of gravity he could not begin to combat sticking the pen fast to its tray.

He had been happy without knowing it. He dwelt with

unbearable poignancy upon the young man who, in a fervour of desire, had planned the takeover of Rommer's in a shabby furnished room; who had read balance sheets with the trembling amorousness more appropriate to a billet-doux. He had recreated that desire in recent months, reading issue after issue of *Der Abend* with premature paternal pride. How tame Rommer's seemed by comparison; he had outgrown it by virtue of becoming the new Herr Rommer, a position that could never be sufficient because he had achieved it with such ease, and because, now, he would never own the entire firm as his predecessor had.

Victor had toured the newspaper's premises which he already thought of as his, mentally refurbishing his office and shaking the somnolent room of sub-editors into life. He had practised the negligent, familiar tone of address used to the burly line of men operating linotype machines in his head. Following Herr Walther's rotund form through the news room, he had found the cynical glee with which the news editor greeted a news-wire catastrophe as intoxicating as the acid inky smell of newsprint and the thundering of the presses. He was an ardent suitor, forcing the pace for a speedy union. He had cajoled the dour bankers into acquiescence, if not enthusiasm; he held Herr Walther in the palm of his hand. This was a romance which had to be consummated; he had only to stave off Ludwig for a matter of days.

Victor knew that his story would make excellent copy. It was precisely the sort of horrific, murky-past revelation the *Abend* liked to splash on its cover in lip-smacking, alliterative capitals. When news was thin, they exhumed the corpses of old atrocities. The human fodder was plentiful: there was always some old SS man, a pitiful white-haired blur hiding his just-recognisable face behind a shielding arm, fool enough to seek an official post in the quiet town of his birth; there was always some ex-convict holding a position of trust in a school or Kindergarten. If Victor became grist for that mill he would lose everything and he had more to lose than any dim-wit official.

He had consoled himself, hitherto, with the lack of evidence: what was Ludwig's word against his? He could already hear himself saying that these were the fabrications of a deranged person, saying it moreover in a kindly, pitying tone. He had thought, too, that Ludwig, himself guilty, would not slay his fatted calf. But now a grim purpose was emerging as this evidence, so spuriously manufactured, rose to mock him. The mother of Wilfried Ferdinand Meyer: a harridan shaking bleached old bones.

Victor sat down at his elegant escritoire and for half an hour scribbled away at his own account of the affair before tearing the useless pages into thin, angry strips. His notes could not begin to equal his enemy's in their complexity. He knew what kind of labour Ludwig had undergone in his maniacal, vengeful zeal. Ludwig had typed a portrait in o's and x's, an uncanny portrayal of the shades and hollows of a face, a demonic and yet still recognisable Victor. He would not demean himself by playing this game; it was better to eliminate the writer and his works with him. He was, after all, a man of action and not a man of words. That facility was one the future newspaper proprietor would develop when it became necessary.

He did have one regret: that he had not already accomplished the deed. How could he kill a man who was having him followed by this nightmare of youth, these parodies of innocence? Even at night they were there, sharp-beaked owls who fixed their vast glittering eyes upon him. It was absurd, a black joke. He thought that he was for the time being in a state of – call it grace. On Monday, Ludwig would advance some proposition, would ask for money. Of course he would not pay; such an admission of guilt would bind them together forever. Today was Tuesday.

Like many householders struck by the sharp rise in crime statistics, Victor possessed a small hand-gun of the type a man might reasonably use to defend himself against intruders. The cold greasy metal soon warmed in his hand. He thought that he could not use it, its number being filed with his licence application, but that a gun could be used as a club. He held it as he read the document again and imagined the further accumulation of detail that must exist elsewhere. It struck him with unpleasant force that nobody in the world knew so much

136

about him or would have taken such trouble over him as Ludwig. It was a compliment of the most threatening kind.

Across town, Ludwig soothed himself smoothing out the soil around his rare Australian orchids. The sharp, peremptory rapping at the door was unwelcome and unusual.

'I know, I know,' Frau Liebmann said, hunched and sharp in the doorway, her sallow face poking through with an annoyed look. 'I know you don't want to be disturbed, but he insisted. Wouldn't take no for an answer, the young –'

She disliked them all, resented their importunate knockings and ringings which obliged her to trudge down two flights of stairs as though she was at their beck and call, and the light bulb so weak that she knew one day she'd fall and hurt herself, not that they'd care. The wall was marked in a hundred places where Frau Liebmann, nervous in her shuffling decline, had reached out a hand to steady herself. She disliked this one particularly, for he did not even contribute to her income. He came and went as though he owned the place. Ludwig went to the wash basin and let the cold water run over his hands. He was wearing a long, ragged grey T-shirt over underpants. Sigi knew that this was not unusual, despite the bitter cold. Like quite a few former and present pupils, he knew about the glass house; Ludwig was, he thought, far less concealed than he believed. Once he had smashed a pane of glass by lobbing a brick from the street side over the high wall when, a wilful sixteen-year-old, acting on an impulse, he had needed to announce to himself that he would never go back.

'How's the heiress?' Ludwig said, turning and wiping his hands, 'What news of Herr Genscher?' That same ironic, smug tone; he spoke to him with the familiarity due an accomplice. Looking at the ugly face which his laughter contorted into a monkey's wrinkled skull, Sigi gave his usual, non-committal reply.

'She's very well. Thriving you might say,' and he curved up the corners of his mouth in a knowing smile. He gave up his scraps of information with some reluctance, which was firstly, simply, because he disliked this bitter man. He thought him a kind of bum, who gave away food to down and outs and thought that made him a saint; who was a sucker for certain

137

boys and by no means the man of iron he made himself out to be. Sigi had seen through him long ago; he had realised that he had, fundamentally, no self-respect. Because he was working for him, all the same, if it could be called work, because he was obliged to deliver something, if he was going to get his money, he found himself picking through the ragbag of tittle-tattle, selecting with care the items which would please and always holding something back. It was a purely instinctive decision.

'I've got something that might surprise you,' he now said.

'My dear boy I wonder if I have that facility,' and Ludwig's face wore its usual, mocking expression, as though he could expect nothing of any interest, yet he always listened with the most extreme care and attention, for all his relaxed poses. Sigi had seen through him all right, but it bothered him, that extreme interest.

'A love story, a tragic little romance,' he said, hearing in himself the faint echo of Ludwig's jeering manner. He watched the little man all but smack his lips over the story of Fräulein Rommer's pitiful romance, he lapped it up and he smiled in a knowing way. He was as eager as an old woman oohing over her neighbours' transgressions; his pleasure was disproportionate and Sigi, finishing, felt a slightly queasy sensation in his stomach.

'Run through it again, dear boy. And you didn't say what year this was,' and, while he listened, he cleaned his black-rimmed nails on the edge of a business card. Fastidious Sigi watched the round worms of dirt coil onto the card and drop to the floor; observed with repelled fascination that he dropped the card back into the drawer when he had completed his toilette.

He had already decided that he wasn't going to tell Ludwig that she never saw Genscher now; that seemed tantamount to wringing the neck of this particular golden goose. Now aggrieved, somehow, at Ludwig's sly pleasure, he began to reckon up the other facts he had suppressed: his credit at the bank. He hadn't yet described her flat, nor mentioned the English friend. There was another fact he had decided need not concern this man, that he liked the girl. There was something endearing about her, the careful way she picked the right word, the little jokes. Yet she was a serious girl, with more on her mind than the next new dress. He would never have described her as pretty. Her features were not regular enough and she was almost alarmingly thin, but she had a beautiful, pale, clear skin. What he thought of as an English complexion, and in contrast to it a great mane of dark curly hair. Her hands were particularly fine. He gazed at Ludwig's bony specimens and thought of her white, tapering fingers with their clean oval nails. She wore no make-up at all and while he approved of this, he imagined she would look dashing with it on. Mentally he applied colour and smoothed the hair.

Ludwig, who had no idea of what was being omitted, seemed to find his remarks a good return on his investment. He shook his head disbelievingly at the restaurant bill, but he didn't quibble, he paid up at once.

'It's good,' he said, 'it's very good, they are close. A first confidence, my dear Sigi, should lead to others,' and Sigi said nothing to disillusion him. The judo master said he had an errand to run and they went out together; in one of those gestures Sigi had grown to loathe, Ludwig clapped his back as they parted in the deserted street.

Sigi walked slowly down the Beckerstrasse in a strange mixture of emotions, for his dislike of the man was transforming itself into a revulsion that he felt more and more strongly. The old Geizkragen had money to burn and he, who had taken it, nevertheless did not care to think of himself as somebody who could be bought. This now seemed to matter more than his long overdue rent. And there was Johanna. What would she think of him, if she knew?

He sat back in the cold bucket seat of the little car, reviewing all that he had said. He had remarked, with some bravado, I've not had her yet, but I will. It was a coarse thing to say, to please Ludwig and he'd said it as men did when talking to each other even though he knew that Ludwig was not, precisely a man; even though he was not that sort himself. Put into a false situation, he was acting the part too well for his own liking. Sigi, who was cocky and streetwise, had nevertheless a certain delicacy. He knew a lady when he saw one.

He turned the key and the motor complained; at the third attempt it sputtered into feeble life. Of course he needed the money badly; he always did. Despite this urgency, he wasn't even looking for a job. He revved up; it took a long time for the heat to begin to penetrate through. At the third intersection he realised where he was going. He was doing what came naturally to him, even at his age. He was going to see his mother.

Vera Schmidt was leaning against the bar, bending down to rub one aching foot with tired fingers. Years of working on her feet had swollen her ankles, pushed out bunions and built corns. Now though she had long abandoned the sharp stilettos of her youth and wore only comfortable shoes, her feet still hurt. On Sundays she would sit for hours with her feet resting on a red Moroccan leather pouffe he'd bought her, but after twenty minutes in the restaurant they would be throbbing as painfully as ever.

Sigi pushed through the door; through the glass he had watched her with the usual mixture of affection and gentle exasperation, the faint twinge of annoyance that she, so expert on what was best for him, wouldn't do what was best for her. She had been offered the easier job of cashier but after a week perched on the high stool had asked to waitress again. She was bored, she missed the tips and she couldn't stand watching the girl who'd replaced her mix the orders up and flirt with her regulars.

'Du bist es,' she said and smiled and poured him a glass of beer. 'It's terrible tonight, Lili's off again, another row with him,' she jerked her head in the direction of the far corner, 'so I'm cooking and serving. Come on, you can stir the pot.'

So Sigi stood in the little kitchen and stirred the huge pot of goulash and watched her wrestle ready-prepared platefuls of frozen snails out of their wrappings and shove them into the tiny oven.

'Twenty minutes at least,' she said. 'Yesterday a regular got them still frozen inside,' and she went out, straightening in the doorway and putting on a smile, a last quick smear of lipstick at the mirror there, a jaunty air.

The Kneipe was almost empty. It was the dead time

between nine thirty when the first wave went home and eleven thirty when the television people up the road came off work and would eat and drink until one in the morning. This lucky chance had kept the place in business, for the proprietor was generally absent, the cook involved in an agonised romance with a Gastarbeiter forever threatening to bring his real family over. They lived upstairs and the man came down for his dinner every night; he glowered in the corner and waited for his beloved, fifteen years older than him. Lili was a fat, good-tempered blonde who was crazily in love. Nobody seeing her in the street with her shopping bags full of onions would have believed that a short time ago it had taken four customers to drag her off her lover, whom she was threatening to eviscer-ate. He looked moody sitting there, but then his dark face was always closed up and incomprehensible.

'She's sobbing her heart out up there,' whispered Sigi's mother. 'It's the change that does it,' and she made a little moue of distaste, for it would happen to her eventually, though she fought it off, sucked in her tummy and wiggled her hips a bit as she walked. The Yugoslav had made advances to her once, but she'd laughed him away. She'd never get mixed up with a foreigner; she knew trouble when she saw it.

The customers came pouring in in one swift wave that filled all the tables. In and out Vera came, laughing, busy, hands quickly scraping off leavings into the pig bin, dumping dishes in the sink, grabbing a fresh tray and off. She knew she was a marvel, irreplaceable, that they wouldn't manage without her. She'd been there for eight years and knew every regular's name. The place was her life, the goings on better than the movies.

Sigi filled the bread baskets, turned down the bubbling vat to simmer and unwrapped the cling-film from a new dish of potato salad, putting it on the side so it wouldn't be too cold. They sold half a dozen dishes, all simple but good, and the place was friendly and even its shabbiness pleasant. He'd always said his mother could make a fortune running it for herself, but she said he was crazy. She had no aspirations, unlike her big-shot son whom she loved and scolded and sometimes, late at night, cried over, blaming herself because

141

he didn't have a decent job, nor any prospects to speak of. She loved him; he loved her; she couldn't in the end think she'd done such a bad job when there were so many kids around who wouldn't even speak to their parents, and vice versa.

By one fifteen the closed sign was on the door and there were only two men left, quiet ones who liked to play a game of cards and drink a few beers after the late shift. Their glasses were full, everything was back in the fridge, big Hans behind the bar polishing the glasses dry and treating himself to a whisky; she sat down with Sigi at the table in the corner, sighed at the relief and eased off the shoes. Pushing a cup of coffee across the table at him, she gave him a quick kiss.

'Thanks. You're a great kid Sigi. How's the flat looking?' He had left home only two months previously, having pulled strings and got himself a cheap but nice place in a big new housing block. He'd bought a lot of stuff she knew he couldn't afford; she put that out of her mind.

'Nice, very nice. You're tiring yourself out here, Mutti,' and his brow was wrinkled up, just like when he was a little boy, and she wanted to smooth it out.

'I'll take you home.'

'Let me sit a bit. I like it when it's nearly empty. I like to sit for a bit, I don't come on again until three.'

Her blue eye shadow was too bright; it had spread into the laughter lines around her eyes, just as the lipstick edged into the little creases round her mouth. He looked at her rough hands with love and anxiety.

'You need money, don't you?' she said. 'Hans will give you thirty, for tonight,' but he wouldn't let her get up.

'Look,' he said, 'I met a girl. A nice girl. Very clever, English, a student. Rich,' and he smiled winningly. 'Didn't you always say I should go for a rich one?'

'Oh Sigi,' she said, helplessly, shading her eyes. He was tender-hearted and very proud; she knew he could be hurt very easily for all his toughness. She and Wolfgang were different, stronger in many ways, they didn't take life so seriously. Sigi took after his father.

The look on her face pierced Sigi with sudden truth; this tenderness, the unspoken misgivings, the anticipation of a rivalry which hadn't yet occurred. His confused general thoughts suddenly clarified under the beam of maternal jealousy. Of course, he thought, now I understand.

'The thing is,' he said. 'I borrowed money from Levison to take her out. I want to pay him back, I don't like to owe him anything, you know what he's like.'

She crinkled up her face at this. She didn't like the man, but he was good to Wolfgang who had nowhere to go after school and who seemed to enjoy the lessons there. She hadn't liked his influence over Sigi and was relieved when he took up the gym instead. She had no choice. She'd have to take a different kind of job altogether to be there for the afternoons, and she looked down at her hands. The hard nails were cracking a little from too many immersions in harsh detergents. She knew she wouldn't give it up.

'You have to pay him back,' she said after a while. 'How much?' and she fished out a bag from under the seat and started to rummage in it. It was more than she'd hoped; it always was. 'Expensive places,' she said, not able to stop herself. 'Look, Sigi, take it, I don't want it back, but you've got to find a job. Any job. You'll get into trouble, you know you will. Please.'

He watched her count out the battered notes, lit a cigarette and remembered how he'd always promised her, when he was a kid, that she'd never have to work again when he grew up.

'I'll pay you back,' he said. She looked older every time; particularly when she didn't smile, when she lost her bounce. He wanted to give her something, to make it up to her somehow. 'I've tried, with jobs,' he said. 'They're never the right ones. No, I know what you think,' he waved her silent, 'it's not that I have to start at the top, it's just that they're wrong. I'm not made to work as a mechanic, with my hands, and I'm not trained for anything else.'

Hans, disliking the silence, put on another tape, her favourite old one, 'Ännchen von Tharau bittet zum Tanz', and the bouncy melodies made her tap her feet, in spite of herself.

'I sometimes think that I should get a proper education,' Sigi said. 'Night school or technical school or something. Get out of that circle. You always said you didn't like my friends.'

She smiled at him, weakly. She could hear the girl speaking

143

already; she could see how she might ruin him. He'd just be a temporary thrill for a girl like that, something different. With his expensive tastes, that instinctive liking for fine things, things he couldn't afford, Sigi would be ruined. And she'd drop him soon enough. There he sat, so good-looking that she wanted to weep, his gentle hands playing with that lighter, another expensive toy. Vera knew that she couldn't say a word against the girl. He looked up now, for encouragement, for hadn't she always told him to try and better himself? One word from some upper-class girl and he's interested, she thought bitterly.

'Come on, you can take me home now,' and the bunion throbbed, even in the sloppy shoes, and she made an effort, straightened up and patted her hair and smiled at big, silent Hans, who winked. Sigi wasn't tired; he loped easily to the door, swinging her bag of groceries, held it open for her. He had good manners that came naturally to him and a good heart. He was good enough for anybody, just as he was.

'Would you like to meet her?' he said, and her heart sank.

'Of course,' she said and, because a sacrifice deserved some return, 'Sigi, will you do something for me? Spend a bit of time with Wolfgang? He hangs around that judo school all the time in his holidays and I don't like some of those boys. That Bernd Aubrecht, you remember him? His mother's worried, he's only fifteen but he's sly and secretive and always out. You could take him out, go to a picture with him. He looks up to you,' and Sigi, driving at exciting speeds through the empty streets, smiled at her and said of course he would, laying his hand on her arm.

'Don't worry so much,' he said, knowing she would. She loved her boys but couldn't control them; either of them could persuade her into almost anything. She wanted to be a good mother but had always left them alone a lot; she fretted about them, blamed herself and atoned with expensive presents she couldn't afford.

'Please,' he said, 'I'll keep an eye on Wolfgang.' He wasn't really thinking about Wolf at all. He was seeing Johanna in his mind's eye. She had leapt unexpectedly into that tight, protective cordon he held around the few people he loved. He thought how odd it was that he had had to see his mother to realise that.

Sigi's matchmaker, meanwhile, being a thrifty fellow, had taken the last S-Bahn to the Hauptbahnhof and made his way through the near-deserted streets of the city centre. Around two o'clock in the morning, he stepped lightly through the back door of Rommer's, treading with extreme care on his crepe-soled shoes across Frau Meier's polished floor. In his pocket lay a set of locksmith's tools, wrapped carefully in a soft cloth so they would not jingle. He was sufficiently practised in the art to be confident that he could open any of these doors, but it was a nerve-racking business all the same and his hands were moist inside the thin gloves, a film of sweat on his brow. He moved his body with the utmost care, with all the trained, cautious discipline of the master, sliding step by step along the long hallway. A strange noise echoed through its empty spaces. He stood stock-still.

He waited, frozen, and there it was, repeated in heavy rhythm. It became clear that this was the sound of a man snoring. It came from the room that opened onto the stairwell; the caretaker's flat. A fat old fool, slow on his feet; his snore that of a man who wouldn't wake in a hurry.

The dark figure passed slowly through the hallway, hugging the wall in case a passing policeman should think to shine his flashlight through the glass door at the front. There, the office door. The glass looked wired, but wasn't. The alarm box proud on the outside of the building was a sham. Herr Genscher's flat, full of valuables, was wired; the rest was not. The building had only adequate locks and the inadequate caretaker to protect its complement of office furniture, regulation chairs and battleship-grey filing cabinets and the instruments of torture belonging to the dentists who rented rooms upstairs. Indeed there was nothing here any self-respecting thief would bother with.

He was inside. He took the tiny flashlight from his pocket and looked around. There was a heart-stopping moment when his foot grazed a metal waste-paper basket placed immediately beside the entrance. He proceeded in complete silence through the empty desks, tried a filing cabinet and

145

found it locked and wasted not a few moments in flicking through a set of dull papers containing various cargo and salvage fees before once more clicking it shut. A large wooden cupboard set into the corner which looked as though it might house a safe turned out to contain a set of coffee mugs neatly up-ended on a piece of paper and tins of coffee and sugar labelled Goldberg, Brinckmann, Schmidt, the latter one ringed by a crudely drawn chain of flowers. The large pictures, poor-quality reproductions of tea clippers, hid nothing and he went on to a smaller row of brownish colour plates depicting quaintly attired tradesmen from long-gone days. Their ugly, finely cross-hatched faces scowled down at Ludwig as the small spotlight passed over them and on in search of richer booty. Nothing there. He was careful, despite a growing feeling that he had to hurry, not to become hasty in his movements.

Very quietly, he opened the door beside the pretentious glass partition that separated a large, old-fashioned desk from the humbler variety. A pile of folders lay on top of it. Herr Tiedemann had even provided an inventory of contents, a slip of a list neatly written in an old-fashioned hand which was taped to the top of the first dossier.

Worthy Herr Tiedemann had departed for Aumühle on the very last train at much the time Ludwig pulled in on his. He had, for once, permitted himself the luxury of not clearing his desk in his anxiety to proceed with the work in hand first thing the next morning. The old gentleman, who prided himself on his discretion, would never have left any important document where Fräulein Schmidt's unworthy gaze might alight upon it, were he not secure in the knowledge that he would be the first person in.

He could not have forseen Frau Meier's unusual decision to run her vacuum cleaner across the carpet first thing; her work revolutionised by an early start made possible by her having spent the night so comfortably on the premises. She had no interest in papers; her ambitions were centred elsewhere and she was in a particularly good mood at getting the office done an hour early. She did notice one small detail, however, as she leant to plug in her machine at the accustomed spot. Most unusually, that stupid Fräulein Schmidt had left the photocopier on all night and with a tut she pulled out the plug and, her labours completed, decided, not without a touch of malice, to replace it as before.

This was the first thing Herr Tiedemann noticed upon his majestic entrance. No little matter ever escaped him and this was puzzling, for he had not seen the glow of the machine in the darkened office of last night. He was obliged to conclude that he himself had committed the grievous fault and, because his obsessional nature was made that way, he found himself dwelling upon it. He was half-inclined to think that Herr Genscher had been in the office overnight and had half a mind to tax him upon it. But in case he had indeed perpetrated that small bureaucratic crime known as over-heating the machine (a fault for which he would have had the secretary in tears) he decided to refrain. He would not expose himself to the censure of Herr Genscher at this propitious moment.

Herr Tiedemann felt positively unhappy if he could not consider himself blameless at every second of his day. He didn't feel right at all today; he was uneasy. He told himself that he had plenty to be glad about. Happy, he thought, be happy. He tried to feel happy. The unthinkable happened; a smile of solitary happiness creased his leathery cheeks and he did not realise it until he looked up and met the astonished gaze of Fräulein Schmidt, busy little fingers for once stilled by the extraordinary event. It felt peculiar; he didn't like it and, while she watched, the corners of his mouth turned down into their heavy, habitual ridges.

By the time the afternoon came, Sigi was flush with borrowed cash; his small store of credit totally used up, he headed for the Beckerstrasse. A generous fraternal impulse took him first into the dingy building, which reeked of cabbage. The small cramped flat smelt of dust and, faintly, of the acrid ozone the fan heaters gave off. The living room had the bleakness and stale chill of a place where curtains had been left drawn all day; where daytime light and fresh air had been ignored. The sofa bore the impress of a lounging, idle body. There was no beer in the fridge. An overflowing bin sat inches from a pile of laundry; there was a pathetic little bottle of corn remover, half-full, sticking to the glass of his mother's bedside table. Wolfgang's room was a litter of clothes and yellow fag-ends. The bed looked as though it smelt.

He took off his watch and rolled up his shirt sleeves, plunging his hands with distaste into the greasy grey water in the sink, finding the slimy blockage and, throat working in faint nausea, soaking the pile of crusty plates. Vera Schmidt, who polished the Kneipe's steel draining board until it shone, had no energy at home.

Sigi was sitting at the kitchen table when the latchkey clinked in the door and, a second later, the telephone rang in the hallway.

'Yeah, I just got back.' His brother. 'Ach du grosse Scheisse. Look I did it, I'll get the money. What's the problem then, I've done it before, haven't I?'

Sigi, sitting quite still, listened.

'Your old man's an arsehole. Yes, yes, I know, reg' dich nicht auf. Me and Heini will do it, on Friday.' A pause. 'What's the big deal about it? Don't worry, you're like an old woman. We'll watch him, we're not going to lose him, I've done it before, haven't – hang on, just a minute.'

The kitchen door opened.

'Oh it's you,' he said in quite a different tone and returned to the telephone. 'Okay, bye, talk to you tonight.'

He gave Sigi a spiteful, malicious look.

'Don't tell me, Mutti asked you to keep an eye on her little boy.'

'What've you done this time?' Sigi sat back, lit a cigarette and watched Wolf's face turn wary.

'Been listening at the keyhole, have you? I've been having fun. I've been a naughty boy, haven't I. Don't beat me, Papa,' and he pretended to cringe away, folding up his lean body into a protective huddle on the wooden chair.

Sigi, who often felt like smashing his brother's head against something very hard, said, 'What now?'

'A little accident.' Wolfgang smiled. 'No wheels now, I smashed up Bernd's bike and no insurance. Got any spare cash? No, never mind, good old Mutti will pay.'

Slowly, Sigi peeled off a couple of notes from his roll; he

148

pushed them across the table.

'Now don't tell Mutti,' Wolf said in an admonitory tone, wagging a finger. 'You know how upset she gets with naughty little Wolfie,' and then, looking down, 'It's not enough.'

Sigi shrugged. Wolfgang's stacked heels found a perch on the table; the body stretched out its over-long legs and yellow-stained, gnawed fingers helped themselves to a cigarette which he smoked in silence, throwing back his head to exhale streams of smoke in the direction of the ceiling. When it was finished, he got up and minced across the kitchen with swaying hips.

'Your old friend Ludwig is getting to like me. I hope I'm going to be one of his favourite boys.' Glass after glass of water was thrown down his long throat; the Adam's apple bobbed up and down.

'Course it keeps me up to all hours. But I don't mind. I just want to be appreciated,' and his voice attempted a Berlin accent.

'You're stupid, Wolf,' Sigi said calmly. 'You don't know what you're getting into half the time. You just follow Bernd around and copy him.'

'Ooh, jealous,' he said, falsetto. 'Course I can't expect to be a real favourite like you. Haven't got the body, have I? But I do my very best to copy you, Sigi, ooh, yes, I do, even when it's very very difficult,' and pleased with his wit, he wandered out of the kitchen.

As soon as he was gone, Sigi reached across for Wolf's jacket and rifled through the pockets. A packet of cigarettes his brother had not thought to offer; a dirty comb and a couple of crumpled Tempo handkerchiefs. He felt inside the zip pocket: a small card. One of Herr Judo Meister's. He flipped it over and read on the reverse, in tiny capitals, the name VICTOR GENSCHER and ROMMER IMPORT-EXPORT HANDELSGESELLSCHAFT with the address, a telephone number, a crude sketch map and up one side the pencil scrawl, unmistakably his brother's: Never out before 9 a.m. Now he heard his brother's clippety-clop down the lino floor of the hall and stuffed it back.

Wolfgang was holding a tarnished gold medallion and chain of the cheapest kind; he rubbed at it with the kitchen towel before handing it over; the thing dangled in grotesque mockery in his hands.

'What do you think?' he said. 'Only DM12.–, it looks exactly the same though,' and he bared his teeth in satisfaction. 'Got it in the market. Here, let's see yours.' Sigi looked at the tawdry little fake, which he would have liked to rip apart and hammer.

'Nice,' he said, with an effort. 'Listen, Wolf, you leave Levison alone. And tell Bernd to keep away from him. You know, he's using you. Don't be an arsehole, Wolf, you always get into trouble on other people's account. Be clever, for once.'

Wolf wasn't even listening; humming, he was fastening the chain around his neck, bent in front of the tiny mirror propped on the window sill to admire himself.

'Naughty Sigismund,' he said, archly. 'Selfish boy. Wanting to keep the best all to yourself. Now you know Mutti always said we boys should share,' and he pranced about, admiring himself, with the medallion swinging on his pigeon chest.

The door, unusually, was unlocked, so Sigi let himself in and closed it very quietly behind him, crossing the great, gloomy room at the edge of the mat. He stood for a moment in the stairwell and heard the sound of the old woman's television above; cautiously, he pushed the office door an inch. Ludwig was not there.

Quickly he knelt at the filing cabinet, flicking through the dusty pieces of paper. All his documents were there. If there was anything to be found, this was the place, he knew his man, and meanwhile he listened acutely, for Ludwig moved like a cat. There was no discernible order. An anarchic sea of paper was stuffed into a couple of files, the remaining blue-black folders hanging limp and rusty, marked in homage to more ordered times with the names of pupils long gone. A yellowing roll of paper set out the oath sworn by newcomers, the 'Gokajo no seimon'; against it lay a thick wodge of xeroxed sheets, all bent

150

at one corner, detailing the timetable of the school. He shoved all this aside and pulled out various documents which he glanced at and discarded: a map of West Berlin in a shiny plastic cover; a pile of electricity bills stapled together; two curling photographs of Professor Jigoro Kano. The white-haired old man stared coldly out of the picture from drooping eyelids with pouches below, hair flattened neatly across the top of his head from a low side parting. This small piece of vanity unreasonably made him seem less, rather than more, human.

He pricked his finger on an unseen drawing pin and swallowed a curse. The bottom of the cabinet was full of old pins and rusting cartridges of staples, rubber bands holding thick, felted balls of dust and the odd hair, pencil stubs and old keys. A thick packet at the bottom seemed more promising and he pulled it out, blowing away the dust. He glanced inside and then stuffed it quickly into the inside pocket of his jacket. He remained for two long minutes on his knees, breathing in the dust and faintly fungal smell of rotting paper that emanated from a pile of Japanese martial arts magazines jammed into the heavy bottom drawer. He lifted them up. There was nothing underneath. He let the wrinkled pile drop back with a thud; a puff of dirt, a mushroom cloud, rose from below and settled on his shoes. By the time Ludwig appeared, he was leaning back on the chair, steadying it by holding his feet flat against the desk. The rackety contrivance was kept in exact balance only by the interplay of thigh muscles and rigidly braced knees.

'Ja, die Liebe ist so schön,' Ludwig sang, in a cracked voice. He took in the rigid pose, the jutting chin. 'Well, what have you got for me?'

Sigi nodded at the envelope lying on the table; there were banknotes inside.

'What's this?'

'It's finished, you've got plenty of boys for your games. I don't want to play any more. Go on, count it, it's all there.'

Slowly, Ludwig pushed it back towards him. 'Oh no,' he said, 'It's not as easy as that. You're involved. You're bought and paid for.' It was rich. He despised Sigi as much for his attempt to get out of his obligations as for his weakness in agreeing in the first place.

'I won't take it,' Sigi said. 'I'm out and you can count my brother out too.'

'Your brother? What has he to do with me? He's your worry, my dear Sigi, not mine. So you're out, are you? You find you don't like the work after all? You don't like my money any more?' His tone was soft and infinitely malicious. 'More fool you, my dear boy, for after all it can hardly make any difference, can it? What you've done, is done.' He gazed at the closed, sullen face.

'Pretty girl, Johanna? Thinking of seeing her on your own account? My poor Sigi, I wonder what she is going to think of you when she finds out how – purchasable you are.' Now his smile was broad; it encompassed a huge scorn of weakness, of failure. Sigi could not even console himself with the thought that he had acted in a just cause; he had no consolation at all.

'You leave her alone,' he said and, jerking himself to his feet, towered over Ludwig, fists clenching and unclenching, 'I want your word, that you won't interfere with her life, do you understand?'

'My dear Sigi, how very ridiculous you are being. Do you want to fight me? With pleasure, but you know you will most certainly be defeated. What do you want me to say, that I promise not to see her, or that I shall never speak to her? My poor Sigi, try to be a realist, as I am. I don't make promises, which I later regret. I don't know what will happen, tomorrow, to make me change my mind. Try to be accountable to yourself and not to others, there is a piece of advice for you.' The boy looked, at this moment, as though he would have liked to kill him; Ludwig tilted up his head and gazed, blandly, at the mottled ceiling.

'Understand this,' he said. 'That nothing is going to interfere with my plans. Not even you, with your newly-active conscience. Do you know, Sigi, I almost find it in me to feel sorry for you? Do what you want, whatever makes you happy, my dear boy. I bought you, and you were very cheap. You're very weak, very soft. A little man, yes, even smaller than I am. No, I don't think I need you, after all,' and he yawned ostentatiously and the lad, standing there with a stupid, bemused expression on his face, a look which recognised the impossibility of his doing anything at all, now turned sharply on his heel and left the room, slamming the door with all his force, so that the walls hummed with the shock and a calendar, hanging next to the door, slipped an inch on its frayed thread.

Ludwig forgot him at once. For, in truth, Sigi was redundant. Ludwig had found Victor's true love and she was a whore. It had taken him most of the night to absorb the information on the photocopied pages. In the early morning he had gone out and found a copy of yesterday's paper. It was a dirty thing, which left grubby marks on the mind akin to the film of black it smeared on the fingers. *Der Abend* set out to titillate, disguising its revelations with the name of decency. He hated its tone of lubricious shock. And Victor wanted to possess this whore; without understanding that, he felt a certain pride in such an overweening ambition, as a parent, punishing a wilful child, could still appreciate its exceptional strength of will. The man gave in to his worst impulses; he courted them with intensity. To redirect such impulses was, to use the *Abend*'s favourite editorialising phrase, a moral imperative. He smiled; it was a piece of poetic perfection, for nothing could have suited his purpose better than this. The pieces of the puzzle were coming together, arranging themselves into a whole with a precision and inevitability that even he, the master, could not have bettered.

Sigi did not have time to examine his prize; the thick packet was jammed against his rapidly beating heart. He couldn't be late. He gunned at the engine in a fury and the little car belched out its fumes with a roar of protest, stopping jerkily not far from a street lamp. The concert was at seven thirty. Twenty yards down the street stood a small familiar figure: Heini, at a shop window, staring unconvincingly at a pyramid of books. The rapid pulsating of Sigi's blood, which beat fast with loathing, above all with self-disgust, slowed to a normal rhythm. Three minutes before he had to leave, a man came through the glass doors of the old building and Heini followed him up the street. The target. Herr Genscher. Tall, good-looking, blond. About forty. With the most extreme and careful interest, Sigi watched his rival out of sight.

# Chapter 10

Thursday, December 18, 1971

It's only six thirty, but I can hear bath water running; Linda always empties Frau Beckmann's great old-fashioned hot water cauldron for the duration. She may scorn Victor utterly, but she would never miss her ritual immersion, Venus in Badedas. I'm pretending to work on my essay, but I can't stop myself listening for her movements. Just now I heard the door creak and found myself spreading out my notes in a horrible, furtive way to cover this up.

I have been on the verge of telling her a hundred times and I don't know why I don't. What can I say? Victor is a scoundrel, you were right. And I don't put it past her to accost him about his dealings and I shan't be there to hear his answers. She would commiserate with me first: equally unbearable. Fraudulent Victor, it's a topic too new, too painful, I can't begin to broach it. The proposition is not yet proven; my eager-beaver brain keeps turning it over and seeking explanations, reasons, for he must have his reasons. He has been out the whole afternoon; Fräulein Schmidt does not expect him back. Please do not trouble yourself to call again, she said with patronising insolence. I can assure you he will get your message as soon as he returns to the office. If he returns. I have called the flat a dozen times and listened to the long dull buzzing tone for minutes at a time, willing him to answer. He's not trying the effect of this tie or that; he's not lathering himself and humming. There is something about the way Linda prepares for the evening with her usual thoroughness which makes me feel slightly sick. She just buzzed in to borrow my silver necklace and pretended not to notice my guilty start. She is making every kind allowance for my vulnerable state. 'How does it look with the purple dress?' 'Terrific. Lovely.' She's even got new make-up to match. God, I must stick to neutral topics. I have an endless evening, hours of privacy to come. Now she's splashing and singing, a warbling mermaid.

A neutral topic. I don't seem to own that rare commodity. My overdue essay, perhaps. Would that be finished, if we'd not gone to the John Mayall concert? Linda's idea, so can I blame her for it? I must stop this. This senseless jealousy is wicked.

The concert. Last night Linda, a veteran of such occasions, dressed appropriately in long Indian silk scarves and an ethnic skirt in heavy felt with little mirrors sewn onto it and gaudy ric-rac. It was at the Kongresshalle and the soberly-clad middle-aged attendants were shaken rigid by the look of the audience. Hamburg's freaks, still clinging to their hippie uniform of stiff sheepskin waistcoats and faded denims, do not often grace those plush seats. Europeans, so good at romantic ballads and folk, don't seem to manufacture rock or pop stars with the same international status. Rock's always English or American, imported, an instant sell-out. When a German group actually manages a Schlager, it's always sung in English. With an American accent, naturally. She durn seema know/Har much ah lurve her. Germans make the best hippies though, for they alone have the necessary seriousness, that Teutonic devotion to the cause. Students who neglect their work do so with great thoroughness. The Mensa is always full of long-haired types in greatcoats cutting lectures but making sure they get full value out of their subsidised lunch tickets. They support each other in studied indolence, majoring in drugs, sex and politics. They are so desperately earnest about all three that it's alarming. English laissez-faire liberalism, our celebrated understatement and self-deprecatory jokes, are all lost on them.

German nature abhors a vacuum. Our worthy professors are always talking about die Gliederung of works, allocating them to their correct place, picking and worrying away at books until they've minced up the meat on them and can form them into the right shape. I can quite see how *Werther* must have shocked the burgers in its day, how Sturm and Drang freaked them out. Now it's safe, just another category. Then, though, the sober citizens smelt a whiff of the French Revolution in *Die Räuber* and how they shuddered in their feather beds. Today's revolutionaries don't, of course, go in for lyrical expression of their case. They get together in organised cells. The Marxist groups study the great man's works one line at a time, taking a whole evening to tease out the meaning. Who but a German could stomach the notion of devoting years to one book? But they get double pleasure out of it, the pedantic study they do so well enhanced and made piquant by its anti-establishmentarianism.

No, it's not true, for there are lots of new plays. Europe is full of earnest young playwrights carefully selecting a grim and static 'situation' to unravel their theories on. There is no humour in this; it's all tension, aggression and betrayal. The emptiness of self: no wit, but heavy irony. In case we've missed the point, which is all too easy when what's unsaid is what matters, they publish their 'discussions'. Spontaneous theatre may seem formless, anarchic, avant-garde, but really it's just the modern expression of that essential seriousness.

The bare-boards, no-scenery school is the one that depresses me most. Static drama: anguished figure centre stage broods in silence; broken soliloquy by tormented outcast, etc. Of course they're saying something, it's 'valid', but oh, the boredom. They're not always young either, for look at Beckett, the worst of the lot, an éminence very grise. How can an Irishman write like that? Easy, he does it in French, he distances himself. The English language simply won't let itself be reduced in that way, unless it has the barrenness of a translation. Its richness subverts.

The new films are to the same formula: jerky, hand-held camera stares coldly at haggard, un-made-up actor staring coldly back. This is best of all in black and white. Spontaneous non-dialogue, meaningful irrelevancies, bodily obsessions. Careful excision of wit, humour, warmth, humanity in favour of bleak inner monologue. Here we go again: more stress and betrayal, touch of the surreal, youthful alienation, bleakness of age, collapse of values and so on. And these intellectual bourgeois European audiences love it, they pay fortunes to sit in their silks and watch it all. I always have the same reaction as the ignorant, observing the flat panels of colour smoothed out in the name of modern art. Give me a box of paints, or rather, give me the minimalist vocabulary, and I'd do you one of those on the cheap.

Now the Germans adopt all this no-nonsense stuff with particular enthusiasm. That's something to do with their taking their pleasures so very seriously. I met a student recently who told us the story of a friend of his who pays rent to his divorcee landlady in an unconventional manner. Every second night there is a knock on his door and off he goes to her room to pleasure her. Never impromptu, never uninvited, never on a different night: it's a business arrangement, there must be Ordnung. As Oma always says, Ordnung ist das halbe Leben. And his friend made the appropriately ponderous joke about this guy being worried about the forthcoming rent increases and we all laughed with the right measure of broad-minded malice.

I laughed too, naturally. In the human Gliederung, I fear I count as honorary German. Worse, German by choice. What do I do, but sieve and collage my miserable little history into more acceptable form, a retrospective Buchhälterin seeking form among the mass. Ordnung, in my case, being always leaving exactly the same margin, always insisting on the same size of book, so they will look neat lined up on my shelf. Sometimes I have the impression that it's my English persona that makes all the mistakes; the German one coldly makes notes and criticises.

Neither of them enjoyed the concert. There was a sudden high-pitched throbbing whine and then a great blast of sound, the muezzin to summon the faithful and off went the freaks in uniform abandonment to jump about at the front. Music to pulsate to, dancing being almost impossible. Half the seats were suddenly empty. Linda went too, that's how we lost her. Sigi was stiff with dislike. Partly, I think, a certain fastidiousness about the musky smells, the drugs, which he doesn't approve of, the trendy rags; partly the feeling I also had of being a spectator when only participants are welcome.

I can't let myself go like that. Too stiff, too bourgeois, uncomfortable without disapproving, yet likely, if alone, to conform and hop about with the rest. We watched and, after a moment, exchanged a speaking look. Then we distinguished ourselves by leaving early. We pushed our way through the thick metal doors past an usher leaning weakly against the cold wall and mopping his head in sheer disbelief at such anarchy. Sigi, who had gone to tell Linda we were going, had spotted her through the mêlée dancing with a group of girls all wearing those semi-transparent Indian maxi dresses and waved, but she didn't see him.

'She'll be all right,' he said, 'She knows how to look after herself,' whereas I, it seemed, didn't.

We went back to his place; it was, as he said, nearer. The moment had clearly come for a proper lunge on his part; by his reckoning probably overdue. And I, understanding this unspoken etiquette, was perfectly ready to give him the opportunity in order then to repulse him. So there was a half-look and a general understanding between us when we went to get the car; a complicity in the attempt, if not the outcome.

His flat is a small, modern one in a faceless but as yet undefaced block in a new housing development behind the Holstenstrasse where two big roads cross noisily. It looks down on a church and beyond the converging mass of Holstenstr. Station. Thin walls and children's crying echoing out into the concrete corridors, but his flat is quiet, soundproofed, anonymous. Every stick of furniture was brand new, bland and modern like a KEPA sitting room. Space-saving units with sliding glass doors; smoked glass coffee table, fitted carpets, large rubber plants. Not a single old thing, nothing from the Sperrmüll, no clutter. It smelt of Pledge and plywood. Lucky you, I said, to get it with all the furniture new, but he'd gone out and bought it all himself on the never-never.

There's one bedroom, a temple to love, with a vast bed on a dais which probably has black satin sheets. Net curtains, even though he's on the twelfth floor and can't be overlooked and other curtains on top. Three books next to the bed: *Und ruhig fliesst die Donau*, a Van der Valk detective story and *Kodokan Judo*. How can I go out with somebody like that? He caught me looking at them. I haven't unpacked my personal stuff yet, he said.

We sat down awkwardly and had tea with condensed milk and brittle biscuits and I was quite rigid thinking oh no, don't lunge, for I couldn't bear it. It was the model cars that settled it: two of them sat on the glass shelves, not even coloured and realistic, but silvery, moulded and totally fake. His lack of a single item I could value and my total physical inexperience. A combination too dreadful to contemplate. The horror of it, to be found lacking by a man who's never read a classic book or for that matter even heard of Proust or James Joyce or anyone that matters. A man who knows the names of football players.

So I sat stiffly and gulped the nasty tea too fast, burning my mouth, and he turned off the main light, plunging us into romantic gloom, and put on 'A Man and a Woman', which is one of my favourites. I heard myself twitter on about how I'd have left home for Jean-Louis Trintignant when I was fourteen and impressionable and he said, but I thought it was Victor you had on your mind and I felt a hot flush of shame for having told him so much; the sensation of being paid back fully for my own stupidity.

Victor Genscher, he said, ruminating, and I sat quite still. I am sure I never mentioned his surname and I have an excellent memory. 'He isn't a bit like Trintignant,' he said. 'Same sort of age but bigger and much more dangerous-looking.' I wish I'd had the dignity to refrain from replying, but, as usual, I was bristling defensively. He said something very odd. 'This man is not reliable, he's not trustworthy. He uses people, he'll use you. You keep away from him.' It was, in the circumstances, a joke, for he doesn't really know him at all. Victor is to him that mythical beast, a friend of a friend. He was inventing it to make himself interesting, as Oma would say, out of some silly jealousy, and I thought that were they ever to meet, which is unlikely, I'd be ashamed of Sigi, of having chosen mediocrity, with the same sort of embarrassment I used to feel when introducing Oma to school friends I suddenly realised were shallow and stupid. Today, remembering what he'd said, I found it uncanny, but I was very angry with him then, I was furious and when he got up I was ready to hit at him. My heart was thudding away with some kind of dread, but he was merely fetching whisky and two glasses. Cut-glass; in a cocktail bar unit. Prost! and I needed the drink, for Dutch courage.

Neither of us spoke for a while. His face was half-lit by the lamp, the eyelashes casting huge shadows down the smooth planes of his face when he drank. We watched each other, mesmerised and immobile, and I felt a little afraid of him but also conscious of how sexy he is, with that face and powerful body and every time he reached for the glass I caught myself holding my breath in anticipation. When he slithered, at last, across the sofa, it was as the snake approaches the mongoose.

'Do you know why I wanted to see him? Because I find it incredible that any man wouldn't want you, do you understand?' and he said it with enormous anger, but very quietly. We stared at each other. Part of me hated him, then, and part was aching for him to touch me, but he didn't, he stopped six inches away.

'I would like to go to bed with you, Johanna. You are a most – exceptional girl. But now would be the wrong time, not now, not today,' and he still was angry, but his face was giving out a different message altogether. I must have had the silliest look on my face; positively piqued, at being denied my refusal, and not knowing what to say, for I was ready to argue, to be cross, and he had just cut the ground away, leaving me both relieved and disappointed. So we just looked at each other and suddenly both began to laugh, and couldn't stop. I must have shrieked for ten minutes. I had tears streaming down my face; every time I looked at him it bubbled up again.

After that we became natural again and pleasant, and it was very innocent. He curled up like a puppy on the sofa and grinning, daring me to say no, put his head on my lap and closed his eyes and promptly fell asleep. I can't decide whether he is very clever or stupid. I must have sat there for an hour, with one leg going numb, and stroked his hair which smelt deliciously of shampoo and he smiled in his sleep.

I didn't get home until very late. I woke him in the end and we drove home without saying much, each of us in our different ways thinking that something was settled. I was ready to assert myself, to say I wouldn't see him again, but he took me so much for granted that he didn't even try to fix a date. Where can it lead to, after all? Sigi the cul-de-sac; Victor the highway to perdition. A Department of Works melodrama.

This morning Linda, the very picture of virtue, gave me a most old-fashioned look. I don't suppose you'll be telling Ingrid and your auntie about last night, she said, miffed at having to clear up; put out by my unusual, early-morning assault with the duster. She wouldn't stay for them. I'll go to town, she said, I'll amuse myself; I got in early, unlike some and, in the same breath, well did you or didn't you?

She's gone. She went five minutes ago in the purple dress with my necklace and black silk stockings, worn for her own pleasure naturally. And shoes he is certainly not fit to lick, black patent leather ones with four-inch heels. For God's sake don't worry, she said with emphasis as she left. This is beginning to be a phrase people throw at me. 'Don't worry', like 'Don't get excited', expressions guaranteed to work anyone up into a frenzy.

I have simply got to see Victor. I want to be a fly on the wall; at the same time I want to be Linda, just for tonight. He gives me the creeps, she said, just you remember that. I'm glad I didn't tell her. It's my job, not hers, to protect the family interests. I have wasted hours of my life dreaming up excuses to see him, compelling reasons to meet, and now that I've got one I feel sick.

I knew something was up as soon as they arrived. Tante Mausi was particularly twitchy. She was laden with cakes and a weighty parcel containing the Bock family's newest tribute to German womanhood's dewy beauty, a range of creams and skin tonics called 'Frühlingsfrische'. She rushed around, still

clutching her parcels admiring everything with effusive kindness. Her faded friendly eyes, rimmed with startling turquoise,
zig-zagged around madly to take in every detail and praise. She
is always nice, the nicest person I know, but so nervous and all
the more so in the presence of the ice maiden. Without uttering a
word, Ingrid manages to put her mother in the wrong.

Ingrid's pallor had a certain glow, which couldn't just be the
bracing effect of the stair temperature between limo and flat.
She was all lit up with news of some kind. I can always tell
when Ingrid's got something on me from her way of tilting
her nose up a fraction higher in order to stare down it more
effectively. She had a good look round my bedroom while I
hung up Tante Mausi's coat, preferring to spread her own
couture offering on my fur bedcover rather than risk it next to
the downmarket rags in my wardrobe. Ingrid suffers slightly
from the knowledge that Rommer's is both bigger and
wealthier than Bock's, a chagrin she has always managed to
overcome by a great deal of spending. 'You look well,' she
said, computing the small cost of my plain, neat sweater and
skirt against her cream pleated affair. She had ribbed cream
tights on, a perfect match of course, for Ingrid's neat muscular
legs are her best feature, and one of those crocodile bags on a
long chain and matching shoes, the sort with Gucci links
across them that are de rigueur in her set. I feel less sorry for
the crocodiles knowing they've found a home from home.

So I opened the first bottle of Sekt and we had soup with
Knödel, the cunning deceptive combination of one of Oma's
glass jars and a packet, which I remembered to hide. Ingrid
sipped at it delicately, spreading her napkin with care to avoid
sullying her perfection. Tante Mausi praised the soup and
started admiring the gold-rimmed crockery, which is Frau
Beckmann's third best set, and would perhaps have gone on to
the cutlery, but Ingrid broke in and said Mama, don't you
think we ought to tell Johanna what we have heard, for she is
not one to shrink from an unpleasant duty. She didn't mince
her words. Victor is in trouble. The bank is refusing him a
large loan he must have to buy, of all things, *Der Abend*. She
pursed her lips up at such a sensational choice. The bank was
reluctant but willing, she said, according to Peter Prick, but

now they have changed their minds. It's the putative best man who's in on the deal. He told Peter that Victor has already bought a considerable block of shares in the open market, not only using his money but the liquid float: that means Oma's money. You see, she said, in a patient way as if talking to a child, if the deal doesn't go through, and it won't, without the bank, Peter says it's unlikely the paper will find another buyer. He says prospective buyers have lost interest because it's losing so much money, only a very rich man could afford it. He says they're likely to close and if they do all the money is lost. I had to warn you, she said, for Oma's sake and yours, but Peter doesn't know I'm telling you. It's very unethical to break a confidence, you must never tell anyone I told you. Ingrid had clearly tussled with her ethical conundrum and altruism won the day. It may have been without a selfish thought in her head that she spilled the beans, but I just wonder if she was thinking about her eventual small share. She added a rider: her clever, knowing Peter had said that nobody in his right mind would buy shares in it now. So that is Victor disposed of.

Tante Mausi, though, had tears in her eyes. 'Of course Peter knew you would tell Johanna,' she said, and Ingrid snapped no, certainly not. Poor Tante Mausi rallied. 'Of course it will be all right, don't worry,' she said, and then 'I am so unhappy for Mutti,' and she quite broke down and it took several more glasses of Sekt to restore her. Money is always a serious matter to Ingrid; the prospect of losing some of her own knitted up those finely plucked brows. She kept insisting that Peter and Uwe can't tell Oma to sell the shares, that it's a breach of confidence and we had to be discreet, whatever we did. I admired my own calmness; that's another of Ingrid's salutory effects upon me. I couldn't break down with her watching.

We sat after that in silence for a while and then, over more drinks, started on old family history. We went through all the ritualised history, that honoured way of facing disaster, as though we were already at Rommer's wake. Ingrid suffered this nonsense with a patient, pitying smile. She never urges her mother to greater feats of memory, as I do. For her the past is dead: a sentimental appendage other people have.

It's nine thirty. I keep picking up the phone to call Oma

and putting it down again. I think the telegram was a mistake: it will frighten her, which worries me, but what is the use of calling when I have nothing to add? I have an unparalleled ability to make things sound wrong. I am clock-watching as avidly as Uwe Schenck. How slowly the hands move; no doubt he thought the same. His inscrutability, his manic hilarity were a deciding factor in the telegram. A panic decision, from the need to do something at once. I should never have wasted my time with him; I should have gone straight to Victor.

He is smiling at Linda now, waiting for the main course. She'll have downed her aperitif and munched a handful of peanuts. Victor will have advised with his usual savoir-faire what's best to eat. He will have selected something both choice and appropriate from the wine list. I know the restaurant well: a smart one, his favourite, with peach upholstery and intimate little alcoves to hold hands in.

I have thought it out very carefully; it's easy, knowing the timing so well. I know exactly what he will do. At eleven thirty he will glance at his gold watch, ruefully, with his charming little grimace – how time flies when you're enjoying yourself – and he will run Linda home in his great car, speeding just a little on the straight stretches of the Elbchaussee. Meanwhile I shall be on my way to his flat and when he gets back I shall be waiting for him.

Nine forty-three; how can it go so slowly?

The afternoon shot by. The instant they left I was on the phone to Schenck, whose snooty secretary hummed and ha'ed and then grudgingly said all right, if you come straight away. I rushed, burningly hot from the over-heated train and in the next moment cold with fear. I should have known.

'My dear Fräulein Rommer, there is absolutely nothing for you to worry about,' he said in reassuring, false joviality. His is a name for a footballer, not a banker. Clearly his parents hoped for better things. We had the most evasive and odd conversation, exacerbated by his wanting to talk about nothing at all and by my difficulty in saying everything while giving nothing away.

What a pleasant surprise to see me, he said, coming right out of the office and past Fräulein Wichtigkeit to greet me like a long-lost pal and he busied himself getting her to scurry around for English tea, that delicate compliment, for an ashtray, then for a lighter, and so on. There were copies of *Horse and Hound* and *Country Life* on his desk. Now wasn't the Ratsweinkeller an excellent restaurant? and he settled back, ready to give up his valuable time in gastronomic mouthings. He's one of those people who smile and chuckle a lot when they don't have anything much to say, filling the void with good cheer, so you have to smile back as though they'd been tremendously witty. No doubt he has an excellent reputation as a good chap down at the club. He had written all over him the knowledge that he knew that I knew that he knew and nothing was going to induce him to admit to a thing. He is taller than I'd remembered and has the onset of a banker's belly under his blue and white stripe shirt, though he can't be much over thirty. He smells strongly of soap and has round pink cheeks and round blue eyes and the effect is of a hugely elongated baby.

We discussed the weather and Ingrid's wedding plans and he seemed quite ready to discourse on the choice of hymns, or, if I preferred, the furbelows of her pure white dress if that would consume his twenty minutes. He kept gazing at the absurd international clock on his wall; a huge plaque with a metal map of the world, the seas done in shiny copper, with a digital clock at the side and chrome name places sticking out in relief and all the international times ever-moving down the side. It's the German banker's equivalent of the sunburst clock, a large executive rattle, and he looked as though he wished he could shake it and magically whisk ahead to Bangkok or Peking time.

'Are you going to Ascot this summer?' he said, just like that, a propos no doubt of ritual clothing, and said, 'I don't like flat racing much myself,' chortling away at his wit and saying that Schockemöhle was his hero, and I had a vision of that belly resting on a saddle, bouncing up and down clippety-clop and the blue eyes staring out from under a hard black cap. He'd been to marvellous point-to-pointing in Gloucestershire, he said, with a little smirk to underpin his savoir-faire in not saying Glow-cester-shire, and I tried to think of something obliging to say back. The only horsy memory I could summon up was the televised Horse of the Year Show with all those identikit men in black jackets jumping Humpty-Dumpty cardboard walls and going round and round a sawdust ring with the Queen watching, and how we used to stampede to the box to switch it off.

He was a brick wall of indifferent good humour; to humour him was pointless, so I said I wanted to concern myself with the firm's affairs since I was now of age and had to be briefed on current activities. Of course, he would be delighted, he said smiling hugely and benevolently, and perhaps he and Victor could take me out to lunch one of these days? I was not – yet – a partner, he said with a little laugh, and it was for Herr Genscher to divulge such information. Victor was not a topic any more; there were no compliments about his superb intellect and no jolly laughs over his brilliance, which perhaps has faded a little. Well, could I have information just on the current major acquisition? and he chuckled at this good joke and denied me in the politest possible way. Really, he said, there was nothing for me to be worrying about and soon enough I would be an active partner, nicht wahr? And then, and I can hardly believe it happened, he said with a sentimental sigh that he envied Peter his bride and how much he wanted to settle down and marry the right girl and he gave me a great, glassy wink and burst into peals of aw-aw guffaws like some loony old delinquent. A moment later his secretary was simpering firmly in the doorway with the next client in tow and, this time, a great sheaf of files under one arm. See you at the wedding! he called out merrily as I went.

It was a farce. I decided on the way home to send the telegram and just made it to the post office in time. I wish I knew what time she'll get it. I was the last to be served and afterwards soothed my nerves with a small, burningly hot and bitter cup of coffee and the necessary cigarette in the stand-up Tchibo opposite.

It is still only ten fifteen. Linda has been persuaded into a pudding. Afterwards she is always on the look-out for the goodies, petits fours and chocolates. In middle age she will be one of those stout, highly finished madams with an enormous pneumatic bosom and there will be a streak or two of peroxide by then on those curls. She'll probably be running a casino in

Rio or on a yacht on the Mediterranean. She'll be terrifically popular and people will say she's a 'character'.

It is not exactly that I don't trust Linda. I simply don't know what goes on in her head half the time. I don't know where she went today and whom she met for lunch. A man, of course, but she was evasive. She does things without worrying, she lives for present pleasures. Enviable, like a child's life, every moment counting. Not for Linda the if only ifs. Perhaps she's right. The rest of us are so frozen in our time warps, Ingrid ever waiting, me picking over my unresolved past. Perhaps that is why I don't, quite, trust Linda not to do some impulsive thing. That is why I am so reluctant to tell her about the shares. She'll know she was right about Victor all along. And since she dislikes him so much, why am I worrying? If only she weren't so very precisely Victor's type, a walking cliché of everything I know he likes in a woman.

I should be thinking about my grandmother. Tomorrow we'll talk; I hope that Victor is going to be very convincing. For all her robustness, she is not strong. She is an old lady after all and how she hates to worry about anything, and money in particular. She has such utter trust in the firm, in the dividends arriving as surely as the sun rises and sets. Her eyes light up when the envelope arrives with 'die Ausschüttung', she saves the opening, a ritual pleasure, for special delectation alongside a good cup of coffee and a tiny, medicinal brandy. Opa never breathed a syllable if he was even contemplating a slightly risky proposition as it gave her stomach upsets. Her generation remembers going shopping with a suitcase full of money; she has a horror of inflation and of debts and studies the exchange rate in the paper daily to reassure herself that she profits by it.

Oma rushes off to the gas board the moment the bill hits the mat, as though to keep it in the house for five minutes would stain her reputation. The word overdraft is as appalling to her as the wickedest vice. She trusts Victor absolutely, that is as far as his business sense is concerned. Our interests are the same, she always says. Herr Tiedemann has standing instructions to invest from her large liquid float in the stock Victor recommends with no need to consult her and she has always been pleasantly surprised by the results.

Oma is a thrifty soul. We have a cupboard full of neatly folded sheets of slightly used brown paper and huge balls of different bits of string, carefully knotted. Her pencils survive to their last inch; she writes shopping lists on bus tickets and marches off with her huge basket in strawberry or peach season to make sure of great mounds of these expensive fruits, at the best price, for her to preserve. The larder is full of her huge glass jars with rubber seals: pickles and jam, apricots in brandy, Sauerkraut, apple and pear mousse and tiny baby carrots with sliced-up beans. It is akin to a scandal in our house to open a tin of 'expensive rubbish'.

On the rare occasions when Oma spends money on herself, it is always foundations. Corsets and girdles, items of lasting value. She is proud of her figure and for years has been having these garments made for her in the latest colours and designs. Twice annually she visits a lady corsetière for a series of fittings; each year both discover with pleasure that she has not gained an inch. For the winter she has long bras that reach to the waist with dozens of hooks and eyes behind; in the summer she wears an outrageously skimpy version of the same. The summer bras, which Linda and I used to call Brunnhildes, have giant sturdy spans of elastic supplemented by cotton panels in lilac and coffee, pale pink and delicate grey. Once, flushed at her daring, giggling like a girl at the wicked extravagance of it, she showed me a garment hidden under a dozen layers of tissue paper in sinful, Folies Bergère black; a set of underclothes which Oma considered the height of decadence and which encased her solidly from the armpits to just above the knees. She budgets, carefully, for these follies. They are, she says, not a luxury but an investment. There is not a day of her life when Oma hasn't known exactly how much money she has in each of her various bank accounts, to the very last penny. Thank God, it's eleven o'clock at last. They will be drinking coffee; Linda will have some liqueur to sip at; she's regaling him with some of her stories and he'll be watching her as he does, smiling courteously but inside sitting in judgment.

I shan't change for him, I'm going just as I am. No perfume, no high heels. I would like myself better if that had happened naturally, if it hadn't been such a conscious decision.

# Chapter 11

As he crossed the road, Victor could feel that their heads were swivelling to watch him. He had grown sensors, which told him that they had moved off, that they followed a dozen paces behind, silent, soft-soled. Sometimes, in the evenings, he would think them gone and then the hairs would rise on the back of his neck and somewhere among the shadows a small, dark mass turned itself into the outline of a boy. There were half a dozen of them, in all, and though he never looked directly he knew them. A series of impressions, of outlines, was stamped into the cortex of his brain. Now, as he walked, he felt them slouching behind, felt the eyes on his back and one hand clenched in the pocket of the navy cashmere coat.

He had a vivid mental image of scything them down; saw the sharp blade whistling towards the thin, animal legs. He had been seeing, in short, bright flashes, a revolver butt beating on a bleeding mouth. The image, in continual action replays, had become imbued with a kind of tender nostalgia. The swift brutality of these fantasies corresponded to his needs.

It was Friday and as the moment grew nearer when he would see Ludwig again, he imagined crushing him, as a foot might stamp down on a beetle and crack it, like a nut. He felt surges of anger that this excrescence should have survived.

The shadows were drawing in, they seemed to him to come ever nearer, and behind their menace lay the broken mouth twisted into a hideous grimace of pleasure. In his mind, he likened Ludwig to a loathsome, flat grey thing found under a stone that remains still for a second as the light hits it and then scuds blindly away, thin veins pulsating on its slimy skin. His sensible, rational mind was full of such images; there had come a moment the previous day when they had ceased to be voluntary and he had felt invaded by them. Standing in the bright bathroom, propped against the bath, he had shaken his head to clear them away and seen a strange, wild face in the mirror, an old man's face. The brilliant light made it look bleak, it etched new furrows in his cheeks. Staring into the shaving mirror he had looked for minutes at the giant pores and traced the cruel lines. Now, as he walked, his tongue like a furtive night animal would dart out and press newly formed ulcers in painful, continuous confirmation of their presence.

He had made the error, then, of calling Heidi; had spent the afternoon in her soft bed chasing away the demons with love-making that had left him satisfactorily blank for an hour. His ardour had awakened new expectations that he would not fulfil. Having set himself to charm her out of her pouting sulks, he found he disliked her more than ever for her feigned coolness, her too-eager subsequent acquiescence.

The bank had called and requested an appointment. He carried a sheaf of papers in his case, which swung at his side with a rhythm of its own, syncopated to each steady beat of his right foot against the pavement. The movement soothed his restlessness. Herr Kortner, like Heidi, wanted to be wooed and comforted, soothed against the risk of his own under-taking. And yet the banker had found the project fascinating. How like a woman it was, to say yes and afterwards seek justification.

As he passed through the revolving doors and placed himself in the custody of the blue-uniformed official who would conduct him up to the sixth floor, Victor was thinking about Linda Davenport. She had a vitality that was infectious; she ate with real appetite like a healthy, exuberant animal; her skin and hair had a sheen that made other women look tired.

She had the directness, almost brusqueness, he associated with the English.

'Well,' she'd said, even in the act of sitting down, 'I'm sure you want to see me for a reason. What is it?'

To be that young had seemed, at that moment, infinitely desirable.

'So, you want to talk about Jo,' she said, and for an instant he'd not understood the soft English dz. 'Good, so do I.' Her fluent, mangled German started each phrase confidently and sidestepped such awkward issues as genders and declensions; her verbs were conjugated with anarchic facility. 'Let's talk in English,' she said, 'I want to be absolutely clear.'

Victor, who had thought to approach the subject with delicacy, had been astonished by her forthrightness; their sudden intimacy. He didn't know any women who spoke like this. She breached the verbal stockade that he took for granted in the male-female war, that barricade behind which each party concealed their evident, but unspoken ambitions, each protagonist considering it a success if he or she nudged the fortifications a centimetre closer to the other side.

'She's mad about you, you must know that,' she had said, and, 'It's time something was done to sort it out once and for all.' He could not understand why she chose to tell him this and to expose her friend so cruelly; he would never have asked that question, but she divined it from his face and answered it directly.

'You know,' she had said, 'I've never liked you very much, I mean, I'm enjoying this evening (here Victor had raised his glass in salute) but I don't approve of you, not for Jo. But you're like me, a doer, not a talker, not a romantic. I care about her, I want her to be happy. And she's, somehow, stuck, she needs to get you out of her mind. I give you due warning, I shan't help you one bit to get near to her. I'm on the other side. But I want something to happen all the same, do you understand?'

'Of course I understand,' he had said and they had both laughed, hers a bubbly giggle, and she had sat back then, with the air of one who had done her duty, and carried on talking, a warm lively girl, silky and perfumed. She had insulted him quite in the English style, without rancour, and even while he absorbed this news, knowing how to turn it to his advantage, he felt a small pang of regret that it couldn't have been her. A part of his mind quite automatically calculated his chances with her and concluded that he had none; this made her all the more desirable. He thought that Linda would not achieve what she wanted, nor as it happened would he.

He had prolonged the evening beyond its usual course with more coffee, another brandy; she had regaled him with stories about a Hamburg he barely recognised, with an amusing series of encounters with types he knew existed, but would never meet. She was perfectly conscious of her own sexuality; feminine to the extreme, but without employing the usual artifices. Yes, she would flirt with him, and enjoy it, but she warned him that there was nothing doing, not with the half-gestures he knew so well how to overcome, but with direct words. Come back to my flat, he had said, I want to talk about Johanna, and she had given him an acute, penetrating look and said, fine, why not, but don't think you're getting anything else. And, unlike most women, she meant it. They had gone, had talked of Johanna, that necessity his excuse, with Linda trying in her inimitable way now to put him off. He had teased her with his sudden interest. He had shown her around, for the pleasure of trying her out in his setting; he compared her with Heidi, with past amours whom he had never brought there. For Linda, he would have been happy to make an exception. She had a brightness that filled a room, that made the chilling, silent wakefulness of the night to come the lonelier.

Victor advanced to greet little Herr Kortner with a smile compounded of all these ironies. In the junior boardroom portraits of long-gone worthies hung on thick ropes and gazed calmly down at their successors. These reinforcements did not today suffice Herr Kortner, who had waxed enthusiastic over the project often enough in convivial tête à têtes with Herr Genscher. My two assistants, he said, and Victor shook hands with the swarthy Herr Holm, pressed the pink palm of Herr Schenck, and turned a mildly surprised eye upon his backer.

Herr Kortner sat stiffly in the uncomfortable, brass-studded chair, removing and replacing the blotting paper in its leather holder, each clumsy movement the signal of an acutely embarrassed man. He opened his mouth, then thought better of it. Pressing his full red lips together he glanced at a document. His face took on an unfamiliar, formal expression.

'I am sorry to have to tell you, Herr Genscher, that the Bank has decided it is unable to proceed with the loan.' His voice, over-confident and too loud in the hush, was obliged to proceed at the same excessive volume and seemed to Victor to boom into his skull.

Silence. The young men stared at the floor, the three of them exaggeratedly still. Victor waited. Herr Kortner, perforce, carried on.

'We have given your application a great deal of consideration,' he said. 'We value our long relationship with Rommer's as you know. But this is a, um, a particularly risky field.' Now his voice was taking on a more confiding and apologetic tone, the wooden phrases modulated as though they were saying something quite different.

Silence; the young men looked expectantly at Victor, who had not moved. He had the impression that they were acting a play for his benefit; that in a moment the curtain would fall and they would become normal again. He waited, now, for Herr Kortner to talk himself out. Kortner licked his lips. He had said to Victor, 'I can't see any reason why it shouldn't sail through,' and, 'Of course you're the sort of client the Bank likes best. Old firm, good name, fine business.' The room was very hot. A ray of sunshine miraculously penetrated the grey clouds and blocked out a bright rectangle on the table; now a million tiny motes of dust pulsated in its path. Victor's eyes rested on this brightness and absorbed the infinite detail of the fine grain; his tongue, tracing the line where two leaves of the table met, pushed hard and deliberate against the inflamed skin of his palate.

Kortner could not bear the silence.

'Our directors have of course the final veto,' he said and, growing voluble, 'Please understand me Herr Genscher, when I say this in no manner reflects upon your own creditworthiness or standing at the Bank. It is the nature of the business which concerns us. We do not see, um, how it can be

173

made to pay.' Again, he licked dry lips. 'We have certainly studied your, ah, documentation very thoroughly, extremely carefully indeed. It is what you might call a leap into the unknown. Frankly, Herr Genscher, *Der Abend* is a very difficult, a very troubled concern and the Bank does not feel prepared to take the risk.' In the deep hush, the sound of Herr Kortner swallowing was perfectly audible, the tiny gulping noise of a frog. 'Personally, I ah, sincerely regret this whole unhappy business. I am sure it will make no difference to the, um, excellent relationship we have always enjoyed.'

At last he was winding up. His colleagues, as though released from imprisonment, were shuffling, crossing legs. Uwe Schenck leant forwards and pushed the folder he held five centimetres towards the centre of the table, as if to say, here, we wash our hands of it, and earned a black look from his superior for his pains. And still Victor did not speak; the two younger men exchanged expressive looks. Both anticipated that in their usual, short unofficial conference some moments hence they would exhibit immature glee at having been in on such an unusual event; at having caught old Kortner with egg on his face. This anticipatory Schadenfreude was restrained by the difficulty of departing; they couldn't just leave him there, like a statue.

'Rommer's has a credit balance. The firm has banked with you for twenty-five years; you may recall a lunch to celebrate that event last year.' Victor spoke so quietly that they had to lean forwards to hear him. Herr Kortner, who knew these facts perfectly well, stammered a little.

'Yes, w-well, naturally we –'

'I myself have introduced a number of new clients.' Smoothly, Victor proceeded. 'You, Herr Kortner, have financed several ventures for us, all highly profitable.' Turning his head now, he fixed him with a look so violent that Kortner involuntarily recoiled.

'Yes, yes –'

'You've had your say,' he said unpleasantly. 'I shall spare your embarrassment by reminding you of your own statements about this project. Your, shall we call it, boyish enthusiasm. Your opinion clearly doesn't count. So one conclusion only remains, which is that something or somebody has interfered. I want to know who. You, Kortner, tell me who.'

Herr Kortner has profoundly shocked, as much by the reference which he took to denigrate his 1.65 metres as by such insolence in his own building. Conscious, moreover, that there was an element of truth in what Genscher said, he was for a moment unable to reply. Looking to his colleagues for help, he noticed with dismay that that fool Schenck was blushing. A wave of pink colour rose from the starched white collar encircling his soft throat and even touched his ears. 'The decision was made by the board of directors,' he said, staring at Schenck, who had taken out a handkerchief as though to mop his glowing face and, thinking better of it, began instead to crease one side into tiny pleats. 'Do you wish to add something, Herr Schenck?' he addressed his junior with heavy irony.

'May I have a word in private?' the unfortunate young man said and let out a trilling, inappropriate laugh.

Victor, left alone, relaxed his face for a moment in a sudden manic grimace. The air seemed thick, a stuffiness of heat and dust and what he thought was the smell of money. His veins throbbed with it, and with an angry rage.

Outside the gentlemen conferred in whispers. Herr Kortner, who wanted nothing more than to be shot of the whole business as soon as possible, vented his spleen upon the idiot Schenck. For once, dedicated career-man that he was, Kortner had actually made a small fuss about this decision; he had been put in his place in a way that rankled. He, as usual, was left with the unpleasant job of telling the client, without being able to tell the truth. The bank knew that this deal would never come off. An in-house rescue operation was in progress and would shortly be announced, pre-empting any outside buyers. They might have said yes to the loan, knowing it would never go through, but that was not how they did things. He could not even give his client the small consolation of knowing that this refusal made no difference to his chances. No outsider would ever get the *Abend*; he had heard it himself from the lips of the editor-in-chief.

They re-entered the room and Kortner tried to smile. 'I must apologise for my colleague,' he said with polite acidity. 'A misunderstanding. Fräulein Rommer visited him yesterday. She was interested in details of the loan, but naturally he told her nothing. He suggested, quite properly, that you, my dear Herr Genscher, were better placed to impart any information, if you so desired. That is all.' He was using the tone of patronising condescension a superior could adopt to rebuke his junior in public; implicit was the understanding that he and Herr Genscher were allied in superiority to the junior men; that they could part on this tone. But Herr Genscher, staring at the light as though transfixed by it, refused to let him off.

'Fräulein Rommer has nothing to do with it,' he said in a quiet, caressing tone. He was even smiling. 'I know who's behind it, I'm not a fool.' The sharp salty pain in his mouth as he spoke was almost pleasurable. 'I've worked for this, I've always made everything for myself.' He leant back, but two hands rested lightly on the table-top. His voice was pitched so low that the three men again craned to hear. 'I'm not dependent on a fat-arsed banker behind a desk. I'll get the money elsewhere. But you're finished, Kortner, I'll make sure of that, and you can forget the special relationship with Rommer's.' The voice sank to a whisper, yet it measured out each word with slow intensity. Herr Kortner sat like a man in a trance.

'Your career's over, Kortner – not mine. You're finished.' He said this with the quietest, surest finality, with his charming, urbane smile, and Herr Kortner could not suppress a shudder. 'Dead and buried, mein lieber Herr Kortner.' They were perfectly still, watching him, as he sauntered from the room; they remained so for a further minute.

Only then did Herr Holm and Herr Schenck dare to glance at one another. Herr Kortner, whose eyes remained fixed on the now-empty chair, on the neat set of fingerprints left on the shining mahogany, finally rose.

'Such language,' Schenck said in his archest, high-comedy voice. Herr Kortner gave him a look of the purest dislike.

'Would you come along to my office, Schenck, right away,'

he said. He had, at least, the comfort of releasing his anxieties in the traditional manner: by creating an equal or preferably greater stress in the mind of his junior.

The chill air, coming from a sky now slate-coloured and threatening snow, was pleasant on Victor's face and he opened his mouth to let it flow in. How simple it had all become. He had to eliminate Ludwig and then find a new backer. No. First Johanna, who could not be allowed to meddle. He had the timetable for action, at last. He quickened his pace, weaving through the crowd of Christmas shoppers, and inhaled great gulps of the delicious, icy air, which seemed to mount into his head with cold, cleansing effect.

It was this rapid progress which drew the eye of Herr Tiedemann. Planted outside the glass doors of the Rommer building, he was scanning the street through the jammed traffic. Fräulein Schmidt, at the office window above, had a far superior view of events. Her mug of coffee rested on the window sill. She was spooning in sugar, her slightly humped back in its bright emerald sweater blocking what little light could penetrate on such a dark day.

She watched Herr Genscher approach with the usual thrill of pleasure, as though he hurried for her benefit. Anna Schmidt was in the habit of embellishing her account of office doings to her married friend, fabricating a romance ever trembling on the brink of accomplishment. Though she always listened avidly, Jutta, looking pityingly at the hump, could not believe that Herr Genscher was as handsome and, well, as interested as Anna said. Fräulein Schmidt looked forward to astonishing Jutta with his magnificence, one day soon.

She confined these elaborate daydreams to her leisure hours and prided herself on her efficiency in office time. She would never have been found gawping out of the window in that vulgar way, were it not for Herr Tiedemann's extraordinary behaviour. He had been taking a long-distance call from England for the past fifteen minutes. She knew it was, most unusually, Frau Rommer, for she had put her through herself. Working her way busily through a stack of invoices, tearing them off at the perforations with a satisfying rip, she had become aware of unusual motion behind the glass partition. Herr Tiedemann's large fleshy hand gestured in the air. He had noticed her looking and then actually turned his back to carry on the conversation. Of course nothing could be heard through the glass wall and for half a minute she had been tempted to pick up the receiver, very gently. She didn't, of course. He had snapped the receiver down so hard she almost thought she heard it; his face had turned that dull brick colour it sometimes did. He had marched straight out without even putting on his coat.

Fräulein Schmidt had listened to the click of his metal-tipped soles on the stairs, an agitated, hurrying click, before rising and going to the tea and coffee cupboard conveniently near the window. He was just standing there. He was waiting for Herr Genscher, something he'd never done before. She stared down at the foreshortened figure leaning forwards, now raising an arm to wave an urgent summons.

Herr Genscher was drawing level. Fräulein Schmidt could see two youths behind him, so close they almost grazed his heels. She saw one nod to the other; they sprang forwards and now walked one on either side of him; she stared in amazement as one darted out a hand towards his briefcase. Horrified, she rapped smartly on the window.

'Aufpassen!'

Behind her, Herr Goldberg rose. He almost had to shoulder her out of the way to see.

Herr Genscher pulled the briefcase tight against his chest; hugging it, he ran straight over the road towards Herr Tiedemann; those hooligans were right behind him and, with the lights about to change to green, all three just leapt onto the pavement in time. They swayed, all four figures in a confused cluster dominated by the blond head; Fräulein Schmidt pressed her bony nose against the pane to see better and another spoonful of sugar slid, half into the mug, half onto the sill. My God, in broad daylight, my God, and she saw a tangle of arms, reaching, and held her breath in alarm and excitement. Now the blond head stepped back; one arm swung the case round aiming for a youth, who side-stepped nimbly. A shriek leapt out of Fräulein Schmidt and condensed on the

window. The cluster suddenly separated out; Herr Tiedemann's mighty bulk was toppling, right into the road and he
crashed, unable to save himself, right into the path of the huge
van and the sudden squeal of brakes penetrated right into the
office.

Fräulein's Schmidt's eyes were squeezed shut. Tentatively,
after a moment, she opened them. Now the scene was
confused, for a crowd was gathering and in it she could see
Herr Genscher, just, but there was no sign of the youths.
Automatically, she raised her hand and sipped the coffee,
which tasted cloyingly sweet. Bewildered, she put it down
and, collecting herself, pushed past Herr Goldberg and ran
across to telephone for an ambulance. She flung her coat across
her narrow shoulders before running downstairs to become
another figure on the pavement in a confused jumble of
people, a babble of voices saying move him to the side, no
don't, give him a coat for a pillow, cover him up, while in a
background rumble the van driver could be heard explaining
to anyone who would listen that it wasn't his fault and irritated
drivers behind, who could not see the reason for the hold-up,
overlaid the whole with a cacophony of blaring horns.

An ambulance eventually inched its way in and took the
immobile figure off in a blaze of headlights and sirens and Herr
Genscher with it. Fräulein Schmidt took it upon herself to
telephone Frau Tiedemann and tell the poor woman that there
had been a terrible accident, but she was not to worry and,
assuming another small piece of responsibility, that she was
sending a taxi to take her to the hospital right away.

Lotte immediately assumed that her Otto was dead, or as
good as. She put on her coat and sat waiting for the cab which,
delayed by the heavy traffic, took nearly an hour to make its
way out of the congested centre. By this time she had drunk
three quarters of a bottle of vodka straight from the bottle and
had to be helped, giggling helplessly, onto the back seat where
she lay in a state of collapse. There was no question of her
being allowed to see her husband, not in that state. The nurse,
a stout Berliner, jabbed her stubby hand into the small of Frau
Tiedemann's back, propelling her with perhaps unnecessary
force into the small waiting room. The doctors were still with

Herr Tiedemann; she could not in any case have seen him, but the nurse with her cynical view of mankind preferred to let the little woman contemplate her own shortcomings during the long wait.

It was very quiet in the office until Herr Genscher returned. Fräulein Schmidt, solemn with self-importance, began to give him her account of the whole incident and was dismissed with a wave as he proceeded on into his office. She followed, after a moment's panicky reflection, and he, lifting the receiver from the phone, gazed at her coldly as she asked after dear Herr Tiedemann. 'It's concussion,' he said, 'he'll be fine,' and dialled. Fräulein Schmidt, who knew her duty, told him that it was a telephone call from Frau Rommer which had agitated dear Herr Tiedemann to such an extent, uttering these words very slowly and deliberately, with a strong note of disapproval.

'Hello, Johanna?' he said and, covering the receiver, motioned her away. As she backed slowly from the room, Fräulein Schmidt heard him say that he would like to go and see that girl. Intent on his conversation, he did not even look up, did not even see her angry moue of distaste. She, who had been heroic, who would appear more so in her account to Jutta that evening, hurried out into the hallway. Safe on the cold lavatory seat, she burst into a passion of angry, frustrated tears.

He was looking at his watch when the phone buzzed; one fifteen precisely. Four hours had gone by. Bloody Wolfgang. His truculence transmuted Sigi's sharp disappointment into acute irritation and he interrupted, brusquely.

'You're a big boy, you're so proud of yourself, you sort out your own bloody problems.'

Wolf's voice turned sly. 'Well I'll have to call Mutti then. It'll upset her. But she won't leave her little boy stranded in town. Heini buggered off with all my cash.'

Sigi exhaled his annoyance.

'Come on Sigi,' the voice said, wheedling. 'Look you can't

just leave me here in the shit can you? What'm I going to do?'

'You fucking arsehole,' and Sigi looked again at his splendid watch. 'I'll come. This is the last time I'm ever going to do anything for you. Where are you?'

Wolf was not one to show gratitude or pleasure, but, getting into the Alfa, he let out a sigh of relief.

'You took your time,' he said. There was a trickle of blood around one nail where he had gnawed at the cuticles down to the quick and ripped away a raw red segment; he had sucked his thumb until he was a good ten years old. The traffic was so slow that they made virtually no headway and Sigi tapped his fingers impatiently on the wheel. The pretty girl in the Volkswagen alongside looked at his handsome profile and smiled winningly, but he didn't look her way. There was a kid in the car, talking with violent gestures into the air. She shrugged her shoulders, she fiddled with the dial of the radio.

Sigi could not find it in himself to offer his brother the slightest crumb of comfort; he wanted him to suffer. He was babbling about it being an accident, but nothing Wolfgang did was accidental. Sigi wanted him to weep and howl. He executed a U-turn outside the shabby building which made the wheels spin, and saw the gangling dolt in his idiot shoes trip on the low step. His head was pounding with anxiety. She called the old man Uncle, and now he was dead or maimed. Jesus, what would she think? He tried to formulate excuses, which even in his head sounded inadequate. He knew that he should have done something to prevent it; with grim satisfaction, he pictured Wolfgang incarcerated, for years.

The telephone stopped ringing when he was one pace away and he cursed, fluently. He had been gone nearly an hour; she might not try again. In the whole bloody sequence of events, this one circumstance emerged as the most important. Sigi's long and successful career with women was notable in one respect: he had never been the pursuer. Girls were attracted to him to the extent of giggling, forward little tarts at discos pushing each other forwards to ask him to dance. She, who had promised to call him, might not want to see him again; she might hate him for giving her the papers. She didn't even know the half of what he'd done to wreck her life. It was five hours since she'd left. Why didn't she call?

Sigi had had dozens of girls, the sort who considered themselves good in bed and liked to squirm and shriek and act, the whole event a performance that they asked to be rated on afterwards. Girls who faked shuddering, dramatic orgasms or cried; girls who would insist on talking when he wanted to sleep; who asked him, off-puttingly, the second before he came whether he loved them. Girls with tricks and techniques and sharp perfumes that smelt as though they must be burning their flesh; who wanted to sleep with him and didn't always expect a meal first.

He'd always been glad to be rid of them, even the ones with model-girl looks who were the envy of his friends. They were the worst. They cried over a spot, asked a hundred times if they hadn't put on a little weight and jumped out of bed in the morning with little cries of horror, rushing to slap make-up on in case, God forbid, he saw them as they really were. He'd never had to try to please any of them. Johanna was so different that she could have belonged to a different species. She had turned up on his doorstep at two thirty that morning, desperately pale, and without a word she had walked straight through into the bedroom. 'I've come to seduce you,' she'd said. Dumbfounded, he had stared at her, seen the smile tremble a little. 'Is it – inconvenient, right now?'

How cold she'd been, like a statue in ice; not just chilled, but frozen in her determination. Something had happened, but she wasn't going to tell him what it was. He thought that he would have refused, had he realised beforehand that this was her act of revenge; for she had used him, blatantly, outrageously; it was a kind of rape of the mind. Moodily, he watered the rubber plants, for the leaves were already turning yellow. No, he would not have refused. He loved her anyway, he simply couldn't help himself. He spent all his time thinking about her. The brandy had warmed her; relaxed her a little. She had peeped at him mockingly over the blankets. It's now or never, Sigi, she said. I'm beginning to think that you've changed your mind. As though he was the reluctant virgin.

He stood up, rubbing his eyes, dragged in the cardboard box of books and started to arrange them on the empty shelves. With grim determination, she had suffered his embraces. He, who had never told a girl that he loved her, who would never have allowed that word to be dragged out of him, had told her over and over again. You really don't have to say that, she'd said, it's awfully nice of you, but you don't have to, you know. I don't mind. As though the word was common currency on his lips; as though that was his stock in trade. He almost felt shocked, at such cynicism and disbelief.

There had been no lovers' breakfast in the morning; no coffee and kisses. He was the one to urge her to stay, uncharacteristically even to plead a little. How anxious she'd been to be gone, efficient and cool, rushing to shower, to dress. And distant, alarmingly so, as though it had all been a dream, making no concession just because they had spent the night in each other's arms. The attitude of a man, he thought, with a small, sour smile. Saying, off-hand, that she'd call him, with that tone in her voice that implied the urgency was all his. There was no reason in the world for her to care about him; five years of eager female flesh were annulled in one night by this cold English girl. She wasn't even beautiful; the whole thing was a joke, and yet he suffered, he sat and waited for the telephone to ring and catalogued, over and over, the list of his misdeeds.

Johanna, who did not care for him, could not be told the story of their introduction; not yet. He shuddered at that idea. He had lain awake in the night, as she slept, one thin arm clutching the pillow tight, and had known that he had to give her Levison's papers. For she had told him, calmly, after they had made love, that her friend Linda was with Genscher. That fact alone had brought her to him; she did not say it so directly, but it was understood. The man's spectre stalked them; it had to be exorcised. He would not have her by default.

While she showered, he had wrapped the papers with care in brown paper the packers had left. He had given her the unwieldy parcel with no explanation. Lying on the sofa, watching smoke rings curl up to the white ceiling, he imagined her opening it. He saw her reading, with that slight frown of concentration, at her desk. He wished upon Wolfgang the torments of hell. He said in his head, please God, please let the telephone ring and listened to the utter blank silence.

A boy was running down the Beckerstrasse at full pelt. His outline, passing the Judo Master's windows, was perceived by Frau Liebmann as a series of black flashes through the stripes in the glass. There was a hammering at the door and she, hunched over her bucket and mop, straightened up laboriously.

'Let me in. I have to see Herr Levison.'

A pink nose; one eye, projected themselves through the letter box.

'Go away. He's busy.'

'Let me in, let me in, it's urgent,' and two fists pummelled at the door, making the panels groan under the assault.

'Wait,' she said, and made her way with deliberate slowness to the office. Herr Levison sat at his desk; he was looking at a picture he kept in it, his head bent low over it. When she clicked on the light, brightening the gloomy room, he gave a start.

'It's a boy,' she said, 'I told him to go away, but he says he has to see you. I don't know who. I can't remember their names,' and she shrugged her shoulders in unvarying indifference.

'Let him in.'

Her progress across the mat was very slow; she kicked off her shoes, bent with a grunt to carry them to the other side, held herself carefully upright on the door at the far end to replace them, oblivious to the hammering on the door and irritating, bleating cries through the letterbox. The lad practically fell on top of her when she opened it, and she pushed him away, clutching at her heart, and he sprinted past. Shaking her head and muttering to herself, she closed the door and drew the large bolt.

Heini looked very peculiar indeed; he was flushed and strangely rigid looking.

'What is it?'

184

'He's dead, he's dead,' the boy gasped, with his mouth all askew, and collapsed suddenly into the chair which tilted back and back and with the ludicrous comedy of a slow-motion farce deposited him with a crack onto the floor. Ludwig, who had felt a sharp shudder of fear, jumped up and went towards him; his shadow fell across the boy's face, which was now, suddenly, perfectly white and he saw with a certain horror that Heini was flinching away, as though he expected to be hit.

Victor, progressing smoothly along the Elbchaussee, glimpsed through a set of gates a woman on the lawn in front of large white-shuttered house. She was sawing at the branches of a small fir tree while a child capered behind, swinging a basket of fir cones. He was rehearsing his little speech to Johanna; it occurred to him now that he would be obliged to spend Christmas with her. For the first time in years, he had failed to make arrangements for skiing.

Curiously, he had forgotten about it completely; had seen the glittering façade of trees on the Alsterhaus without making the connection. And yet everywhere glossy-leaved garlands with bright ribbons hung on doors. The Christmas trees were set out in serried ranks outside the ugly face of the Petrikirche, where the Christmas fair had spread its colourful manifestations and stallholders offered wooden decorations, Lebkuchen and almonds. For some years now he had avoided the family celebrations of friends, those gatherings to celebrate the season of goodwill when even the greasy goose, the roast carp and exchange of costly gifts did not obliterate the faint animosity garnered during the year. He hated these occasions; too much Sekt, a present for him in the bright pile and a pitying glance when the children came in to see the tree, as though he had the slightest desire to duplicate the event on his own behalf. It was a hangover which perpetuated itself, faintly, for a week, until the bright hilarity of Sylvester, the streamers and din and wet, drunken kisses put paid to the whole business for another year. He wondered what he and Johanna would do; he thought with distaste of the extraordin-

185

ary vulgarity of the English counterpart and remembered how shopkeepers covered their plate glass windows with black tape and sprayed fake snow into the corners. A nation which ate dry turkey and wet vegetables and listened to its monarch; there, even the Rommers hung lights on the great grim fir outside the house in twinkling homage to their neighbours' brightly bedecked windows. The weight of these future occasions oppressed him. Feeling in his pocket for the ring in its little case, he allowed himself a last, ironic smile. He would make the pretty speeches. He closed his fingers tight around the gun; transferred it to the glove compartment. He thought that, after all, he had his Christmas present to look forward to. First Johanna, then Ludwig, then the great glittering packed parcel, that most expensive of indulgences, *Der Abend*. He would have it, whatever it cost.

The telephone rang and rang. Finally it was picked up. Silence.

'Are you all right?' he said. Her voice was small and hollow; he could barely make it out.

'All right? No. No. I'm not. What do you think I am?'

'You've read it.'

'I thought it was a present, isn't that funny. I thought you'd given me a gift, a souvenir, well I suppose that's what you might call it. Very memorable, your souvenir. I only opened it an hour ago, I forgot about it.'

'I see.' She sounded very peculiar indeed; now he could hear her yawning into the telephone.

'I'm tired,' she said, 'but Victor's coming over. He wants to see me, he said, about business and other matters. So I'll just have to stay awake.'

'You let him come? You said he could come?'

'Oh, don't get excited about it. I hadn't opened it then, I didn't know. And I have to get it over with some time, don't I? I wish Linda was here. We had an awful row and she's gone out.'

'Jesus bloody Christ,' he said. 'Look, I'm coming. I'm coming over right now,' he paused; she didn't say no. That

186

was something. 'Johanna, would you have rung me? Tell me. Quick.' Very faintly, he could hear the tiny, tinny ring of animated voices talking on the line, as though on another planet.

'No. Probably not.' A faint sigh whispered down the line. 'I'm sorry Sigi, but no.' It was a ghostly little voice, the English accent very pronounced. Click. He dialled again in a fever of anxiety.

'Don't tell him about it, do you hear? Don't do anything about it, just pretend, right? He's dangerous,' and he slammed down the phone before she could reply and ran down the stairs; he cursed the little car when it wouldn't start first time. Herr Victor Genscher, he thought, must have a good half-hour's start on him, maybe more. Embroiled in the rush hour traffic, realising that he had left his cigarettes at home, he beat his hand upon the wheel in disproportionate thumping rage.

# Chapter 12

Half a dozen typed pieces of paper had carefully been placed edge to edge, as though for purposes of comparison; as a scholar might examine a manuscript. The remainder were heaped in an untidy pile, any old how; a long green ribbon snaked carelessly across it. The desk was littered. Barely a square inch of its mahogany surface peeped out. A bundle of pencils jostled an ash tray; a vase of brackish water containing flowers which were shedding their brown, furling petals over the whole overhung a coffee cup in which pollen floated.

The diary lay open on the top right-hand corner of the desk, its edges exactly aligned with it in neurotic pedantry. It was a hard-cover exercise bok, not a printed diary at all. It was the sort of handsome book, neatly bound, which would command a good price in a stationer's shop, but which would always prove disappointing, later. Once opened, there was nothing to distinguish it from the cheapest kind of exercise book: the same green lines ruled across slightly too-thin, yellowy paper and the same double, wavy red line across the top of the page. The date was hand-written, neatly, above every entry and the margins, not ruled but nevertheless straight and identical, controlled by that same exacting eye. A shelf full of identical volumes bore witness to past industry, no doubt subject to the same format.

No formality constrained the content of this book, however. ' . . . had all the intellectual bite and subtlety of the playground,' the page began.

'Did/Didn't, but with adult venom and bile. She accuses me of obsessional paranoia; wide-eyed innocence and reproach is something she does rather well. "Of course I was there; we were talking about you, and that's the Gospel truth." A consummate performance and that bit cleverest of all, for it hurts. She's gone out to get her ticket home. "You're completely wrong," she said. "I'm not going because of anything I did, but because if you can't trust me there's not much of a relationship left, is there?" Why does she pretend? I even saw the bedroom light go on: as though they were having coffee in there, it's a farce. She denies and denies: guilty as hell, can't admit she's choking on a great slab of it, remorse with Schlag. She thought I'd never find out.

'It's a bit of fun for Linda, that's why she did it. She doesn't need to like a man to sleep with him: proven fact. It's just a mechanical response to a situation. Fuck her, and he did. She wasn't to know I was lurking around outside. I thought I'd been too clever, for the windows were dark and I wasn't going to wake him, so I hung around in hope and dread, with my entire attention fixed upon the watch: another minute and I'll go, and another. It's a phobia, the timing thing, like rearranging the letters of signs in alphabetical order, over and over. I do that, too. Then they arrived. Pretty, the two blond heads, standing at the balcony windows. The first glimpse I've had in two and a half years. A nightcap, what could be more pleasant? Except that he never took me home at night: inviolable territory. Not for Linda, though. I knew through every bone and fibre of flesh that he had taken her home to make love to her. It was quarter to one in the morning by then, and bitterly cold. I gave them another minute, then another, sixty revolutions of the hand went by and I knew, then, that she wasn't coming out. It was as though my whole insides were filled with hot sourness, like that Chinese soup. It was unthinkable, to just go home and wait. I wanted to punish them, to spite Victor. Like a tart, needing a man, any man, but of course there was Sigi. And I thought that I could have

189

described myself as fortunate, if that is the – '

No hand moved to turn the page. The typed documents were not in fact consecutive, though at first glance they gave that impression.

'I, Ludwig Jakob Levison, born 1928, by profession teacher of Judo, self-employed of 48 Beckerstrasse, 2-Hamburg Altona, am writing this testimony after long and careful thought. This document is a record of events that happened nearly twenty-five years ago and some might say that old history is better left alone: let the dead bury the dead. But I feel that it is my duty to tell the truth. No one, apart from myself, knows exactly what happened all those years ago.

'My position is an unusual one, perhaps. For I am guilty, by association; not guilty of any crime, no, but blameable in a moral sense. In these pages, I believe I have made that much apparent. This is a document devised to trace that borderline between remorse, of the type we all suffer, and real culpability. There is a difference between what I term "physical" and "moral" outrages. I must, perhaps, first explain that these are issues which concern me, closely, every day. I teach the young. I uphold, in so doing, the old-fashioned virtues of discipline, of pride and integrity in honest labour, of humility in victory and of continual striving for self-improvement. Our sport contains all these lessons and many more beside. I try to lead my life along these lines, which nowadays some people would call unfashionable, or no longer justifiable.

'I have reached a point in my life when I can no longer justify silence. I see a man walking through the streets of my adopted city, not just living, where I thought him dead, but flourishing where he had no right to prosper. A man who has committed the worst of crimes, murder, and never been brought to justice.

'What kind of justice am I talking about? This is not a letter to the police; this is not the dry language of official documents or of legal testimony. This piece of paper is a mirror, in which a man, this man, should see himself, should recognise what he was and what he has become. And there shall be justice, real justice, the sort which does not merely punish, but remakes the world as it should have been. Perhaps I should call that my notion of justice. I am writing this without the aid of a lawyer and entirely of my own volition. It is a true story, it is also my story, and I must tell it in my own way. I have had to overcome something in myself before writing this down.'

'This man was once my protégé. I raised him, if anyone could be said to do that, from the age of ten years old. At that time I was known by a different name, Levi, that of my birth. If that seems an admission of guilt, then I must admit it. For I say that he is guilty, and he is, but I am not blameless. His faults are mine. His problems are also of my doing. I admit that freely. It is one of the ironies of maturity that it is possible to look back and see how acts of stupidity can pervert the course of simple, straightforward things. Many bad, even wicked things, are brought about, not by wicked men, but by a combination of errors that, in happier circumstances, might only have produced a small mishap. But I am anticipating my story.

'I was, at the time of the events I mean to describe, in charge of a hostel for the homeless in Berlin. War orphans, misfits, the children nobody wanted, all made their way to me. It was not an official place. I ran it myself, to give these children shelter. Nobody cared, in wartime, what became of them, particularly those who could be described as simple. Many children, indeed, were simple: children abandoned by parents who were relieved, perhaps, to be rid of them.

'I had seen many such children rounded up and taken away; their destinations unknown. Those who had eluded the dragnet lived in terror, lived a half-life sheltering by day in the basement which also served us as a bomb shelter. We know, today, the deadly nature of the buses which took them away, and which brutal sanatoria took them in for the last moments of their short, unhappy lives. One of the consequences of the events I describe was that I, too, was forced to abandon them; I do not know if any of them were able to make any sort of life for themselves. Unable, as they were, to distinguish right from wrong, innocents who nevertheless were living proof of their parents' afflictions and wrong-doing, I fear our society, which had elevated the crude basics of survival and, later, the more luxurious artifacts of living into its tribal totems, would consider them the disposable rubbish of the new affluence. I had enjoyed a measure of success with these simple souls, succeeding often in training them in basic skills where others had failed. I take no credit for it; fear had sharpened even dull wits and the most backward of them could understand a simple ritual, performance of which ensured a piece of bread and a bowl of soup. Today, such methods sound harsh, perhaps. I do not apologise for them. In those dark days, an existence could rest upon the satisfactory performance of a simple greeting – '


'. . . the community was divided, accordingly, and those who had some form of work had special status. They, who contributed a part of their income, had better rooms and food. Their presence gave the hostel a semi-legitimate status; visiting relatives were kept away from the crowded attics and back-rooms where the children slept.

'Among these "normal" children, whom I can term such only by virtue of the fact that they suffered from no obvious disability, Victor was exceptional. He was so very different from the rest; intelligent and alive, quick-witted. A child who had all the virtues, all the possibilities within him. It was not surprising that I soon discovered that I loved him more than the rest; an affection which made me uncritical, which overlooked faults. This was my fault, my error, which, although I did not see it at the time, was to exacerbate his problem, for it blinded me. Growing fond of him, I excluded him from the continual search for foster-parents, which was one of the main purposes of the mission. It was not, at first, a conscious decision; later, realising that I did not wish to be parted from him, I considered it and decided that he could benefit more from the care of a just, but loving parent, a father, for I saw myself in that role, than by living with a family. It was true, that I cared for him more than strangers ever could, but the decision was nevertheless wrong. I believe that Victor has suffered all his life, continues to suffer, from the lack of the parental bond, from the need for close ties to a loving family. It is a measure of my grave fault in this that he, forced by circumstances into early independence, has grown a shell so thick that he does not even recognise that lack. My decision, however wrong, was soon justified by events, for it soon became clear that no family would wish to take this boy.

'For Victor was a thief and worse; he used his acquisitions to buy himself special status and to dominate others, not just exacting obedience, but sexual submission. This did not immediately become apparent; for it was the sickness of the age. He was roaming the streets, sheltering where he could when I took him in. By eleven years old, he already seemed mature for his age. He was quiet and did not speak much of his past. That he had survived by stealing was evident; there was no other way to live on the streets. He carried on taking things, for the old habits died hard, but he committed the sin of taking from the hostel. We had practised, through the war years, a moral code which some might term hypocritical, but which conditions made necessary: it was one thing to find or barter outside, and quite another to take from fellow-sufferers. Inside our shabby little house, there was order and discipline. This phenomenon was by no means unusual; I believed that the atmosphere of our house would influence him, in time, and so for a while let him be. This boy had the face of an angel. It was hard to believe that he was intrinsically capable of wrong.

'By the age of fourteen Victor was very tall and strong and precocious for his age. He was already having sexual relationships – '

'It was a time of change. I had succeeded in moving our family to a house which could accommodate all of us. Emerging from the cramped, cold basement in which we had huddled, learning by rote, into a bright classroom was at first disorienting and strange. Like moles emerging from their burrows, the children congregated in the familiar safety of the corridors. The city was not safe and I imposed a curfew; one from which our three new lodgers, among them Wilfried Meyer, were exempt. Nevertheless there was an excitement, a new optimism, a sense of change. It is hard to believe how little things could delight us then, what certainty I had that a better future had already started to happen. To walk upon a' carpet was a luxury few of my poor orphans had known, but soon there were books, too, and I even began to fear that a return to prosperity would undermine our simple, pure regime. Many people believed that a new world could be built upon the ruins of the old, as though overthrowing one tyranny would obliterate the beast forever. The survivors, the widows and children of the millions who had died for ideologies, could find comfort in that belief, could see a virtue in the senseless slaughter. It was a beast of a different sort which killed Meyer; a wild thing hitting out at anything which stood in its path. The wilfulness, the abstract evil of that murder haunts me; it is not too extreme to say that it has destroyed my life. I was the keeper of the beast; I was the one who failed to train it and it hit at me. I bear the scars today and I accept them, my punishment for a failure. My misdeeds made evident upon my face, and they are ugly things which make people avert their gaze. Just as there is no justice, no consolation for Frau Meyer, there is no justice in a world that allows Victor to walk abroad, unblemished, a personification of handsome health, of the new order, of esteemed, respectable sobriety. He knows, as I know, that it is a sham, that I am his dark shade, the true delineation of his deformity. I cry justice, not revenge, that is the prerogative of the innocent. Let the beast show itself, let it atone for evil by doing good, let it acknowledge and expiate its sins. I do not believe in the possibility of redress in another world, I cannot abdicate responsibility so easily.

'For I failed him in so many ways. He broke the curfew; knowing that, unable to exact obedience, I set a child to follow him. He was eluding me in every sense, straying into a world of corruption, of flesh. Victor chose as his object a young girl who could satisfy his carnal desires and, daughter of a butcher, could contribute to his black-market profiteering. Perhaps I should have informed the parents of this girl, I no longer know. I had a reluctance to become involved with the father, whose greed was known, who refused sustenance to the starving. . .'

'By holding aloof, by permitting Victor to corrupt the girl, I let him slip into a world which was profoundly tainted. He was only fourteen. For all his strength and precocity, he had not the inner resources to face evil, when it surely came, and I, his teacher, had let him slip too far. I know, now, that a good father must be stern, must root out corruption and inculcate strength with a disciplined regime, must face unpleasant tasks. My love for him made me weak.

'There were riots in the city and a crude mob, demanding justice in their own fashion, stormed shops and looted. This poor girl, her name was Charlotte Bamberg, paid a penalty for her father's greed. A man asked for meat and, refused, killed the butcher, killed the girl. Victor came upon the scene and my young boy, following him, terrified, ran to tell me the story. I remember waiting for him to return, uncertain what course to take, walking up and down. With my grief on his behalf was mingled the knowledge that the time had come for him to face his life and what he had become. Too late, I decided to play the role of the stern father, to upbraid him, but gently, with a father's love. To make him strong. He came carrying a gun and accused me of her murder, not understanding that in reality he accused me of failing him. I remember his young face staring at me, the piercing gaze of his eyes which could not cry, which had outgrown childish sorrows, and indeed his sorrow was that of a man. I remember telling him that, that he had to be a man. How he punished me for that, for his boyhood, my failure to raise him to the stature of an adult.

'He broke my jaw, using the gun, and smashed my teeth. I was good-looking once, as a young man. He turned his gun

195

upon Wilfried and shot him through the skull. He died within minutes. I held him in my arms, blood streaming from my face onto his, unable to speak as I was for months to come. His eyes were terrible, frantic and uncomprehending, and I had not the ability to offer a word of comfort. His was a cruel, a pointless death. It is the weak, the vulnerable who suffer in this world for the transgressions of others and my children paid a heavy price for Victor's. He vanished; I believed, later, that he must have killed himself. I cannot live so lightly with my guilt, but Victor, if he has a conscience, does not display it. He gives money to orphans now. I wonder if he thinks of mine, whom he rendered homeless, for Meyer's mother, hysterical with grief, instigated an investigation into the death which brought severe penalties. My premises were closed, the children dispersed, taken away from me, and I was not told where. Too ill to fight my case, found guilty in absentia, as was Victor, we were both made outcasts, condemned to wander. A strange chance has brought us both to this city, and allowed our lives to link once more. Our story is not ended yet. I believe that I have been given the opportunity to remake history and this time I shall not permit any weaknesses to hinder me – '


'Today he is thirty-nine years old, a respectable business man. Victor is the managing director of the old-established firm of Rommer Import-Export Handelsgesellschaft, of which he owns a fifty percent share. He has been working for this company for over twenty years and is now a prominent citizen in Hamburg's small, well-to-do business community. He belongs to a number of clubs and associations, including some formed for charitable purposes, and it is known that he gives generously in support of waifs, orphans, refugees, the homeless and abandoned.

'That he is an orphan himself is known; the remainder of his life cannot be common knowledge. I venture here into the realms of conjecture, for it is impossible for me to know how much Victor confides in his close friends. I believe, however, that he does not in truth possess a close friend. I believe that he has told no one of his early life; that he lives a lie and shuns situations so intimate that confidences could not be avoided.

'Victor is not married; his predilections may be unchanged. Hamburg is a city in which many encounters of a louche type can easily be arranged. Many men in his situation marry; he has chosen not to. He is often seen with women, pretty women of a certain type. Women who dress expensively, who are perhaps married to particularly complaisant husbands or separated; who enjoy a social life, furs, jewels and fine clothes in return for their favours. This sort of cold-blooded arrangement, whereby each partner receives precisely what he bargains for and expects no more, is the basis upon which his network of relationships has been constructed. In short, if he were to lose his position, all would be lost. If this man could not buy a friend or lover, he would have none. He is incapable of a relationship of any other sort. Even as a boy he was skilled at using possessions or threats as a means of obtaining sexual compliance.'


A sheet torn from a student block, one covered in tiny squares, partly obliterated this last page. The writing on it, identical to that of the diary, had set out a series of short, cryptic statements down the left hand side of the page, each one neatly separated by four spaces from the next:

L Levison/Sigi/phone boxes
Possessions or threats = sexual compliance
*Homosexual*
Buying women/cold-blooded arrangement
Proof (1) Frau Meyer (2) Levison

The note-taker had laid the pen upon this piece of paper; it was held in position by the further, substantial weight of an unused round glass ashtray. Under its round base, the words 'proof' and 'sexual', hugely distorted, curved in upon themselves, but there was no eye looking to appreciate the phenomenon. The room was empty; it was also extremely cold. A window near the desk had been opened and a half-drawn curtain now flapped into the room, the bitter northern wind lifting up a billowing fold of the net curtain snatched at the papers and sent them sliding among a flurry of brown petals and rippled the black liquid in the cup. The door slammed to.

# Chapter 13

Frau Beckmann, twitching at the lace curtains, saw a white Mercedes draw up and park grandiosely and illegally on the narrow pavement directly under her gaze. A good-looking man emerged from the car and locked it. She watched from her perch as he walked to her front door and just made out the bell shrilling in the flat above. She strained to hear the sound of footsteps ascending the stairs. This was, as far as she knew, the first male visitor Fräulein Rommer had ever received. Her curiosity was perfectly natural. Undecided whether to remain sitting at the window or to station herself nearer to the door, she wandered about the room in vague, circular movements. Even turning up the sound level of the small hearing aid to full; even listening as hard as she could, she could make out nothing. There was complete silence.

Above her, Johanna stared at the desk, at the papers so carefully laid out which rippled in the stiff breeze with small sinister flappings, like an animal trying to crawl. Two polite rings at the bell were succeeded, now, by one more urgent tone. Suddenly she stooped, gathered together the whole in an unwieldy mass and stuffed the bundle into a drawer that, for an agonising moment, refused to close. She jammed it shut; banging down the window she could see the car that must be his and ran, frightened that he might go away, to let him in.

He carried his smile before him up the two flights of stairs until his dark bulk dwarfed her and they shook hands awkwardly. They stared at each other for a moment and then both looked away. He had made a small motion, as though to kiss her cheek and she, recoiling slightly, found herself awkward, gauche.

'I'll make coffee,' she said, 'please sit down,' politely and was startled when he laughed.

'Marvellous,' he said. 'It's incredible. I do believe you've got a Hamburg accent. Say something else.'

'You make me sound like a talking monkey. I'm not going to gratify you, you're the one who's come to talk. Milk, no sugar, is that right?' and she thought that's it, that's the right tone, and came in and out with coffee cups. He was examining the room, scrutinising her. Shrugging off his coat, he lounged, now, at his ease.

'I like it here. It's charming. Peaceful. What a long time it's been, Johanna. I must have startled you when I called,' and he crinkled up his eyes ruefully and, with that familiar boyish gesture, ran a hand through his hair.

'No,' she said and, 'I was expecting it,' and without a tremor filled their cups. The reality was never as bad as the anticipation of it. They both knew how to behave; there would be no histrionics. And yet part of her felt almost paralysed by the shocking fact of his presence. He had aged. His hair was beginning to grey at the sides, the white so close to the gold that, as yet, it barely showed. More apparent were the furrows on the forehead and deep creases round the eyes. Veins stood out on the back of his hands.

Victor, as though unconscious of these changes, curled up the corners of his mouth in the old, self-deprecatory, charming smile. The Victor of old was still there, the one who had had the ability to make her heart lurch so violently and unfairly. As the room began to warm up, she detected the faint smell of lemons.

'You're going to explain, aren't you, but really it should be to Oma. The deal's going to fail, isn't it?' and, because this was so bald, she added, 'Of course you had to get in touch, sooner or later,' giving him a thin smile and then, regretting this,

'You're not going to let her lose all that money, are you?' And Oma's investment was minor, compared to that she had made in Victor. Was that a flicker of irritation in his face? He sighed a little and leant forwards.

'I should have spoken to your grandmother, I fear you've alarmed her unnecessarily. There are two issues here. Firstly, as far as consultation is concerned, I'm sure you know that I am empowered to invest as I see fit, a system which has often allowed us to act swiftly and reap high profits. But you couldn't know what was going on, I do see that. If you'd come to me, I could have explained everything, and that's the issue, that we have had no – lines of communication. My fault,' and he clasped his hands on his knees and watched her as he talked, full of sincerity. 'I can't reproach you for not coming to me, can I? What reason could you have for trusting me, after all? I can't tell you how happy I am to see you today, oh not just because of this silly misunderstanding with the shares. Because we've opened communications, haven't we? Now we can speak honestly to each other, we can put everything right. It's a new beginning, don't you feel that too?'

Johanna sat perfectly still, staring at him. While her ears absorbed this message, an unmistakable churning of the guts warned her of what was coming; she understood perfectly the nature of the bargain he was expecting to strike with her. And yet this was so unlikely that it couldn't be true; she must be misunderstanding him, and for a moment she faltered and didn't know what to say. She clattered at the coffee cups with sudden, manic abruptness and looked up to see him smiling intimately at her, at his eyes watching her eyes with a sort of satisfaction. They were so very blue.

'Honesty, that's right, that is what matters, isn't it Victor? To tell the truth? That's why you came here, isn't it,' and because she was willing him to tell her everything, because she couldn't help wanting the truth to be the real one, she added, quickly. 'I ought to tell you Victor, perhaps you don't know this, but I told her she should sell those shares straight away. We can't afford to be involved with this – newspaper of yours, can we, we can still pull out.'

'You think I've let your grandmother down, I know. Tell

me, Johanna, who has told you about this deal? What is it that makes you so certain that it is going to fail?'

'I, um, met Uwe Schenck,' she said, after a slight hesitation. 'From the bank. At a party.'

Victor nodded, with a kind of amused contempt.

'I fear he has been remarkably indiscreet. But, Johanna, I don't think he told you that the deal would fail, merely that it is not going through his bank. The young man has jumped to conclusions. And I believe he, quite properly, then referred you to me.'

'But it is going to fail.'

'Why? I have backers, the deal is virtually accomplished. You can discount Herr Schenck, he's a petty official. You know, I have a great deal of money riding on this purchase and I don't intend to lose a Pfennig of it. If your grandmother wants to pull out, she can. She has already spoken to Herr Tiedemann about it, didn't you know? She will do what she wants, of course, but I can tell you that if she sells now, it will be at a loss. On the other hand, she stands to make a considerable profit when the purchase goes through. Do you think I would involve her if I wasn't certain? It's a marvellous project, Johanna, it will put Rommer's on the map and I'm very excited about it, very confident,' and now he was animated, smiling, his hands gesturing. 'But I don't want to persuade you into something you don't like. Your grand-mother has the matter in hand, we don't need to discuss it, or rather Herr Tiedemann has everything organised, as always, you know he always does what Frau Rommer wants. You can take my word for it. This time. Is that what you've been thinking, that you've not always been able to take my word? No – don't look away – didn't we agree that today we could be honest, at last, that we could be open with each other?'

For she was blushing and, made miserably self-conscious, could not look at him. Against that frankness, that open, confiding air, she felt horribly duplicitous. She, who was ready to accuse, was being made to feel that her lack of confidence was something discreditable, that she was letting him down.

'You should be talking to Oma, it's her decision,' she said.

'Oh no, for you both must decide. And I like to talk to you, I prefer that by far,' he said caressingly. 'I've missed you, Johanna. Very much. Seeing you now has made me realise how much. Do you know what I feel? It is the chagrin of the collector, who has held a rare and beautiful piece without recognising its worth, who has let it leave his hands and never ceases regretting his mistake. We can all make mistakes, my dear girl, even banks can,' and he smiled wryly. 'I don't believe in dwelling on past mistakes. Regret, self-blame, those are pernicious, destructive emotions, they weaken us and sap our strength. I believe that we have to live in the present, to have confidence in our actions, to choose our course and follow it.' She was watching him now, as though mesmerised; he broke off and, rising suddenly, paced across the room. 'I'm not, quite, coming to the point, am I, dear girl? Do you know why? I shall be frank with you, it's because I am a little scared. I am afraid of failure. How many years have we known each other? Fifteen, sixteen years? And yet I can't at all guess what you are thinking now, what's behind those big brown eyes of yours,' and he gave her a particularly sweet smile. 'You are an honest person, Johanna, you have a certain integrity. I admire that. And I know too that you no longer feel that you can trust me and I have only myself to blame for that. Once I told you that you were too young and the truth of it is that I was an old fool, and a dishonest one. I lied to you. But you know that already, don't you?'

The big brown eyes were fixed on him, sharpened by an extreme attentiveness. He was speaking hesitantly, picking his words with care, talking in a way that was completely unprecedented. He was opening himself to her; she had not expected it and felt as though they were on the brink of the revelation she had long ceased expecting. Speaking like this, he surely could not be lying, not now. In the drawer of her desk, somewhere among the papers, lay the accusation that Victor was a compulsive, congenital liar. 'He lied easily and fluently and had an unusual ability to convince himself and other people that he spoke the truth.' She believed that document, she had accepted it, all its shocking entirety. She had read it twice with the utmost care. On the second reading,

203

she had realised with a sad, sinking, sick feeling that it was not just an accusation but a love letter. Why should the words of a man she didn't know be so very believable? But she knew that man was telling the truth, or thought he was.

Did she trust Victor? A small, incredulous voice in her head said I think he's a murderer, but I'm going to hear him out. I believe him, too. What's wrong with me? She had a sudden, vivid knowledge of herself as a creature so weak that it did not have the power to distinguish the truth. The material was so anarchic, that she could not form it into any kind of order inside her head. She found herself wishing that she could write down what he was saying; that she could analyse and annotate on paper, in a way that was impossible in her head. In a sudden anguish, she realised that she was going to be forced to make a decision.

Victor was leaning back against the window. He looked tired, his face intent with effort.

'I understand a lot of things now,' he said. 'That summer – in '68 – I suddenly realised that I would have to change. I wasn't prepared for that. I was, how can I put it, naïve in my expectations. When you came to Hamburg I realised at once that I wouldn't be able to continue leading the same sort of life, that I couldn't after all change you, make you more like me. Oh, it sounds cold-blooded, I know,' and he screwed up his face in a grimace. 'The truth isn't always pleasant. I wanted your love, I enjoyed your youth, your energy, but I didn't think I'd have to work at deserving it. I felt – exposed, suddenly. I didn't like it. That was what finished it, Johanna, and when I said you were too young I was really saying that I was too old and selfish for you.'

He looked at her and Johanna, who could not yet trust herself to speak, nodded, twice.

'It was despicable, wasn't it? But I don't need to tell you that. I couldn't find the words to explain to you exactly what I felt, I didn't even try. I don't think I even understood it properly myself. So many things have changed since then. I have had occasion to examine my life, to decide for myself what I want. I surprised myself, Johanna, by finding you were there, on the top of the list. I miss you, you know, and more than that, I need you. I respect you, I think I understand your independence, your way of seeing the world. I wouldn't try to change that. The need is quite the reverse, you know, I want you to change me, I want you to teach me how to live a better life. No, wait – ' for she had made a motion, as though to speak. 'This is the old selfish Victor speaking, who wants to be heard out. I have an opportunity to do great things, with this newspaper. I believe in that, I know I can make it work, that we can make it work and enjoy it together. To create something fine, oh, I suppose a kind of memorial, something that will last. You know, Johanna, I believe there's nothing I can't do with your confidence, your trust in me. I – lay myself open to you. Believe me, I have never spoken to another person like this.' He moved slowly across to where she still sat, perfectly motionless, and stood looking down at her.

'There's something else, isn't there? Yes, I know there is. I spoke of honesty, didn't I? Well I mean to be perfectly and absolutely honest to you.'

The world had condensed down to his face, the mobile mouth and the soft, persuasive voice. Her legs were trembling; she could not have moved an inch. In her head, a little voice was whispering this is real, this is it, this is the truth.

'There is a word missing, I know. I haven't spoken to you of love. I haven't told you that I love you. You're thinking, what kind of man is this, to ask so much and promise so little? Well, I can't say that I love you, in the conventional sense. Oh, it would be easy enough to do, but you mean too much to me for me to lie to you. I feel for you – the most tender friendship and affection, the most urgent need. I don't believe I have ever used that word and meant it, I don't know exactly what it means. But I am certain, Johanna that we can, we will love each other, that what we have is so very precious, that from it love will grow. You will teach me how to love.' Now she was ready to speak, but once again he forestalled her. 'Wait,' he said. 'Don't speak for a moment, reflect. I want you to marry me, Johanna. I want you to do so with conviction, with certainty. I think, well, I have an idea what you are feeling. I must be honest about that, too. I know by now you must have spoken to your friend and she will have told you how much we talked about you. You know she acted with the best, her uttermost convictions in telling me as much as she did. I'm glad she's not here today, I know she doesn't approve of me, she told me so quite frankly. Wait, what is it? – no you mustn't be embarrassed – she said nothing you wouldn't be pleased to hear – ' he broke off. Johanna, conscious of the blood draining from her face and thinking for a moment that she might faint, got up. With a quick, fluttering gesture of one hand, motioning him away, she walked jerkily out of the room. Behind the locked door of the bathroom, grateful for its icy cold, she laid her burning head on the tiled wall which seemed to throb in time with her pulse.

Victor could hear the sound of running water in the bathroom. She had been in there for an inordinate length of time. He walked about the room, studied the photograph of Frau Rommer on the desk and noted the family resemblance, which was increasing as time passed. Johanna was prettier than he had remembered. Her pallor had something distinguished about it, something fine. He was beginning to imagine what it would be like to lead a life together. It was imaginable, it was possible. He could make it work. She had changed; she was of course older and less ingenuous. Grown more mature, wary of him and less trusting. That was perhaps inevitable, though he regretted it. He had a nostalgic image of the little girl with thick pigtails and solemn brown eyes who had sat upon his knee and listened while he told her a story. An age of innocence had passed.

Restless, he paced up and down. What was she doing in there? He kept looking at his watch, conscious that so much had to be accomplished in so short a time. In mentioning Linda, he had made a mistake, he had embarrassed her deeply. Unused to so many naked emotions, he had forgotten the profound vulnerability of a young girl.

This was the marriage that was always meant for him, that had always been inevitable, and he delivered himself up to it with good grace; better, with a genuine willingness to please. When had he talked so frankly or for so long about himself? He had offered more of himself than he had ever given anyone. He did not love her, that was true, but then perhaps he was no longer capable of loving anybody. Theirs would be an honest, an open relationship; he would profit immeasurably from that kind of intimacy with another human being and he saw now that he needed it. He had been alone too long. A bright bubble of optimism was kindling itself in him: perhaps he would grow to love her after all. It would help to have children. He could not help wishing just a little that she was prettier, more obviously attractive, more suited to being the wife of a newspaper magnate, a public man. It was an ignoble thought and he suppressed it. What was she doing in there? He began to calculate the time it would take to drive back to Altona.

He thought he heard a noise, a gentle swish of short skirts against the doorway, and he turned. A gaudy woman stood at the entrance to the sitting room, cheeks brightly rouged. Her lips, outlined in cerise, were smiling brilliantly at him. She was so altered that for a moment he stared without recognition and with a kind of sudden horror. He could not help himself; she looked extremely ugly.

It had taken some time for Johanna to compose herself. She gave the obligatory second's pause before making an impressive entrance and in that instant, when he thought he was unobserved, she saw him looking at his watch, wearing a frown of impatience. He looked up and it smoothed itself at once, to be succeeded by something far worse, a look of the purest, nastiest, sheerest dislike. The lines on his advancing face were a web of deceit she hadn't seen before and he pulled her close to him and the real Johanna, who was not the one he wanted or thought he needed, looked with the most damningly exact eye upon the folds of his face, the open pores, the little lines around the mouth, and shuddered. Misinterpreting that little quake, he bent down to kiss her and she allowed it to happen. Frozen, she waited for some surge of emotion to blank out her brain. Dry lips on hers, a hot breath through his nostrils, his tongue in her mouth and she nearly gagged and pushed him away, suddenly, with a rude strength that made him stagger.

'No,' she heard herself say it loudly and then, stupidly, 'Sorry.' She sat down abruptly and looked up the grey perspective of his elegant waistcoat. 'I can't, I mean the answer

207

is no.'

Frau Beckmann, dozing in the comfortable chair, was jerked awake by the loud roaring of a car screaming round the corner, brakes squealing even over the roar of the throaty exhaust. A little red car shrieked to a halt behind the white Mercedes. Bang. The door slammed behind another young man, one with dark hair. She barely got a decent look at him as he hurtled to the house. She heard the thundering of his footsteps as he scaled the risers and then silence. A noise had to be very loud or very near to penetrate the old lady's auditory passages.

She waited for several minutes before arming herself with a duster and issuing forth, a fine flowered apron tied around her ample bulk. She made much of dusting the banisters and then the small vase of dried flowers and grasses near her door. With enormous stealth, she crept up the stairs to Fräulein Rommer's door, a few steps at a time. Still, and another shake of the head did nothing to help, she couldn't hear a thing. She advanced. Another step saw her with her good ear pressed to the door, the duster still in her hand as she steadied herself against the genteel striped wallpaper, her matronly heart beating away at a slightly higher than usual rate inches from the wooden panels.

Sigi stormed into the room, stopping short when he saw Victor standing there. His fierce look, his clenched fists were comical and inappropriate. 'Sigi Schmidt – Victor Genscher,' Johanna said in a weary voice; they made no motion to shake hands.

'This, I suppose, is the boyfriend,' Victor said, eyebrows raised, in a tone that implied that this explained everything. Calmly, he went to pick up his coat, put it on gracefully, wrapping a silk scarf around his throat and, offering her a hand, bowed his head slightly with a formality she had seen Herr Tiedemann use. He was encased and distant; the mental retreat was effected and swiftly succeeded by the actual one.

'Thank you for seeing me. Good-bye Johanna,' and his eyes were looking somewhere over her head and he did not smile, though he spoke with his automatic, impersonal courtesy. She was already obliterated; the last hour might not have hap-

208

pened. Mutely she watched the elegant back retreat. The door met a large, soft obstruction. There was a faint shriek, a vision of Frau Beckmann clinging desperately to the banister. Victor passed by her and was gone. Johanna watched without understanding as the old woman scrabbled herself back into an upright position and retreated down the stairs. She closed the door and there, with a hangdog face, was Sigi.

'You – bloody idiot.'

'I'm sorry, I came as quickly as I could. Have you got a cigarette?'

'Go away and you can take your – horrible papers with you,' and she tore them from the desk and threw them at him, and they fell heavily around his feet. 'You've spoiled everything, why did you have to give me those? You knew all about him, didn't you, you and your clever phone boxes, you bloody liar,' and she was forcing her arms into a coat, throwing a scarf around her neck with a violent gesture. 'What right have you got to come in here? You get out, I'm going out, you can just bugger off.'

The process of explanation and expiation went on all the way up the steep hill, along the wooded seclusion of the Bismarckstein, that destination, never attained, of Bismarck's imposing memorial. He tried to kiss her in the dark seclusion of the little tower – which, far from being rural and gothic, smelt unpleasantly of urine – and was savagely rebuffed. He told her about Levison; she hardly protested at the manner of their introduction, staring at him in dislike, her sufferance suggesting not so much that his explanation was adequate, as that she didn't care about him and so it didn't matter. The street-lamps, flickering on, revealed their faces; she pushed him away at the moment when a white Mercedes passed them. It wasn't him; a pretty woman with a dark curly mop of hair smiled at the lovers' tiff, parked in front of the old patrician villa at the end of the row. Johanna talked and talked and he had the impression that she was talking to herself; certainly she treated all his remarks with scorn. 'I could have been happy with him, not knowing,' she said, and, 'I would have made myself believe in him, I'm good at that, at projecting the attributes that are lacking. J. Rommer the projectionist, sending out pretty pictures of what she wants to see, seeing them reflected on his face. But the power's been shut off, no beam. The screen's empty. A tabula rasa. Do you know what I mean? No, I suppose you don't.' He told her that she was too complicated. She said something else: 'When I sensed a deficiency in myself, perhaps it was just a rip in the screen, a hole showing the void, the blackness. Perhaps all I'm doing now is projecting another version and making it believable, perhaps this is false too. The reality could be quite different again. We're all just blank human beings, when you take away the reflections of other people's needs and desires, that's what colours us up. We're just mounds of flesh, cold and uncaring, that's what real is. The rest is imagination.' He, who had such simple, such very understandable needs, attempted to expound them without success. It was a cold tramp back, the steps were slippery. It wasn't until they were the length of the beach from her flat that he told her about how it was an accident with Wolf and old man Tiedemann, and then she broke away from him and started to run. He sat, silent and useless, while she telephoned her grandmother in England. He poured her a brandy and she took it. 'Your brother's a thug, like you,' she said, 'an interfering bully,' but her heart wasn't in it; she was still talking about Genscher. 'He lied to me, right here, he didn't even tell me about poor old Otto, but it's part of the con, do you see? All he wants is his bloody deal. Not me. I still believe that he told me the truth. Some of the truth. Perhaps he doesn't know it himself. Perhaps that is asking too much,' and she sat for a long time staring into space as though he wasn't there. When he took her hand, she smiled sardonically. 'I suppose you think you've got me now, well you haven't, you're going when Linda comes home,' but she didn't take her hand away. For a long time they sat in the darkness like exhausted combatants in the sudden silence that follows a battle; who know that the war must rage elsewhere, but have no stomach to seek it out.

# Chapter 14

The white Mercedes executed an illegal U-turn and headed back into town, escaping by one minute the return visit of a policeman who affixed a ticket to the windscreen of the red car, such being the unfairness of life in general and of traffic policemen in particular. Frau Beckmann, twitching at her net curtain, did not fail to notice the misdemeanour.

Victor drove with great care, to avoid attracting any attention. He was fully occupied in reckoning the advantages and possible disadvantages of his position; he did not have it in his character to view events in terms of defeat, or failure; he saw them rather as episodes which presented further choices, further decisions. Thus Johanna's refusal, her strange behaviour, had positive consequences. He was now certain that she knew nothing of Ludwig; he was free of any commitment to her. He knew that in Herr Tiedemann's absence, the shares could not be sold by anyone but himself; days would pass in which nothing would be done, and in that time he would secure his deal. The old man was old, tired, he might not recover. Victor thought that a lengthy convalescence and an honourable retirement were now in store for Rommer's oldest and most faithful servant. A new clarity and order was manifesting itself, to which the only obstacle remaining was Ludwig. He had no plan, other than to confront him; he did not waste his time in imagining what difficulties there might be. He was perfectly collected, prepared for an ugly scene, for the necessary violence. And yet his hands, gripping the wheel, were shaking slightly.

He observed them with a certain dismay. Upon the face reflected in the broad-angled driving mirror, he noted new and unpleasant manifestations of the passage of time. His flesh was sagging, decaying inside his mouth, gums lifting from the teeth. The surface was beginning the inexorable process of moving away from the bone beneath, the sack of skin loosening in anticipation of its fall. The years had barely touched him until the observers came, to witness his dissolution. His youth, his strength, had stolen away and turned tail and they mocked him in the shape of a boy in a blue anorak. He understood that he would age at this accelerated, unnatural rate until the watching stopped, until Ludwig was destroyed.

Ludwig was sitting cross-legged upon the mat in the quiet house. Upstairs, Frau Liebmann would be sleeping, refilling her small reservoir of patience for the evening class. The weekends released her to practise a form of semi-hibernation. She spent the hours cat-napping in her small, dark room, waking to stare at the screen with a concentration which left her heavy-lidded on Mondays.

Frau Liebmann was as inaccessible to Ludwig as the most perfect stranger. He knew nothing at all about her; he had never asked her a single question. This arrangement, so admirably discreet, suddenly seemed impossibly bleak. Had she ever, perhaps, wanted to talk to him, needed a human contact? It was too late now; it was unthinkable that he should, for example, knock on her door, for a purpose as minimal as seeing another human face. He would pass the next days like a man on a desert island. He, who didn't care for company or for idle talk, felt with a pang that after this class there would be nothing, nothing until Monday. Tiedemann was dead. There would be no Bernd, this Sunday, to make his tea. There would be no glass house; he had no better way to punish himself than to deprive himself of that. He already lived in solitary confinement, in prison conditions. No vengeful agency could starve or beat him with greater vindictiveness than that he exercised against himself. Punishment, for him, took on a more refined, more elegant form. He was tied to an acute consciousness of self, a thinking mind which revolved endlessly on its arid circuit, denied release.

He thought that the worst suffering he could inflict upon himself would be to abandon the Victor project, condemning that mind to ceaseless re-enactments of the same, sterile speculations and regrets. Against this he balanced the fact that its continuance was a duty, his way of benefiting others. Thus, to punish himself would be selfish, if it deprived them. He took this casuistry a step further. His mission was a form of charity, which others might construe as being devised for his greater glorification. Yet he could not remove himself from the equation; he was the linch-pin upon which it all turned. The mission was the object he most ardently desired; it was also his opportunity to do good and the latter must always outweigh the former. There were good precedents to support this view; he thought, with irony, that the Church in its wisdom knew to take an expedient view of charity, whatever its motivations.

Ludwig was a man who manufactured his own doctrines. He examined the succession of past events with a pragmatic eye. Where did this train of events start? A minor occurrence, an accident with a motorbike, which had hurt nobody. Two boys larking around on a slippery back-street had found nothing better to do with themselves than to smash up a machine they particularly prized for giving them mobility. Bernd's father had confined him to his room for this; so Wolf had taken his place and precipitated the 'accident' that was no accident at all. Blame Proto-Neolithic man, who first saw the virtues of the wheel; blame the internal combustion engine; blame the ice upon the street. Ludwig would not take a simplistic view; his dark eye, inward-looking perceived more.

There was another interpretation: that this was a piece of summary justice which, in striking down Tiedemann, was punishing him in a particularly apposite way. An innocent suffered in his place: that was a torment chosen very particularly for him. Was that insufferable vanity, to believe that there might be some destiny at work, rather than a succession of trivial incidents? He contemplated the chain of events and saw in it an emotional house of cards that had toppled flat. Ludwig's coldness to Bernd, that unavoidable necessity, had made him set his friends on to snatch the briefcase. That fitted too, for it was a worthless object, a symbol of a businessman's prestige, nothing more. They had ascribed to it a different value: they had seen it as a bribe. Bernd would have brought him this empty, shiny thing and expected caresses in return. Ludwig saw that, since he had never admitted anyone into his confidence, they could never have known that it held no value for him; he could not deny that he coveted Victor's wealth, in a manner of speaking. Their actions, grotesquely, mirrored his; he could not blame his boys. It did not even end there; there was a further causality, another link in the chain. Their stupid, juvenile amorality, their mindless brutality, seemed justifiable to them, indeed they did not even question the nature of the activities he had asked them to perform. They did everything for his benefit. The judo teacher could not complain, because his class had learnt its lessons too well. Force used against itself. He looked into the darkness and saw the emptiness of the skills he taught, unless a thinking, warm humanity controlled them. He, who had given them the opportunity for evil, could not marvel at the consequences.

Another illumination came: that the boys had not the capacity to learn, to profit from their mistakes. That was one of Ludwig's redeeming graces: why had he not taught it to them? For he had seen on Heini's face, not just fear, the dread of punishment for pushing a man who now was dead, but something greater. Ludwig had seen that the boy's strongest emotion was, quite simply a naked terror of him. Not the pangs of remorse, not the anguish of guilt, but fear of his teacher. It could not be possible, surely, that that was all he had taught them?

There was a thick, sour taste in Ludwig's mouth. He would not drink, to wash it away. He would not drink or eat at all that day. History was repeating itself and it was a frightening thing, to see how each event engendered another so uncontrollably. What historical inevitability had brought Bernd to him, with that poignant resemblance? What had made him decide to force himself upon Ludwig? The judo master knew that he had fought against the likeness and, in so doing, he had repeated his mistake, albeit in a new variant. In guarding against loving too much, he had loved too little. The irony of such determinism did not escape him.

Ludwig had forged these chains which bound him so securely. He could not have been more safely imprisoned. And now he smiled to himself and showed the darkness his deformities. There were no choices left. No, he would not abandon Victor, for that meant that he was abandoning himself to all the consequences of his errors. He would not condemn himself to suffer with no hope of redress. He thought that while he retained some ability to think and to reason, he was obliged to use those powers as best he could. From the back of his mind the phrase 'moral imperative', as though it had been lying in wait, now drifted up to mock him. How neatly he had seized the expression from the inky pages of the *Abend* to justify his aims; now he saw what poor shelter the ambiguous phrase gave.

An elegantly dressed man was not, after all, such a novelty for the Beckerstrasse, where the bourgeoisie rubbed shoulders with the working class in common pursuit of a skill which each thought would help to defend them against the other. It was already dark and no light shone through the legend on Meister Judo's window. The man stopped, looked through the thin transparent stripes in the glass and then, stepping boldly up to the door, rang the bell. It jangled in the distant office. His dark grey suit blended against the doorway; over one arm he was carrying a coat. Now the door opened and swallowed him up into the blackness beyond so swiftly that his mass seemed to absorb itself, as though the façade had assimilated him.

They faced each other, standing on the mat. Reflecting the sudden brightness of the lights above, its whiteness made their outlines sharp and threw a pallor onto their faces. 'So you're alone,' Victor said softly. 'That surprises me. Where are your watchers? They didn't follow me here.'

Ludwig, curiously, was smiling. Twenty years had taught him to use that gesture, not to signify friendship or pleasure, but as a means of exercising control. He was small, thin and ugly. He was looking at his physical opposite, a man who all his life had rejoiced in possession of the visible indicators of what was considered desirable and good; to this formidable armoury, he had added the accoutrements and powers of a powerful elite. Knowing that the splendid edifice was a sham did not make it less attractive or less deceptive; Ludwig looked through the blue holes in the face and thought, for an instant, that he glimpsed the creature scuttling inside the hollow chamber; thought that he had provided it with a grievance, a cause. Instinctively, he adopted the classic, loose-limbed position for combat. The elegant man in front of him laughed.

'Oh, have they deserted you?' the soft voice said.

'I am alone, apart from the old housekeeper. Nobody can hear us, if that is your concern. I didn't expect you, and yet I should have known that you would come. Action, reaction, nothing alters under the sun.' The harsh lights gave Victor's hair an almost unbearable brilliance. Ludwig turned and beckoned him towards the office.

'Come, we'll talk in here,' he said and turned his back upon him. The time of manoeuvring for position, of taunts, of veiled threats was gone and now the moment for openness had come and he glanced back over his shoulder and said, with almost tenderness in his voice, 'The end of the game, isn't it?' and saw a strange, a haunting smile upon his adversary's face.

Ludwig did not see that the coat, negligently flung over one arm, had now slid back to reveal the muzzle of a gun. Coyly, it peeped out. He did not see it until they were in the office and he was sitting behind his desk and had placed that barrier between himself and Victor. This mistake, indeed Ludwig's absurd simplicity, his error in walking away as he did, his subsequent, ludicrous look of surprise, so akin to the tragi-comic grimace of a clown, milking a situation for all the cheap laughs he could force, all these things made Victor, who now held the balance of power, laugh out loud.

'Yes,' he said, with an effort, for the impulse to mirth was almost insuperable, 'All over,' and, 'The end,' and then, pulling himself together in an instant, 'Give me the papers, hurry. Your delightful autobiography or whatever you call it, where is it?'

'So Tiedemann's dead, I see. I wasn't sure.' Ludwig made no effort to move. He stared at Victor's face and then at the gun and back at his face with a flickering movement of the eyes which made Victor wary and cold.

Victor was not going to enlighten him.

'Shut up,' he said. 'The papers.' And slowly he cocked the gun, letting the coat fall to the floor, and now held the weapon with both hands; it was aimed at Ludwig's mouth. The man just sat there, looking at him, as though he didn't even know what a gun was. It was very difficult to control the urge to pull the trigger, it was such a very small movement, such a very fine thing. Victor was aware that it could go off in his hand, right now, and that he would not have pulled the trigger; it would have been an accident, a slip of the finger. With slight regret he concentrated on controlling the small tremor; he thought that the noise would bring the old woman down. It was like trying to operate somebody else's hands.

'Hurry,' he said and Ludwig rose slowly. He walked over to the filing cabinet and knelt in front of it. The drawer scraped and creaked in protest as its weight was pulled forward and the whole cabinet swayed for an instant, as though it might topple on the small man. With maddening slowness, he began to pull out a stack of magazines, one by one.

And Ludwig started to talk now, glancing back over his shoulder. 'You understand, my dear Victor, that the story is exactly the same. Do you see that, how curious it is that history should repeat itself so neatly and offer us the same set of choices. You see that, don't you, that I have made choices?'

Victor, watching his hands, did not reply.

'I am not a vindictive man,' the voice said, 'I have never thought, for example, that you should be made to suffer physically, that you should taste blood. I wonder if you know that feeling, to gag on warm blood running down your throat, your own blood that you can't stop.' The pile was growing, there were barely half a dozen issues left in the cabinet which now settled back upon itself in a little jolting movement, achieving a new balance. 'No, probably not,' Ludwig said and now the thin fingers were feeling through a maze of rusty folders. 'Do you see how redundant that thing in your hand is? How can that be a solution, to permit violence to engender more violence? The preferred solution of the morally and mentally deficient. Is that what you want to demonstrate, Victor, that you still have a capacity for violence? I think not, for we all have it. Our strength, our goodness, lies in overcoming it.'

Now the cabinet was half-empty and he leant forwards and began with scooping movements to bring out handfuls of things; the debris and odd items that lay there, dirty, dusty paraphernalia which stuck to his fingers. His movements seemed to Victor to be growing increasingly frenetic, but the voice continued in its calm, its insufferably arrogant manner. Craning forwards, looking into the blackness of the empty drawer to reassure himself that Ludwig was not concealing anything, Victor sat back again and watched Ludwig repeat the process with the drawer above.

'I believe in intelligence, in a moral intelligence, that gives us the capacity for choice,' and the thin arms reached with nervous energy, pulling out folders and dropping them around his sides, so that he soon sat in the centre of circles of objects, which grew out concentrically from his bent back. 'What difference is there, between Meyer and Charlotte Bamberg, or in Tiedemann's death? Sudden death, in the midst of life, shocking and needless, but even that can be a catalyst for change.' Now he turned and looked at Victor with his cunning, inscrutable eye. 'We're the same, you and I, now more than ever. Meyer's death taught me something, I learnt what my responsibilities were. I was made to see what I owed to others, not just to myself. And you're going to learn that now, do you see it? The old man's dead, but there is a – legacy he leaves.' He stretched himself now and turned back and pulled out the topmost drawer.

It was only at this point that Victor realised that of course Ludwig wasn't going to find the papers; that the occasion suited him, gave him the chance to produce his complex little pieces of self-justification, so neatly woven around a travesty of the truth. At the same moment, Ludwig feigned a weary sigh; he rubbed a dirty hand across his brow.

'They've gone, I don't understand it, I don't know who –' and he made as though to walk across to the desk.

'Stay where you are,' and Victor almost wanted to applaud; it was the performance of a life-time. In the Schauspielhaus he would certainly have stood to salute a performer of this quality. 'Would you like to know what I've learnt – the, as you term it, legacy of the old man? I don't have your sophistry, Ludwig, your cunning to twist the facts. It's a little simpler where I stand. You've brought violence with you, and death, you're an agent of destruction, I see that quite, quite clearly. I think you also like playing the fool with me, Ludwig,' and as he spoke he kicked open the drawers of the desk and glanced at the miserable contents, finding nothing of interest. 'A cautious man like you makes a copy of his documents, puts it in a safe place, isn't that what blackmailers do? "To be opened in the event of my sudden demise",' and he smiled at him with a gloating feeling of his power. 'Well, Ludwig? Where is the copy of your masterpiece?' and now he was feeling his way round the room, never turning his back for an instant, flicking over the calendars, looking behind the chair, even, with a grimace of distaste, flicking back the shabby strip of carpet and looking underneath it. 'Are you going to make me search the whole miserable place? No, I think you will search for me, I shall merely keep this – redundant thing in my hand. Where shall we start?'

'There's a copy at my lawyer's,' Ludwig said, simply. 'He's probably left for the weekend, I shouldn't think it possible to obtain now,' and he said it with such a tone of regret, such quiet sincerity, that Victor rapped the knuckles of one hand sharply on the desk in the traditional, student salute.

'Bravo, bravo!' He gestured with the gun towards the telephone. 'But shall we try, however? I had forgotten what you are, Ludwig, I've wronged you. You have the cunning soul of a Jesuit, the tone of a holy man, I do believe you were born out of your time. Come, hurry,' he said, and now he banged the gun against the desk, one, two, three, in a gesture of impatience, suddenly bad-tempered at the way it was stretching out, for they could be interrupted at any time. He was standing around where he should be acting; he had been too easily taken in by the amusement value of Ludwig trying to evade responsibility for Tiedemann's supposed death and it now occurred to him that they could be surrounded, that the boys could be standing all around the house and he hurried to the window, wrenched it open, and looked outside.

It was almost a shock to see nothing but darkness where he expected a circle of eyes and, staring into the gloom, he saw that there was a high brick wall at the back and that there could be no way out there.

'There is nobody here, is there?' and for a moment Ludwig looked steadily at him and did not reply.

'No, we're alone,' he said, looking up from the finger dialling and giving him that vulpine smile. 'I could say yes, couldn't I? A small choice. I am not going to lie any more, that is over. The enemy lies within, my dear Victor, that is the one to vanquish, not me, for I am not your enemy, nor those poor children even if they make mistakes, as we have.' He had a power to do good, to change everything; he felt it surging through him.

The telephone rang four, five times. It was ten minutes past five, a Friday afternoon; people went home early.

'Ja?' A man's voice, irritated. The tony of somebody with his coat on, with a briefcase hanging heavy in the other hand. He was annoyed, he demurred; it was the weekend, couldn't it wait until Monday? Staring sardonically into the muzzle of the gun, noting that it was trembling just a little, Ludwig said no. Grudgingly, the lawyer said he would have it dropped round. He would call up a motorbike messenger, a good firm, the one they used for genuinely urgent matters, and the angry voice stressed the last three words with heavy irony, that tone of voice which clients foolish enough to evoke paid for dearly.

They waited, Victor sitting behind the desk, resting his arm on it, which enabled him to point the gun without any strain; Ludwig sat cross-legged on the floor and watched him. 'When you've read it,' he said, 'I think you will understand what I planned for you, you will see what our aims should be. You will understand yourself better. You have no idea how active your shadows have been, what a lot they have learnt about you.' He watched him very carefully, for there was something strange about the way Victor was staring into space, for seconds at a time, and then his eyes would focus again upon Ludwig and he was taking aim at different parts of his body, first the face, then the knees, then the groin.

'Force always turns upon itself,' Ludwig said. 'Don't play these games.' He saw that the face, under the naked bulb, was harrowed and he spoke very gently. 'There was no other way, do you understand? You see how entrenched in your life you are, how cold? I can help you, I can build a new life, we can start again. It's not too late for that, to remake the past. Put down the gun, Victor, that is not a solution. There shall be no more killing. You are the product of false values, do you hear me, of empty materialism, of meaningless acquisitions. So many good impulses gone wrong, perverted, that can be put right. Open up your mind, think of all your wealth can do, think of yourself as a force for good. It's not too grandiose a word, I can show you – ' he flinched as the gun crashed down onto the metal table. The noise was very loud; it did not, however, go off.

'Spare me your fine moral judgments,' Victor said. 'You make me vomit, with your clever justifications, with your talk of virtues. You've not changed, you were always the same, using power to pervert, adept at finding excuses for yourself, for your perverted lust. Fine words to excuse blackmail and murder, but you forget, I'm not a boy any more,' and his voice was a slow and deliberate, rhythmical tone. 'You couldn't bear it, could you, that I should succeed where you failed? You're still a little man, in every sense, a hypocrite, who talks about morality and finds excuses to put his arms around little boys.' Pausing, he lifted an interrogative eyebrow. 'You don't deny it? How can you,' and his voice became quieter, until it was almost a whisper, a flat trickle of venom. 'You forgot something, Ludwig. I'm a man, I know your kind and I've dealt with them before. Anarchists, wreckers, who talk like you of materialism, of false values, who hide their aims behind big words, but who don't shrink from violence and terror, from blackmail, anything goes, doesn't it, you justify any act to advance your cause. But you don't have a cause, Ludwig, what's your excuse? Is this the new world, the new order,' and he swept a hand around and smiled. 'We're the new order, we're stability and prosperity. I've built an empire, you know that don't you, and you think you want a share in it. You actually thought I would help you finance your dirty games,' and now he laughed, throwing his head back.

'You don't understand,' Ludwig said, and spoke louder. 'Listen to me, Victor, you don't understand, there is a new order, we can change everything,' and he was shouting now, over the terrible noise that came out of Victor's throat, 'I am talking about a mission –'

The noise of the motorbike outside was loud; they both hushed. A moment later a peremptory rapping on the door was heard. 'Open up,' Victor said calmly. 'I'm right behind you.'

Ludwig had become aware, as the minutes passed, of the hard floor under his coccyx; the small deadening of nerve ends. That was life, that was what living came down to; small, definite sensations and their absence. The brown paper parcel was nearly empty. Victor had rifled through its contents, glancing at and abandoning the worthless documents that made up Ludwig's life: the deeds to his house, his will, his passport. He was now engaged upon burning the testimony of Frau Meyer, page by page. He did not read it.

'You're a fool,' he'd said, picking up the first page and looking at Ludwig over the room, and he had giggled. 'What made you think I'd want to read it?'

The pages blackened, curled, fell in plumes of grey ash to the floor. Victor's face was beaded with sweat, his shirt stained with it, but he was perfectly concentrated. The gun lay on the desk. Whenever Ludwig made the slightest movement, Victor reached for it. Ludwig sat very still and imperceptibly tensed one muscle after another. A match hissed and flared in the violent silence; the piece of paper curled in the white hand, which allowed the flame to lick almost to the fingers before letting it drop.

'Who told you about the newspaper?' Victor asked; Ludwig did not reply.

'Have you given this to anybody else?' and, when he said nothing, added, 'Where's your openness now? You're a kind of devil, there's something uncanny, evil about you,' and then he stopped, abruptly.

Watching him, alert to his slightest motion, to each flickering muscle on his face, Ludwig thought that Victor was quite eaten away inside. Behind the façade of this man there was, after all, perhaps nothing left of the boy and he said to himself that he had made a mistake, but that he could not regret it and he thought that Victor, whose hands trembled uncontrollably, could not sustain his effort for much longer.

'You'll never know what I've said, will you? You will lie awake worrying about that, my dear Victor,' and Ludwig laughed. He knew so much better than Victor how to control a fight. 'My poor Victor,' he said, goading. 'How are you ever going to find out? What if there are another five copies? What if there are ten?'

In an odd way, Ludwig pitied him then, as much for his brutal indifference to everything that mattered as for any other reason. He would survive even this; yet, as a private joke with the God he knew didn't exist, he recited the Sh'ma in his head and with equal irreverence the Credo. He felt preternaturally alert; he was trusting in his training, his own religion, to perform the work of personal salvation. 'Will you finish off the old lady, upstairs?' he now said. 'She's deaf, she might not hear a shot. But I wouldn't let that influence you, if you want to be secure. An important man like you needs security.'

'I should have killed you in Berlin,' Victor said in a conversational tone. 'I had too many scruples. I still couldn't hurt a woman, I'm not like you. Remember Charlotte? I should have finished you then, I could have spared you the trouble of being alive so long. Your life for other, more valuable ones, doesn't that make sense on your moral balance sheet?'

Ludwig sprang to his feet and in the same instant threw himself to one side. He rolled, came up again, cracking his head against the desk and, hearing the loud report of the gun being fired, thought for an instant that he must have been hit. He seized the weapon, which Victor held limply as though he couldn't believe that his shot could possibly have missed. With all his strength, Ludwig hurled it backwards out of the open

223

window; it hit against the top pane which smashed under the assault.

He lunged across the desk for Victor who ducked and aimed a clumsy punch. He had him by the shirt front and one arm, but could not get at him from this position; he kicked and shoved at the desk to get it out of the way and Victor, suddenly nimble, darted around the other side of it and made, not for the judo room, but up the stairs with Ludwig just behind him, their feet hammering against the wooden risers. He caught up with him in his bedroom, as Victor thrust his head through the window. Ludwig knew there was no way out from there; he pulled him back roughly. Staring up at him in the instant before he closed in, the thought formed clearly that it was a waste, a tragic waste of a man, of the time and love and effort he had put into this human being. They wrestled, in silent, blind, tussling fury at the open window.

The room was dark, the only illumination the orange street lamp outside which shimmered around two unequal silhouettes, one so much larger than the other; it lit up a profile for a split second and glinted on pale hair on a head that bobbed and wavered. It showed a small black arm, reaching forwards. The dark man, springing back, had the agility and sure-footedness of a monkey. Ludwig gained, in that instant, the space he needed for a backwards throw. He grasped tight, but the big man took hold of him, lifted his slight body into the air and with a grunt propelled him into the void. A confused shape hung at the window, a two-headed monster with flailing arms and legs; and then there was nothing there at all but the misty night and its artificial, orange moon. For Ludwig, with his trained, rigid grip, did not let go. Even in the act of falling, even in the free, cold air, he twisted his body to take Victor with him, toppled the other man backwards, falling down. Unlucky Victor, not to have reckoned with this; unlucky Ludwig, who had not the time to say as he badly wanted, despite everything, to do, that he had had nothing to do with Charlotte Bamberg. That some crazed Pole or Hungarian had killed her and, yes, he had not regretted it, insane with jealousy as he then was, but God knew he was not a murderer.

An explosion woke Frau Liebmann; a few minutes later

there came a tremendous crash of breaking glass. She crept downstairs in trepidation and looked through the ground floor for signs of breakage. There. The window of Herr Levison's office was indeed broken and the room now chill as the cold wind swept the warmth away. Walking closer to inspect the damage, Frau Liebmann could not understand how such a small window could have made such a noise.

It was only when she went upstairs looking for Herr Levison, who must, surely, be in the house somewhere, that she understood. His window was open, as it always was, but through it her eye caught a flash of colour. The whole grey expanse of glass below was smashed, its jagged edges revealing a brilliant patch of green, in stark contrast to the concrete and brickwork all around. In this riot of foliage, there among the bright blossoms, her weak eyes just made out two figures. One lay in the centre, on a bed of plants, and was, she thought, moving. The other lay quite still on the hard stone floor. Tutting with excitement and distress, Frau Liebmann hurried up the stairs to get her glasses before she did anything else.

# Chapter 15

Rain dripped through the dark laurel leaves, soaked into the small card fixed onto them and obliterated the spidery script. The men carrying the coffin had turned up their coat collars against the drizzle. Persistent, the water found its way through thick leather gloves, infiltrated their shoes, beat in treacherous gusts against their raw-chapped faces. Rivulets ran across the shiny pale wood of the coffin and found their way down to the freshly-turned earth, which glinted yellow where the spade had struck patches of clay. Clods of it clung heavily to shoes. Surreptitiously, one of the men tried to scrape it off against the neighbouring gravestone, a marble slab, marring its rain-washed pallor with an ugly crust.

The principal mourner, dressed in black, her head perfectly concealed under a scarf, observed this process with a cold eye. She stepped forwards and dropped a flower onto the coffin, from which the wreath had been removed. This gesture released the bearers, who now hurried to the gravel path, stamping feet against the cold, before proceeding in a more measured way back to the relative warmth of the chapel, where the next funeral party waited. But the woman remained there, quite alone, as though unconscious of the cold, her head bent down. She might have been crying, but at this distance it was impossible to tell.

When every figure had disappeared from the landscape and she stood, the only living, breathing creature among the cold stones, she began to speak. This was not the eulogy that had been lacking in the short and badly-attended funeral service, but a hopeless, angry interrogation of the dead man.

'Well, is this it? Are you really there, in that box? Over, finished, all gone? And what am I to do without you? What becomes of me?'

A day or two later on the other side of town, the neurosurgeon charged with the delicate and probably impossible task of reassembling the broken pieces of a badly injured man, was interrupted in the very task of scrubbing up. With the patient weariness of a busy man with not an instant to spare, he addressed his laconic persecutor. 'This really won't do, there is nothing I can tell you now.'

'One question.' The Kommissar's ears stuck out behind the mask; he looked for all the world like a bloodhound, subjected to the ignominy of a bath and now wrapped up in a sheet

'Just give me an idea of when I can speak to him.'

Backing away from possible contamination, his gloved hands raised protectively, the surgeon began to utter the ambiguous and vaguely soothing phrases he more usually employed with anxious relatives. 'Always hope . . . too early to tell . . . have known remarkable improvements to occur . . . understand your concern . . . assure you we are doing our utmost . . . ' and he disappeared smartly behind a door marked 'Strictly No Entrance Except For Authorised Personnel'.

For a long time the patient seemed perfectly unaware of the regular visitor seated at his bedside. His physical condition, which the surgeons spoke of amongst themselves as a triumph of their delicate skills, seemed to the policeman quite hopeless. He lay perfectly immobile and never spoke, staring vacantly at the white wall or the shiny door for hours at a time. He showed no sign of responding to, let alone hearing, the questions thrown at him.

At last the spring came, the season of growth bringing its familiar rituals. Two weddings took place on the same day in the Hansastadt, two ceremonies of very different types. There was a grand affair in the Michaeliskirche; the wedding party, substantial as it was, still dwarfed by its massive vaulting arches. No bride could compete with the splendour of the massive altar with its pink marble columns, nor with the brightness of the fresh gilding on pilasters and above doorways.

Across town, Herr Frisch and Frau Meier tied the knot in a purely civil ceremony. The bride, bony hips and well-muscled, scrawny arms veiled in cream chiffon, bore a smile of genuine pleasure. Herr Frisch seemed less delighted, which was no doubt due to the tight new shoes he wore, so uncomfortable that he longed to sit down. The bride carried a small posy of artificial silk flowers and took care to toss these in the direction of Fräulein Schmidt, who showed unexpected agility in scrambling after them.

At the reception, the Fräulein was seen to annex a bottle of Schnapps, which she used to keep her glass perpetually full. The groom, whose round face was flushed with heat and excitement, was about to refill his own glass for perhaps the third time, when he felt a sudden sharp pinch in the fleshy part of his upper arm. Turning his head to discover the cause of this odd manifestation, he was astonished to see his charming new wife looking at him with an unfamiliar expression. Her look was so hard and penetrating and so completely novel, that his jaw sagged.

'Nein, nein, nein, das kommt nicht in Frage. Das muss sofort aufhören,' said the new Frau Frisch adding, sotto voce, out of delicacy, 'Enlarged liver,' and two fingers closed like pincers over the neck of the bottle and removed it from his slackened grasp.

Perhaps the consequent increase in liquor supply for the remaining small circle of well-wishers was not altogether desirable. Fräulein Schmidt was to be observed, an hour or two later, hiccuping tearfully into her glass. She sat next to a stranger, introduced to her as Frau Frisch's former brother-in-law, who started at this point to stroke her knee under the table. This sensation was so novel to her that it took her some time to realise precisely what was happening and a further age passed before she decided to register a protest. By then this quiet, middle-aged man had somehow worked his way up to her thigh and had the good spinster in such a state that she had neither the strength nor the desire to resist and simply stared at him in amazement at his audacity, in pleasure and in fear that he might desist.

The other, grander, wedding was characterised by that particular, faintly sexual and hilarious atmosphere always present when a young couple is solemnly and ritually adjured to go forth and copulate. The reception offered that classic and curious mixture of envy, innuendo, a consciousness of money spent and the onset of headaches from too much alcohol, from smiling and talking too much; the guests, having gossiped and drunk to excess, drove home in silence, wondering whether they would be held to the invitations issued in rash bonhomie to other couples they only ever met at weddings.

In short, a memorable affair, complete with top hats and tails, dear Ingrid so marvellously calm and composed, so suitable, so worthy of her happiness. Indeed the new Frau Schwantz was perfection itself, splendid in a frothy white confection; so wonderfully controlled that on this, the happiest day of her life, she didn't once avail herself of the bride's traditional privilege of being unpleasant to her mother. Mausi Bock was nevertheless overwrought. She wept during the ceremony and was ecstatic and unintelligible afterwards, irritating the waiters by wandering about and attempting to serve the guests herself. Her husband, who shrank from any public exhibition of his country accent, relegated his honours to Herr Tiedemann. The latter spent much of his time furtively examining the notes in his pocket for the speech he had in any case been determined to make and which proved as long-winded as those who knew him had feared.

This was, naturally, the perfect occasion at which to discuss the affairs of the house of Rommer and ogle the participants in the drama. Jovial Uncle Otto could be persuaded to give his version of events, one which proved disappointing as it concentrated interminably on the details of his concussion, his convalescence and the lucky escape he had had. Fortunately the 'shocking tragedy' of Herr Genscher had not set him back too much; he had found the strength to shoulder his new and important responsibilities. Not for anything in the world would he have let dear Frau Rommer down in her hour of need.

Frau Rommer, seemingly unconscious of any special interest, chatted amiably with everyone and was overheard in deep discussion about foundation wear with that funny, timid little Frau Tiedemann. Nearly everyone noticed the pretty English girl, who laughed so much and danced so well and was followed wherever she went by a young American in an ill-fitting suit with the shortest of crewcuts. Somebody said she was studying drama, in London, and certainly that seemed to suit her; somebody else said the American had been a monk, but of course nobody believed it.

Dear Ingrid's quiet little cousin, that studious, rather odd girl, also had an admirer, good-looking but dreadfully common, and it was said that the family did not approve. Some people whispered something about an involvement with Herr Genscher, for they all remembered the broken engagement a few years back, but that was generally held to be mere speculation and unkind too, given the circumstances. Dear Ingrid took special care to throw her pretty bouquet for her cousin to catch, but she turned her back quite rudely and it was the lively Linda who caught it. That witty young man, the banker, Herr Schenck, who had made such an amusing speech describing Ingrid as a pretty filly brought to bridle, watched this little scene with a most sentimental look and was heard to utter a deep sigh.

The following day at nine o'clock sharp, when the bridal party were engaged in the appropriately self-congratulatory post mortem, a woman carrying a bunch of spring flowers walked briskly through the gates of the cemetery and made purposefully for the distant corner. Something untoward made her pause for a moment and then accelerated the rhythmic crunching of stout shoes against gravel; she was straining forwards to see what it was. A dark silhouette was hovering over the grave, still and ethereal, an angel cut out of black marble.

Frau Liebmann blinked. At a distance of ten metres the divine became mortal, a lanky boy who started into life, darting, veering, then turning suddenly and racing past her with an averted face, a blur. A shorn head, the tip of a nose. It was a blind, instinctive retreat, the panicked rush of the young animal confronted by a predator. Guilty, thought Frau Liebmann grimly; carefully she examined the newly-planted shrubs for signs of any disturbance. Shaking her head, she drew a small mat from her large shopping bag and knelt clumsily, leaning forwards to poke inexpertly at the earth with her trowel. Everything seemed to be in order. With satisfaction she contemplated her handiwork, tweaking with motherly solicitude at the leaves of the puny-looking winter flowering jasmine. Staring sightlessly at the fine new marble slab, she knew that she knew that boy. There was something distinctive, memorable about the vulnerable nape of the adolescent neck. The hair, the long hair, that was it. It hadn't fooled her. Now she remembered how he had hidden behind it, in the chapel, concealing a tear-stained face. She sat back on her haunches, slowly she rolled open the paper cone of flowers. His grief had astonished her; he had left the service before the end with his head hanging low. She looked down at the bright tulips and thought he'd got his come-uppance then, hadn't he. Without knowing exactly what she meant by that, she began to clip the stems, her face a frown of concentration. Against such single-mindedness, the boy's face, so formless and innocuous, was soon to fade.

Frau Liebmann had found the will herself, lying in a pile of dirt and ash on the office floor; she had been going about the work of clearing up in a dreary and half-hearted way and had picked the papers up before she realised what they were. Hurriedly glancing through, she had finally made out her own name in the blurred print and had fallen to her knees in gratitude. The house was not worth a fortune, but it had bought her a place in a decent old people's home and a colour television and she was deeply grateful.

In due course the plants she had selected with such care put out tender new shoots. Their roots groped down for nourishment. They fastened upon the lid of the cheap wooden box and prised it open, inching down to the rotting matter underneath. Their forked tangles, always reaching out and

231

intertwining in the small space, finally achieved a rearrangement of matter which would have pleased Ludwig, had he known of it.

With reluctance, the Kommissar closed the case. For a long time the file on Victor Genscher hung around in his office, the neat manila folder growing grubby around the edges, the few papers inside leafed through so often that they became quite ragged. The file remained prominent, becoming at first the mat on which his coffee was placed and then a perpetual reproach in the pending tray. At last it disappeared in a stout bundle of folders, tied with twine, down to the permanent files in the basement where so many unfinished stories were left to moulder.

There were no witnesses and no proof; there was not sufficient evidence to bring a charge. The Rommer family maintained its obdurate, albeit charming silence, maintaining to the end that it knew and understood nothing. The firm's employees seemed equally ignorant of their boss's affairs. The whole issue of the newspaper, which had seemed so promising a lead, dwindled to nothing. *Der Abend* was the subject of an internal take-over and later the shares in it were sold by the family at a small profit. The Kommissar had never managed to establish Levison's authorship of the strange document found in Herr Genscher's safe, a piece of blackmail if ever he'd seen one, with its explicit references to theft and sodomy, its lamentable absence of detail on the date and place. The Kommissar had taken the unprecedented step of pulling strings and using influence to get this job, as eloquent in its pursuit as another man might have been in his manoeuvrings for promotion. Now he feared that the Genscher business had left a small black mark on his blameless career. He would, unsolicited, have done his utmost to save the man, to find mitigating circumstances, once he knew the truth, but he was denied the facts, denied an opportunity to render service. He felt outmanoeuvred, excluded and bitter; more than any single fact in the unsubstantial mess of half-evidence, this feeling of being cheated convinced him of the man's guilt.

And then there was the man himself, victim or aggressor, the powerful Herr Genscher. He lay day after day in his silent room, beneficiary of the best possible medical care. The doctors described his recovery as remarkable: he was, it seemed, fortunate in terms of paraplegics in being able to move one arm and his head; matters could have been so much worse. He broke his silence: he talked about the weather. Daily the Kommissar had taken his melancholy face to the invalid's bedside where he would sit with his notebook open on his lap, observing with a jaundiced eye the efficient and protective ministrations of the well-paid staff. The room became as familiar to him as his own sitting room. Patiently, he questioned the stricken man. And Herr Genscher would reply, turning his placid face towards his questioner, perfectly lucid. 'Altona?' he would muse in his pleasant voice. 'I don't make a habit of going there. It's not a good district and I always remember to lock the car doors when I drive through,' and he would smile with faint irony, with the slight puzzlement of a man who was too polite to inquire why he was being asked such things. The name Levison was completely new to him; the word blackmail provoked his melodious laugh. Occasionally the Kommissar, growing irritable, would shout and accuse, and then Herr Genscher would retreat into a faintly wounded silence, waiting for the display of bad manners to cease. Nothing moved him. Nothing provoked any kind of defence or explanation. As far as he was concerned, nothing whatsoever had occurred; he did not even seem to wonder what he was doing there, in the crisp white bed. Scrutinising him carefully, the policeman could not detect any hint of conscious deception. He had gone away each time with his notebook empty, a frustrated man.

June 11, 1972

Victor is going away, to live in Switzerland. Oma has worked out a deal with the bank to buy him out of the company. She is jubilant, for that means she can go home at last. She is taking all Levison's documents with her; for months she has carried

233

them around with her in her great, unwieldy ostrich-skin bag, afraid to leave them anywhere. She calls them our insurance policy, though nobody thinks Victor will ever be active again. He is imprisoned in that immobile body; a sufficient punishment. Switzerland, as a solution, pleases everyone. Victor will be well looked-after and able to afford a complete entourage of servants; with care, they say he should live for many years.

He is very strange now. He sent Oma a formal letter of resignation, thanking her for past kindnesses and saying that he intended to pursue a different path, but would always wish her well. She has been to see him several times and has tried to wring the truth out of him, but he gives nothing away. He actually laughed, when she asked him about the judo school; he said skiing was his sport.

For some strange reason, I suppose for old times' sake I went to visit him today. He gave me an odd look but was as courteous and polite as ever. He waved his good hand towards the seat at his bedside and I could see that in his mind's eye he was standing, that he pulled the chair forwards and helped me to sit, as he always has.